TALL IN THE SADDLE

K͏ Rocklin's trade was cattle. Rocklin arı s at the K C Ranch to becomes its for an, but when he finds that the owner of ranch has been killed and that the ran is run by Clara Caldwell, Rocklin refu s to work for her. He does agree, how er, to obtain a letter from Judge Ga y proving Clara's ownership of the ran . Rocklin arrives in Garley's office just afte Garley has burned the letter. With a croc ed judge, a pretty girl with a grudge, and back-shooter on his tail, Rocklin does 't stand a chance ... or does he?

TALL IN THE SADDLE

TALL IN THE SADDLE

by

Gordon Young

The Golden West Large Print Books
Long Preston, North Yorkshire,
BD23 4ND, England.

British Library Cataloguing in Publication Data.

Young, Gordon
    Tall in the saddle.

MA   05/13

WESTERN   £15-99

    A catalogue record of this book is
    available from the British Library

    ISBN   978-1-84262-935-2 pbk

First published in Britain by Gardner

Published in Large Print 2013 by arrangement with
Golden West Literary Agency

The Golden West Large Print is an imprint of Library Magna
Books Ltd.

Printed and bound in Great Britain by
T.J. (International) Ltd., Cornwall, PL28 8RW

CHAPTER ONE

A tall man in a wide white hat got off the train at a place townsite plat makers had miscalled Garden City. He carried a big new cardboard valise and had a folded coat under his arm. Heat flashed with shimmering dazzle from the small red depot, and the sun hit so straight and hard that he made only a spot of shadow as he walked down the cinders to where the baggageman had dumped a saddle in a gunny sack.

He heaved the saddle up, upside down, to rest on his shoulder and balanced it awkwardly by holding to the horn as he walked uptown with the short, tiptoeing steps of a man in high-heeled boots. The heels clacked the board sidewalk as sharply as a hammer when it searches for a studding.

The old stage-company agent ran an inky thumb under his suspender, let the suspender snap. 'Santa Inez? Seventeen-fifty. Name?'

'Rocklin.'

The agent's mild, faded eyes had watched men come and go. There was a range-bred toughness about this fellow; he had a horseman's lean hips and high shoulders, and the new store clothes, now wrinkled and soot-stained by train cinders, had not settled to his body. The trouser legs were held in firm cylinder shape by being drawn down over high boots. The white hat was not new. A lean fellow, with the hard tiredness that saddle work gives men, even young men, and the burn of an overdone biscuit on his face, he had the tight, hard eyes that men get by peering afar through sunlight.

'I'll book you up with the driver if you want.'

Rocklin moved his hat far back; the hair was a dark red. He dipped a tobacco sack from the vest pocket and said, 'Thanks.'

'Don't thank me yet. Dave's mad. His last trip. He hates quittin', but he had a row with Harolday. A couple of drinks and he'd row with his grandmother! Old-timer, Dave is – and a grumpy cuss.'

Rocklin's voice and manner were deliberate, almost not friendly, but he said, 'I like grumpy old cusses. Hope to live long enough to be one.'

Dave fingered his beard, peering at Rocklin, and said, 'Git up on the seat.' There was a whisky stink on Dave's breath, and he faced the agent again, quarrelsomely.

Rocklin got up with foot to front wheel hub and folded the coat behind him on the seat. A hostler in bib overalls languidly held the horses' bridles, and up the street heat shimmered in a flowing haze and sweat-stained idlers lounged in the hot shade to watch the stage pull out and grinned at Dave, who was trying to row with the agent.

A fat man in a leather apron came out of the Boot and Saddle shop with flat-footed plop of hurrying. 'Dave! Dave!' he called. 'I near forgot. Tell Miss Harolday her saddle ain't come, will you, Dave?'

Dave turned with round-shouldered bulkiness and from under the floppy hatbrim stared, then turned his back. The idlers' grins widened, and the fat man said with no anger, 'Crazy old coot, you!'

Dave put out a claw-shaped hand and gathered the front of the agent's shirt into a fist. 'This is the stage-comp'ny office, ain't it? Ain't it? Then why ain't they here? Women, just 'cause they're women – why make me go pick 'em up?'

The agent sighed and spoke mildly. 'They're at the hotel, Dave.'

'Two block on'y, and they got laigs, ain't they? Ain't they?'

The fat man in the leather apron came into the dust and rounded the stage to ask Rocklin, 'Will you tell the agent over at Santa Inez to tell Miss Harolday her saddle ain't come? Will you, mister? I don't want her mad at me.'

Rocklin nodded. 'I'll say that.'

9

'Thanks, mister. And hang on with both hands! When Dave's had him a couple of drinks too many you can hear the passengers prayin' for miles!' Then the fat man gave his heavy body a lift on tiptoes to urge, 'An' try to hold him down, or he'll scare the women to death and jolt 'em bad!'

Rocklin looked down as if sighting over a rifle. 'I never feel sorry for anything that happens to a woman!' It was as carefully spoken as if summing up an old decision.

Two women came down the warped porch steps of the hotel followed by the hotel man and his fat wife, who was mad. The hotel man slouched along; the weight of the swollen carpetbags dragged his arms out of the sweat-wet shirt sleeves, and his head bobbed in rhythm with his plodding walk. An iron-bound oval-top trunk had already been dragged to the roadside.

The passengers were a girl and a tall, old, high-nosed woman who carried her head up and wore a black hat that looked lacquered. Her black, sharp eyes, scrouged behind a network of wrinkles, peered at Dave and Rocklin, and she said sharply, meaning to be overheard, 'They look like ruffians!'

The girl begged, 'Oh, please, please don't!' It was a subdued pleading, conscious of futility, and she offered a quick, apologetic smile toward Rocklin, but he ignored her.

She had large dark eyes, was rather shyly childlike, and looked very tired. She was pretty in a pale, timid way, and there was a kind of loneliness about her.

Dave gave Rocklin the reins and got down to stow the trunk, and the hotel man's angry fat wife kept at Dave's heels, also meaning to be overheard. "Tain't offen I feel spiteful, but, Dave, that old Miss Martin there is the meanest critter I ever seen! I wouldn't want you hurt, Dave, but I hope you overturn her 'cause–'

The girl was already in the coach, and the high-nosed old lady was just getting in with the boosting help of the hotel man. She took her seat stiffly, then cocked her head to listen to the fat wife's shout. '–just tried to hurt people's feelin's – like callin' you boys ruff'ans!' The old lady smiled as if breaking a porcelain mask.

The hotel man wanted to help with the trunk, but Dave told him, 'Git away!' and upended it by a one-handed pull, crouched, heaved, and with spraddle-legged steadiness carried it to the end of the stage and lifted the trunk to the boot. His deft, claw-shaped fingers whipped on lashings, jerked down the canvas, making it fast, then he went back to the seat.

Before Rocklin was settled Dave's whip spun a thread of movement above the horses' ears and cracked; and, cued by the whip's

11

snap, they hit their traces all together and their feet splashed dust into a smoky roll that the stage wheels swirled higher. Rocklin's head went back with a jerk and he barely saved his hat.

Presently Rocklin looked back and down. The stir of dust was swirling with the draft through the open sides of the coach, and the women were trying to fasten the canvas curtains that swayed and flapped like live things fluttering to escape. He smothered down the feeling of wanting to help.

Red Rock country lay ahead with switch-back climbs to the rim. Some splotches of far-off color had the redness of campfire coals, and there was a heat in the wind as if coming across hot coals. The stage rolled by a fallen-in shack where some fool nester had marked the earth with plowings that had turned into weed patches; even the weeds were dead and brittle.

Rocklin knew the way of old-timers and didn't disturb Dave's glumness. His thoughts drifted about, remembering, *Hard on women and horses, the West*. He thought, *I'm sorry for the horses*. The women were Easterners, as plainly as if branded, and the paleness would soon be scorched out of the girl's face and old lady's wrinkles would look like those of cracky leather.

There was the muffled rattle of harness

and whimpering creak of stage springs as the horses plodded with loose reins and heads down on the long upgrade. *Nobody has prayed yet,* Rocklin thought.

Dave said, 'I've druv stage thirty-odd years.' His eyes were on the road, and his hoarse voice had a brooding mumble. 'Druv in Californy. On curves where you could use the boot for the lead hosses' nosebag.' He said it without humor. 'This is my last trip. They say I'm too dang old. Me!' He turned his head, peered from under gray bushy brows at Rocklin. 'Don't git old an' wore out and useless.' That was the best advice he knew.

'Who're them as say you are?'

'Harolday for one. Owns the stage-comp'ny. Owns a couple of ranches. Dead men's ranches. Mebbe he hopes to git another'n! Put nuthin' past him. Nuthin'! I figger,' Dave added matter-of-factly, 'the devil owns him.' He spoke as if reading a brand.

Then Dave took the lines into his left hand, cleared his mouth of tobacco, and drew a full half pint from his inside vest pocket. 'Nip?'

Rocklin said, 'Thanks.'

The bottle was unlabeled. Bar whisky at its reddest. Rocklin drew the cork, tipped back his head. The raw whisky sent out shudders like a rock plopped into a pond. Rocklin said, 'Ah-hmm!' which was as much of a lie as any other form of praise. He wiped the mouth of the bottle with stroke of palm and gave it back uncorked.

Dave drank, held the bottle to the sky line measuringly, then drank again. He said, 'Oogh!' and blew as if his mouth was scalded. He extended the bottle for the cork that Rocklin thumbed in. The bottle went back, half empty, into his pocket.

Dave grumbled, 'Women and whisky – ever think how much alike? A man can't handle either, and both fool you. Ever think? Sometimes for a while you git along fine. Then, too bad! Ever think?'

'Lots. Especially about a friend of mine and how he's hardened toward women – at last.'

Rocklin stopped, and Dave waited, then said, 'Let's hear. Talk shortens miles.'

Rocklin tightened his mouth with a wry smile. 'All right. The first was Hazel. As a youngster he rode into town with three months' wages. Hazel said he mustn't be foolish and throw it away like other boys. Hazel was sweet and said she loved him. 'Let me keep it for you,' she said. She kept it, taking the first train out with a pimply young tramp. He never told anybody about Hazel; that is, just me.'

Dave nodded. His neck was short and thick. 'Lucky to be shut of her.'

'Then there was Alice. Nice girl, men

thought. He thought so, too – this friend. You can never tell. Soft and quiet with blue eyes. His heart hurt like it had been tromped on when she married a well-fixed old man whose wife had just died. They hung the old man for poisoning his wife, but Alice was pretty and could cry to melt iron. Leastwise, the jail door opened and she disappeared. It was her furnished the poison for the well-fixed old man, but it was this fool friend of mine that got the poison for her from a wolf hunter. She wanted it, she said, to mix with sugared water as a flytrap.'

Again Dave nodded with understanding. 'That orta cured him – on'y nuthin' does.'

'He's cured, but it was Judith did that. Just lately. Now if he saw a woman bogged down in a mudhole he wouldn't throw a rope. It'd be a trick, sure.'

'Most likely, sure,' Dave agreed.

'Judith was the daughter of a man that run stock on old Mel Milton's range and she lived on the ranch. I've worked for Mel Milton near all my life. That's how I happen to know so much. A man had to like Judith if she wanted him to, and she did him.

'There was a bad bunch in Tahzo headed by an outlaw named Highman who run off horses and cows as a side line. Old Mel Milton turned this fellow – this friend of mine – over to the Cowmen's Association. He knew the country and laid for Highman, but

15

somehow never met up with him, and he never guessed why. You never do when you trust a woman, not one like Judith.

'One day he told Judith he was riding alone up to a place called Craggy to see about something that had nothing to do with Highman. Judith got him to wait a couple of days. She could get a man to do anything. She kissed him good-by and said how much she loved him and would he hurry back.'

Rocklin quit talking and gazed toward the far-off mountains that seemed to be floating in the horizon's haze, and his face had the hardness of something forged and hammered.

'I'm awaitin',' Dave growled.

'You can guess!'

'Not about a woman.'

'Mexicans like this friend of mine – probably because he likes them – and he met one on the road that told him Highman was already at Craggy. Even then this fool man didn't think what it meant, but he cut across and squatted on the back trail and waited. Sure enough, Highman got tired of waiting and come along with a couple of riders. When it was over one had got away, one was dead, and Highman was out of the saddle, dying. When he saw who'd shot him he gave Judith a cussin' that spilled the beans.'

Dave said, 'Somethin' in the Bible about one like her, ain't they?'

16

'Mebbe, but there's worse. Judith then wanted the reward. Money with blood on it – she didn't care. That's a woman for you! Cure any man, don't you think?'

Dave meditated, shook his head. 'Not 'f he's got the weakness. Headaches don't cure taste for whisky.'

'He didn't tell anybody but Mel Milton, and old Mel run her off the ranch. He's cured now, for good.'

Dave said, 'Of Judy, mebbe, but not of May and Jane and Sue. Just like whisky. You'll see.'

Words died away, and each milled his own thoughts as a mile of upgrade crept away under the wheels; then Dave broke the silence. 'I wonder why a young feller who don't have to wants to come into this God-danged country?'

Rocklin's hat was between his knees and he was rolling a cigarette in the deep crown to keep the wind from stealing the tobacco flakes. 'I've been hired, sight unseen.'

'What doin'?'

'Riding for the K C.' He bent forward with the cigarette in his mouth and touched the match flame in the hat's crown. Dave squinted at him, taking a long look. Rocklin sheltered the cigarette between thumb and finger with the fire toward his palm. Rocklin asked, 'Big outfit?'

Dave drew a walnut-sized piece of tobacco

from his lower vest pocket, eyed it, rubbed some of the pocket's lint and grit off on his pants leg, put the lump into his mouth. The stage dragged on. When Dave had softened the tobacco he leaned from the seat to spit, wiped his bearded mouth with the back of his hand, and asked, 'You know about old Caldwell bein' killed?'

'Never heard of him.'

'Owned the K C.'

'Caldwell, hm? That was my mother's name. She died when I was born. I don't take after her much. She had gold hair, they say. Look at mine!'

'I have looked.' Dave divided the lines into his claw-shaped hands – hands that thirty-odd years of line-holding had cramped until he couldn't straighten his fingers. 'Caldwell was the best-hearted an' worse-tempered man in the country. He had redder hair'n yourn. He'd been over to Garden an' was killed comin' home. Somebody shot 'im out of the saddle. From behind.' Dave leaned over the side and spit, added, 'Safer that way. Five, six, seven months back. He wasn't very smart some ways, but he was honest and not afraid of nuthin'.'

Rocklin asked, 'Who's Jim Brotherton?'

'Jim? He's runnin' the ranch.'

Then Dave withdrew into a sour glumness and wouldn't talk of the Caldwell ranch.

When the stage reached the rim where,

18

southward, there was a view of the country as if from a cloud, the horses stopped for their rest before Dave said, 'Whoa,' but he grumbled, 'Whoa,' anyhow, giving permission. Then he drew the bottle, silently offering it.

Rocklin said, 'Thanks,' and nipped again, lightly. Dave swigged it empty and gave the flat bottle a fling. It spun through a colorless flash of sunlight and fell out of sight beyond the ledge.

Dave told him, 'Get off an' stretch yore laigs if you want.'

Rocklin went to the ledge and gazed as far as eyesight could carry. A heat haze hugged the earth, but above the haze was a wind-swept clearness. The Catana Mountains hovered there at the edge of the earth, their foundation floating motionless in the haze that looked like water.

Old Miss Martin's head came out between the canvas of the coach window, and she demanded shrilly, 'Driver? Driver, what's the matter?'

'Nuthin'. Restin' hosses. Git out an' stretch yore laigs if you want.'

The women got out, not easily, for the step was high. The old lady's voice went up with: 'No, I don't see anything beautiful about it!' Then: 'Driver! Resting horses, are you, and let passengers burn and blister?'

Dave turned his shaggy head, glowered

from the seat. 'You in such a hell-fired hurry, lady?'

'Certainly we are in a hurry!'

'Well, pile back in. We'll hurry some!' He called hoarsely at Rocklin, 'Climb up!'

Rocklin came back, and when he lifted his foot to the front wheel hub to step up and across he happened to meet the pale girl's eyes. She had helped her aunt in and now held her skirt ankle-high, helplessly, for it was a long reach with foot, and arm, too, and there was no humble hotel man to steady her.

'Will you, please?' Her voice was timid.

He stepped down and helped her without speaking. The aunt, from the shadowed depth of the coach, said, 'Gentlemen don't need to be asked!'

Rocklin didn't care what she said, but the girl cared, and turned, bending her head below the coach top to smile. 'Thank you.' Her dark eyes had a velvety warmth and lingered as if wanting just a bit of pleasantness. His grudged 'Welcome' was lost in the snap of the closing door.

Women, pretty ones, were like that – kitten-soft and snake-mean. Caught in their meanness, they would lie, beg, drip tears, and blubber. He knew; knew, too, that even when you hated them they could make you feel bad.

Dave shook the lines. 'Git up!' The horses

walked. 'I've been poky. Last trip. I reckon I'll go freightin'.' That was as if a cowman thought of plowing. 'In Californy I usta tool six an' sometimes eight at a– I'll show you! Goda'mighty, come on!'

The whip went skyward in spinning curves and exploded. Then the horses broke from their easy lope as the whip fired again and they ran as if running away, headlong. The rackety beat of shod hoofs pounded through dust and struck the roadbed's rock, and the coach bounced and swayed with heaving lurch; not creaking now, it had a sound of muffled bellowing.

Rocklin thought, *No wonder they pray!*

The stage rocked and bounced with a grinding slide of iron on hairpin curves that put the boot into an overhang. If a horse should fall, a spoke snap, a felloe wabble, a dislodged boulder lie around a curve– Under the hard jostling that shifted his weight on the seat the folded coat worked loose and flew away.

The snake-crooked rim road was too narrow for the passing of any other vehicle except at some widened-out inside curves, and from his seat on the near side Rocklin could look down over the rim's edge, sometimes felt that he hung in space over it, and often the jolting stage flung its near-side wheels across the rut marks right at the drop-off's edge. A bit of crumble under the left front wheel and Dave's expertness would be sodden jelly three hundred feet below.

Rocklin knew the women were being knocked about; however they braced themselves, there would be side bumps. He hadn't heard a squawk so far; maybe they were too scared and prayed silently. More likely the wind whipped away their cries that were half smothered by the coach's rumbling groans. The pale girl's half-sad dark eyes hung before his thought, and he could not be pleased if she were bruised; but he hoped the old mossy-horned heifer was getting enough hurrying to suit her.

The leaders swung sharply and for an instant were out of sight around a wedge-shaped turn, then the skittering coach whipped out with a jerk and followed on the teeter of two wheels, just barely not overturning. A bearded freighter had heard the coach coming and put his high-loaded wagons and six mules into a turnout, hugging the bank. He raised his hand in a slow, unstartled greeting as the stage rolled by in a swirl of red dust.

Some miles of this, then Dave sang out, 'Ho, boys! Ho, now – ho-o-o!' with quieting hoarseness as he pressed down the brake and tightened the reins, not jerking and sawing, but with the powerful pull of steadying hands. The horses knew, trustfully, and came to a jogging trot, still nervous, with ears back, but he soothed them down to a walk; then the wheeler blew dust out of his nose with a rippling snort.

Dave turned inquiringly, proud and childish in the wish for a compliment. There was an ache in Rocklin's fingers from holding on; he would have been off and over a dozen times if he had not held fast to the seat iron, and he said, 'Dave, you sure had me wishing for wings!'

Dave peered at him, and the beard drew back to let the pleased grin show through. The horses turned slowly around a curve, and there was the downgrade, zigzagging steeply. Dave pulled the horses' heads up and set the brake blocks squealing; then a shrill voice came up from below, fiercely.

'Now what is the matter?' The old lady's anger vibrated into the defiance of: 'Why are we stopping again?'

Rocklin looked steadily ahead, not smiling. Dave hunched his shoulders. The old lady was lying, of course, but she knew how to make a fellow mad. Rocklin sensed that Dave was half minded to throw off the brake, lash the horses, send team and stage tumbling down the zigzag – smash everything. Give her enough of hurrying.

CHAPTER TWO

Sundown brought the stage to Stan's Place for a supper stop and another change of horses. Stan was stockkeeper and ran a measly roadhouse in the lonely adobe with ramshackle outbuildings near by.

A little Mexican shuffled out of the sundown shadows, his big hat flopping limply, and he called a soft *'Buenas tardes, señor,'* but Dave surlily ignored him. Rocklin answered in rippling Spanish, and the little Mexican took off his hat and grinned from ear to ear, pleased to be addressed politely in his own tongue. He began unhitching the horses.

Dave got down and moved with a lurching, stiff-kneed walk to the side of the coach and opened the door. 'We stop here,' he said gruffly.

The old lady leaned forward and peered out as if she meant to be on guard against traps and tricks. 'Why do we stop here?'

''F you wants eat and stretch yore laigs.'

'Will you please stop referring to my legs!'

'You got some, ain't you?' Then Dave snorted, turned away, and lurched toward the house with sandy scuffle of broad-heeled boots.

Rocklin, still on the seat, thought he had never seen anybody quite as bad-tempered as that web-wrinkled old lady, and his look idly followed Dave toward the squat adobe. Now that he was drawing nearer to Santa Inez he was wondering more than ever why Jim Brotherton had sent for him, had sent money; and he was the same as hired.

The old lady marched toward the house, and her back was as stiff as if a pine board were strapped under her corset. *Tough!* Rocklin admitted. He had his own muscles and joints to tell him how the women's must ache. The girl's silhouette moved wearily through the coming darkness, and her skirt trailed and her arms hung as if broken. A minute later lamplight glistened against the 'dobe's dirty windows.

When Rocklin went in, Dave was at the one-board bar in the corner with a bottle before him and his back to the women. They sat on a bench at a table covered with scabby oilcloth and the yellow glow of the smelly tin lamp on their faces. The splutter and greasy odor of something being fried came through the doorway behind them. The floor was beaten earth and long unswept.

The pale girl was already wind-burned, and her sad tiredness seemed pleading for bed and sleep; but the old lady looked along her high-arched nose at Rocklin, making ready to speak. He turned his back on her

25

and lounged his forearms on the flimsy bar by the side of Dave.

'How far from here to town?' He didn't care about the distance but was breaking ice, or trying to.

Dave growled, 'Leave me 'lone,' and poured more whisky into his tin cup.

Rocklin's glance dropped toward the bottle. Men didn't grow big enough to take drinks like that and see straight.

Stan was poking the fire through a pothole and right off told Rocklin, 'Supper's purtnear ready,' as if answering before the question could be asked. Then Stan grinned, jerked a thumb, and dropped his voice to sly lewdness with: 'Ain't that girl a somepin'!' Rocklin's look straightened him up, and Stan mumbled, 'I mean jus' plain purty!' Rocklin didn't say anything, and Stan prodded the frying steaks with a wide-pronged fork.

The coal-oil lamp had a rusty reflector behind it that was made from a tin can and threw down light from a shelf. The flour sack about Stan's waist was dirty, and Stan was gangling, loosejointed, loosemouthed.

Rocklin hadn't said a word and didn't now, but he eyed the frying meat. Then his look turned from the sizzling pan to the fresh chunk of veal on the whisky barrel's head that served as a meat block, and the next instant he caught Stan's wavering eyes and held them accusingly. In cow country veal nearly always means stolen meat and a buried hide.

Stan one-handedly fumbled the flour sack as if wiping his hand. 'Friend of mine roped a yearlin' and broke its neck. He give me a quarter.'

Rocklin took the lie as if he believed it. None of his affair, and if Stan hadn't been watching guiltily he'd never have known Rocklin's guess. But Rocklin's quietness was hard with dislike of Stan and Stan's kind. He said slowly, making it a command, 'Hurry supper on out there to stop Dave.' Dave's drinking was some of his concern.

Stan drew in a relieved breath and skimmed sweat from his forehead with a finger. 'Yeah, sure. But you all can put up here if he gets too drunk.'

Rocklin gave him a look and went out.

Dave was still at the bar, now mumbling thickly in his beard. The quart bottle was another half-pint down. Dave wouldn't drive this night. *I can,* Rocklin thought. He took off his hat, picked up a stool, set it by the table across from the women, and carefully did not look at them.

The old lady said, 'Young man?'

He looked at her now. The lacquered black hat had been well batted about in the coach and had lost its crisp shape and gloss but was again straight on her head. Dust that hard water and soap could not reach had stenciled her wrinkles.

She poked out a bony finger toward Dave's back, 'That driver is intoxicated!'

'Is he?' He didn't like her and wouldn't pretend, and waited with indifference in case she wanted to say something more.

She said it. 'You are a fool!'

'Frequently.'

That made her stiffen her neck with a jerk, then she turned to the girl. 'Clara, the rudeness of the people in this country is appalling!'

Clara's face was wind-burned with a look of blushing, and she was ghastly tired and hadn't the pride not to appear tired. Her very white hand that a cotton glove had protected moved aimlessly about her forehead, and as Rocklin watched her the velvety dark eyes gazed at him with a weary longing for friendliness and she smiled a little, but his unresponsive stare killed the smile. Rocklin could be mean as hell without frown or word.

Stan shuffled in with his hands full. 'Now help yourselves, folks!' he announced as if to a crowd, and set down the meat platter, the gravy dish, the plate with its chunk-like slices of bread.

Rocklin jerked his head toward the bar, and Stan called, 'Dave, supper!' Then Stan went closer and touched him. 'Dave! Supper's on!'

Dave didn't move but said, 'Go to hell!'

Stan's look asked Rocklin, 'Now what?' Rocklin said, 'All right,' admitting nothing more could be done. Then Stan told them cheerily, 'I'll bring coffee,' and shuffled out.

The old lady picked up the tin fork and iron knife disdainfully. 'Silverware!' She leaned forward stiffly to peer in distrust at the grease-brown steaks, the dirty gray of the gravy. 'And I have dyspepsia!' It sounded as if she thought 'dyspepsia' was a good cuss word. Then the women ate a little with nibbling uncertainty, but Rocklin was hungry. He chewed with a sidelong stare toward Dave and hoped the whisky would flatten him out; that would be better than having to argue about driving.

Two men came in, and Stan nearly choked up in saying, 'Howdy, boys.' A deputy-sheriff badge dangled on the elder man's vest, and he scowled at Stan and fingered the scraggly mustache that overflowed his mouth. The other man was young, rail-thin, hatchet-faced, and his mouth was open in a lax grin. The deputy said, 'Stan, we just found somethin' out there in the straw!' Stan began wiping his hands on the flour-sack apron and swallowed hard, and the rail-thin man sniggered at him.

Then the deputy took off his hat and told the women, 'We hate to bother you ladies, but–'

Dave had turned with fuddled glowering,

and he waggled out an arm that looked tired and told them in a loud voice, 'She ain't got no laigs!' He peered through his haziness and saw the men well enough to grumble, 'You fellers, huh?'

There was a long moment's solemn hush before the old lady snapped, 'Don't look at us that way. We aren't monsters! Nor cripples!'

The rail-thin young man grinned at the girl. 'From how Dave spoke, f'r a minute I wondered!' His laughter was a kind of cackle.

Dave staggered up with spraddle-legged weave of body. 'Fourflushers, both you fellers! Worser'n that, you—'

Rocklin left his stool to keep Dave out of trouble, but Dave pushed at him, trying to get by. Rocklin held on. The burly old stage driver was a big handful.

The deputy crowded up, saying, 'Crazy drunk!'

Dave shouted, 'Shore I'm drunk! Tell truth on'y when I am drunk – too much sense other times, you—' It was the West's fight-ingest word, and Dave teeteringly wanted to fight.

'Too bad!' the deputy told Rocklin, as if sorry about it; and Rocklin said, 'I'll help get him off to bed somewhere.' Dave pulled away, drew back a fist, but went off balance and lurched sideways in a helpless stagger to steady himself. The deputy pushed Rocklin away with: 'Me an' Bob'll look after him. We're his friends. Come on, Bob.' The rail-thin Bob was already there. The deputy said, 'Careful, now, don't hurt 'im, Bob!'

The powerful Dave fumblingly tried to scuffle and did cuss, and waved his fists about but didn't get them in anybody's face. Bob's slack mouth was half open, as if amused. He said 'Whoa up, now, Dave, don't be so rambunctious!' Dave's drunken weight was hard to handle.

Dave roared at Bob, 'Keep yore hands off me! You try to be ornery as your jailbird brother an' don't know how, you–' That only made Bob laugh.

The deputy coaxed through quick breathing, 'Don't act up this way, Dave! They's women watchin'!'

Dave's floppy hat fell off and was stepped on. Rocklin picked it up, dusted it with slaps against his leg, laid it on the bar. They now had Dave by each arm and hustled him out of the wide-open front door.

The Clara-girl's anxious glances fled about, seeking reassurance, and settled on Rocklin as he rolled a cigarette because he looked as if nothing much had happened; but the old lady was stiffly tense and asked sharply, 'What will they do with him?' She aimed the question equally at Stan and Rocklin, but Rocklin wouldn't talk to her, so Stan mumbled, 'Oh, lay him down some'eres and

31

let him sleep it off.'

Stan had a hangdog uneasiness, and his eyes fluttered about his feet then wavered guiltily up to Rocklin. Rocklin let the match burn away from the cigarette and bobbed his head toward the kitchen. 'That it?'

Stan mumbled listlessly, 'I been a damn fool!'

The match stung Rocklin's fingers. He dropped it, stepped on it with grind of toe, lit the cigarette with another. 'Penitentiary?'

Stan pointed a finger at the steaks now lying in cold grease on the platter. 'I orta knowed better, but a feller give me a hunk of yearlin' an' even skinned 'er here!'

Rocklin pitched the broken match toward Stan's feet. 'Penitentiaries are hard on fellows used to having all outdoors for a back yard.'

Something was going on here under the old lady's nose that she didn't know about, and she peered at the meat platter, at Rocklin, at Stan, then she demanded, 'What are you men talking about? "Penitentiary"? The meat isn't poisoned, is it?' She didn't think it was poisoned, and wasn't pretending that she did, but just said it.

Stan fidgeted and would have talked, but the deputy and his man Bob were coming in, now less stiff-legged, and both grinned. Rocklin thought he liked the look on their faces better when they didn't grin.

The deputy pulled off his hat again. 'Sorry to have a ruckus before you ladies. He went right to sleep as soon as we laid him down.'

Bob's grin widened. 'Sleep, you bet!'

Then the deputy flapped his hat lightly against Bob. 'Dave he's too drunk, but Bob Clews here'll take the stage on in.'

Bob nodded at the Clara-girl, his mouth grinningly half open. 'Be glad to, you bet!'

Rocklin's shoulder lounged against the wall. He took the cigarette from his lips and said, 'I'm driving.'

The deputy jangled his spurs as he turned, and Bob, too, had another long look. They had sized Rocklin up once, now were reconsidering, and he passively faced the scrutiny. Then the deputy threaded anxiousness into his voice. 'But 'f anything happens to these here ladies, I'd feel to blame!'

Rocklin said, 'Don't.'

The deputy wasn't sure he liked the way Rocklin said it, but decided to leave it up to the old woman and asked her, 'Do you ladies want him to drive?'

She stiffened a bony finger at Rocklin. 'He is going with us anyhow, so let him drive.' She spoke as if making a choice without approval and hurrying it because there was something else to talk about. Her black eyes took aim on the deputy's face. 'What's this about the penitentiary and that man?'

'He,' said the deputy as he surveyed Stan

with a tightening stare, 'has throwed in with rustlers an'–'

'Rustlers?' she asked quick as a flash. 'What are rustlers?'

'Cow thieves,' said the deputy. 'And we just found the hide down yonder in the shed under straw before we come on up here!'

Bob elaborated. 'It was a K C yearlin'!'

Rocklin had reached his hat from the peg to go out and see that the stage was ready, but veal with a K C hide in the straw appeared to be definitely some of his affair. Brotherton of the K C had written old Mel Milton that he wanted, needed, a man of Rocklin's reputation, and some of Brotherton's money was now in Rocklin's pocket. He set the hat on his head and came closer, and the calmness of authority was in the question. 'Do you mean from the Caldwell ranch?'

Bob grinned loosely. 'Yeah, you bet!'

Then the old lady drew back her head, put the tips of both hands to the edge of the table, and demanded sharply, 'Do you mean that you intend to send this man to the penitentiary for stealing a cow from the Caldwell ranch?'

'Yes'm!' said the deputy, and looked sternly at Stan.

'I never stole it!' Stan mumbled, adding with feeble lift of voice, to make the distinction seem important, 'I just knowed it was stole!'

'Anyhow,' Bob said in an eager, pleased way, 'Jackson here is goin' to send you to the pen'tent'ary in spite of hell an' high water!'

Old Miss Martin slapped the table. 'Young man, don't swear in my presence!' She had listened quietly to Dave's hoarse profanity, probably aware that she couldn't stop it. Then her voice went up, sharp and vibrant. 'What is more, young man, and you, Mr Officer, he is not going to any penitentiary!' Her black eyes shone with triumph. 'It happens that the Caldwell ranch belongs to my niece here! It also happens that we dined on a piece of that cow. My niece may do as she pleases with one of her own cows, may she not? What do you say, Clara?'

The deputy, Bob, and Stan were knocked silly-dumb, and the old lady liked that and smiled a little, but with a look as if smiling hurt her face. Rocklin suspected that she had banged that surprise at them more to thwart the deputy than as a favor to Stan, for she seemed to have that kind of cross-grained contrariness. Rocklin knew right off that K C hides were now none of his concern because he wouldn't work under that old woman's high-arched nose and bad temper, but he would have to go on and say so to Brotherton, and there was also money paid out for fare that would have to be refunded.

The deputy and Bob got their breath and

35

blurted at the same time, 'Are you that Caldwell girl?' 'You're that Caldwell girl?'

Stan gulped hard and trailed with: 'You old Red Caldwell's niece?'

'Of course she is Clara Caldwell!' Then the old lady snapped, 'Do you think I would lie about it?' Bob mumbled something about being damned, but she didn't anticlimax her scene by jumping on him. She said, 'Now, Clara, inform these men how you feel about sending a man to prison over a cow!'

The excitement brightened Clara's headachy weariness, and her soft voice earnestly told them, 'If it is one of my cows, of course Mr Stan is not to be punished!'

Deputy Jackson and the rail-thin Bob looked queerly at each other, and Bob cackled, 'The joke is sure on you!'

The deputy did not see anything funny, and he told Stan, 'You're a fool for luck!' That was all he said to Stan. Rocklin could think of lots of things that ought to be said, no matter what the cow owner thought about it, and he would have liked to tell the girl what a mistake she was making, for she looked helpless and he guessed that the old lady wanted to keep her that way.

The deputy plucked Bob's arm. 'Come on, let's be ridin'!'

Outside the door Bob's voice could be heard, again saying, 'The joke is sure on you!'

Then there was the clatter of hoofs leaving.

Stan fumbled at his flour sack and mumbled about being grateful, saying he didn't know what to say. Rocklin, on his way out, heard the old lady tell him, 'If you don't know what to say, keep quiet!'

The little Mexican had brought up fresh horses, harnessed and ready, and left them at the hitching-rack. He squatted patiently on the ground with a lantern beside him.

Rocklin said in Spanish, 'My little friend, Stan will break your neck for telling the officer where to find that hide.'

'Señor, please, I did not tell!'

'Then who did?'

'They rode up and took my lantern and went at once to where the hide was covered by straw!'

'Who brought the cow?'

'A man I do not know.'

'My little friend, it is bad to lie – unless you do it well!'

'But, señor, I do not lie! I speak truth. I am a stranger here, before God!'

Rocklin gazed down through starlight at the small dark face, and the Mexican youth took off his hat and held up his head as if wanting his face read. Rocklin was not thinking of that; the face was merely an object for his gaze to rest on while he figured things. If they came after dark and found the hide so easily, they had been told where to look; and

Bob's 'The joke's on you!' could mean that the stacked cards had slipped out of the deputy's fingers. 'Fourflushers,' Dave had said, perhaps knowing.

Rocklin asked, 'Where is Dave?'

'Come, señor!'

Dave lay face down on the ground around the house and behind the corner near the wash bench, and the little Mexican carefully held the lantern so that it showed the blood on the old man's tangled hair.

'Señor, the tall one hit him with the barrel of his revolver, and he laughed!'

Rocklin squatted down, remembering how they had laughed. 'Went right to sleep,' the deputy had said. He thought, *Fourflushers, hell!* Dave's other names for them were more accurate. And while tussling they had seemed friendly. 'Don't hurt him!' the deputy had said. Strong, proud men like Dave were at the mercy of such sneakiness.

Rocklin stood up. 'My little friend, do not tell anybody what happened. Let Stan think he fell and bumped his head. But now go in and tell Stan that I want him out here. This man has to be put to bed before I drive on.'

CHAPTER THREE

Under midnight starlight the town lay like a lot of low block-shaped shadows, and the horses, knowing the trip was over, wanted to lope. Rocklin gave them their heads, sure that they would go straight to the stage-company stables.

The night wind came down from the mountains with a faint chill, refreshing now, but it reminded Rocklin that his coat had blown away, and he noticed the many trees and thought, *Water!* Not wholly with approval. Water drew plows, fence posts, barbed wire.

Near the center of the town the horses turned to the right of the street and stopped where a lantern hung under a wide archway sign that curved overhead. He could smell the hay and horsy mustiness, and far back behind the buildings a horse nickered.

A sleep-weary figure shuffled out of the darkness, unhooked the lantern, and, seeing Rocklin alone on the seat, called, 'Where's Dave?'

'He had an accident over at Stan's Place. Some women wanted to come on.'

'A wonder he didn't drive anyhow; bein'

drunk don't stop him.'

Old Miss Martin opened the door, put out her head. The stiff bonnet was over to one side and she was probably boil-sore, but she wasn't licked yet and she asked, as if looking for trouble, 'This isn't the hotel?'

'No'm, lady,' said the stableman.

'Where is it?'

'Up the street a piece – the best un.'

'And are we expected to wander about at this time of night, carrying heavy bags?'

The stableman lifted the lantern to her face. 'Well, now, I reckon not.' To Rocklin: 'You want to drive the ladies on up? Just a whoop and a jump.'

'No. I want a room, but not at the best hotel. I'll take my war bag and leave the saddle. Where's the best chance for a room close by?'

'See on the corner across the street down yonder – the saloon? Rooms there over the Sun-Up. Ask the barkeep.'

Rocklin reached back from the seat and unlashed the valise that he had called the war bag. As he stepped down he could hear the old lady saying in a lowered voice, as if not wanting her gentleness overheard, 'Wake up, Clara. We have arrived. Come, wake up, child!'

The bartender turned from the poker game he was watching and met Rocklin before the

40

bar. He was a tall, strangely expressionless and nearly bald man who moved with a jerky stringhalt gait, and the valise let him guess, 'You come on the stage? We heard it go by.' His voice was flat, his face blank as his palm. 'Like a room?'

'And a drink.' Rocklin set the valise on the bar and glanced at the players – four men, one much younger than the others and cheerfully noisier and with too much finery for Rocklin's liking. A wide silver band was on his hat, and he had a calfskin vest and a silk handkerchief; the gun he wore was pearl-handled. *Spoiled kid,* Rocklin guessed. The others looked like ordinary, all-right people. A lot of chips were on the table, most likely as dimes or less.

The bartender put out bottle and glass. 'Who come in with you?'

Rocklin tipped the bottle, not filling the glass. 'A Miss Caldwell and aunt, of the Caldwell ranch. Dave stayed on at Stan's; that's why we are late.'

'Judge Garley was saying she'd be in the next day or two. And so Dave got drunk this trip, hm? Seems a shame.' The 'shame' ran along the bartender's thoughts and came out with, 'That's Clint Harolday over there. The young un.'

'Dave had his row with him?'

'No, with the Old Man. And Miss Arly. Sure bad luck to quarrel with that girl!'

41

Rocklin said, 'I'm ready for bed.'

The bartender walked jerkily to the end of the saloon and pulled a dangling cord. He came back and pointed overhead. 'That rings a bell up in Mrs Bruce's room. Go out and round the side. You'll see stairs and she'll be waiting. Night.'

It was a railed outside stairway with a landing before the door. Mrs Bruce, fat and with sleep-swollen face, waited in a faded wrapper with a lamp in her hand. Gray hair fell loosely down her back, and she was barefooted and peered without friendliness. 'Night or week?'

'Not sure. Week, mebbe.'

'Three dollars. You can have a front room.'

Rocklin closed the door of his room and sniffed at the stale air. The patch of old carpet in the center of the room looked mange-eaten. Not that he cared. He rolled up his sleeves and turned to the pitcher in the washbowl; it was empty, and gritty dust had rimmed the pitcher's bottom.

The windows were down and struggled to keep him from raising them; then he squatted to lean on the sill and suck in the night's coolness. He was tired, all right, but suddenly not sleepy, and hazy thoughts jiggled any way they would. Dave with blood on his head and why. He didn't know but guessed that had been a hell of a long way for a K C cow to go and get skinned; probably other cows had been driven on. No doubt of it, they had planted the hide on Stan, most likely to let that deputy make an arrest and show up good. Stan could be made to talk, of course; and Brotherton would know what to do when told; and that high-nosed old lady would change her tune when she found out what rustling meant. If Brotherton wasn't honest, that girl would lose hair, hide, and horns. A pretty girl, just barely full grown and sadly gentle. He thought, *Anybody would be sad with that old woman on your neck!*

Rocklin was dust-grimed and felt sticky; also he wanted a big drink of water. For no reason at all he thought of Miss Harolday's saddle and wondered if she were the 'Miss Arly' who brought bad luck to a man in a quarrel. He thought bitterly, *They bring worse luck when they say they love you!* Judith was so fresh in his mind that the memory of her still bled, and he wondered how a man could be such a fool. *No more, ever!* he resolved. His mouth was dry to his tongue's root, and he meant to get a drink and wash up if he had to go clear back to the stable. Plenty of water there. But he would ask downstairs in the saloon.

Rocklin showed his hands to the bartender, who was again watching the game. 'I'm looking for water.'

'Go right around back of the bar, help yourself. Towels on a shelf there at the end.'

43

Then a small, weather-beaten man at the poker table tossed a hand toward the ceiling. 'Mister, there's a barrelful up there, but Maw Bruce forgot to tell you. I live up there.' His name was Gene Dyer, and he was a prospector who had crawled afar over mountains, groping with tap-tap-tap of hammer for the hiding-places of gold and silver. A fall had lately broken his leg, and he now walked with a cane and had the unhappy dread of a perpetual limp.

The coal-oil lamp that hung from the ceiling on a chain had a cone shade that spread the yellow glow over the players' faces. One of the players was a graybeard, Pap Fossler. His hard-working boys ran the Emporium, and the old man stole pocketfuls from the candy bucket for kids and lost sleep in poker games.

Sam Haynes, who ran the feed-and-grain part of the Emporium, was on Pap's right, and he yawned, thinking of 6 a.m. 'We waded out too deep tonight, Pap. Got not only our feet but our shirttails wet! You,' he told Clint Harolday, 'must be catchin' your rabbits in a new corner of the graveyard!'

Haynes turned toward Rocklin, who had paused after washing to look on. 'Set in, mister. Mebbe another hand'll change the run.'

Clint urged in strident eagerness, 'Come on in!'

44

Rocklin estimated the money on the table; the game's stiffness was beyond beans, and he was thinking how much better he would feel if he could say to Jim Brotherton, 'here is all your money back.' Probably he couldn't make it, but he asked, 'Who is banking?'

'Me,' said Gene Dyer welcomingly, and he shifted his seat to reach back and hook his cane's curve on the rung of a chair, dragging it up. Rocklin sat down and gave Gene a five-dollar gold piece.

'New blood,' said Sam Haynes, whose round brown face glowed with good nature. He looked at his watch. 'I'll just about get to bed in time to get up.'

Rocklin played poker as if he knew how, and he was hard to figure; he seldom called but either dropped out or raised, and his raises were stiff, and sometimes he was bluffing.

The time came when Clint, playing a pat hand, raised more than Rocklin's stack, and Gene Dyer said, 'Table stakes, Clint.'

'Not if he wants to dig!'

Rocklin dug, raising. Clint called and found his flush topped by king high, and he slammed his cards, squirmed in his chair, sullenly recounted his diminished chips.

An hour later Pap Fossler was dealing, tiredly. Sam Haynes, with a week's salary on the table, went out, leaned back, stretched his arms, said, 'By rights, I oughta be lucky in love!' Rocklin and Clint were battling before the draw, and Gene Dyer, whipsawed, tossed in his cards. 'No place for a cripple, Pap.'

'Ner a granddad,' said Pap, throwing away his hand. 'Wisht I was in bed.'

Rocklin, to the left of Pap, said, 'One,' and got it. Clint lifted a finger, also said, 'One,' and was tense about it. Pap yawned and fumbled Clint's card over; it fell face up – a queen. A gleeful look came like something splattered on Clint's face as he put it into his hand.

Rocklin studied Clint, then said quietly, 'Don't you know that queen is dead?'

Clint said challengingly, 'I can take it if I want it.'

'Sure, if you want; but you'll have to beat my hand with four cards.'

There was a hot look in Clint's eyes. 'I'm playing these, mister!'

Rocklin glanced inquiringly along men's faces, and Sam Haynes turned to the bartender with: 'How about it, Cap?'

Cap spoke tonelessly. 'I'm not settin' in.'

'Yeah, but what's what in a case like this?'

Cap said, 'Ask Pap; he's played enough poker.'

Pap stroked his beard, shook his head. 'I've seen men take or refuse a turned-over card, just as they liked.'

'That goes for me!' said Clint, and shoved

in chips, betting. He was excitedly betting out of turn, for he had a way of losing his head when stirred up. 'Call or get out, you!'

Rocklin's eyes crossed the table, went by Haynes, studied the bartender accusingly. Cap pretended not to notice. Then Rocklin looked inquiringly at Gene Dyer, and Gene shook his head. 'I never read a poker book.' Sam Haynes reached out to suggest, 'Why don't you split the pot?' He knew the Harolday temper and sensed the hardness of Rocklin, and his own unquarrelsomeness had soothed many a wrangle.

Rocklin said, 'He's playing only four cards, but I'll split.'

Bad temper flared in Clint's face and he made the chips bounce with a fist blow. 'Split, hell! I've bet my hand. Are you calling?'

Rocklin paused to say, 'No.' Then as Clint reached out with arms extended to pull the chips toward him Rocklin added, 'I'm raising – and you are playing four cards unless you pitch that queen and draw another.'

Haynes protested, 'Now listen, boys–' but no one heard him. Clint was raising back, nervously shoving in all of his chips. Rocklin said 'Dig!' and upped the bet. Clint dug, bringing up silver from his pocket and not enough. He called shakily at Cap, 'Let me have some money!' Cap scratched gingerly with a fingernail behind his ear and shook

47

his head. 'Sam?' Clint demanded, but Sam Haynes showed empty hands. 'You, Pap?' Clint begged. 'I'm good for it – you know I am!' Pap said, 'You better cool off, Clint.' Then Clint looked at Gene Dyer, but Gene spoke first. 'You're in deep enough.'

After that there was nothing Clint could do but glare at Rocklin and tell him, 'I've called for all I've got.' He spread his cards. 'Full house!'

'No good,' said Rocklin with unsmiling quietness. 'Kings up. Your third queen is dead.' He laid out his hand, spreading it to show kings and eights, then raked for the chips.

Clint lurched up out of his chair, making it skitter back and overturn. Pap's old eyes stretched wide as he gasped, 'You damn fool – put that gun down!' It was leveled at Rocklin's head. Gene jumped up to clutch for Clint's arm, but the lame leg turned under his weight and he grabbed stumblingly at the chair's back to keep from falling. Sam Haynes yelled, 'Don't do it, Clint!' and rolled sidewise out of his chair, slipping to a knee, then got up and started around the table, his voice anxiously too high to be soothing. 'Now, Clint! Clint!'

Clint shouted, 'Keep back from me!' The revolver was cocked. 'I'll learn him something about poker!' Clint was blind mad; old-timers knew the Haroldays were like that from their mother. 'You, Mister Smart Stranger! Get away from that table – get your hands up, you–' Clint used names it was hard for a man to take.

Cap had moved back on stringhalt legs. 'I wouldn't talk that way, Clint!' he said, as if trying to show excitement and failing, and he wasn't looking at Clint; he had his eyes on Rocklin.

Clint's voice went up so high it almost cracked, and he told Rocklin, 'Get the hell out of here! Maybe from now on you'll know a full house beats two pair, fourflusher!'

Rocklin hadn't said a word and didn't now, and his hands were palms out, shoulder-high, and his look was steady. His face was tired to the bone and he had the tenseness of a stubborn man, but he moved deliberately, stepping back three or four times, then he dropped his hands and turned and left the saloon. He didn't look back and he didn't hurry.

Clint's hand trembled as he holstered the gun. Anger always did that to him. 'No man can run a bluff on me!' He wanted approval, and their faces were solemnly not approving.

Pap Fossler summed up with a grave: 'He wasn't armed. And you mighta killed a man – over cards!'

'Cash me in!' Clint told Gene Dyer as if mad at him.

Cap said, 'I don't like to tell men how to play cards unless I'm settin' in, but I mebbe ought've spoke up. That queen was dead. And you, Clint, you'd better be out of here when he comes back.'

'Comes back? How'd you know?'

'He's the kind,' Cap said wearily.

Less than ten minutes later Cap, behind the bar, stiffened awkwardly in a look between men's heads toward the door. Cap's flat voice droned ominously, 'There he is – back!'

Clint splashed down the whisky glass that was halfway to his mouth and turned as if jerked about, then his hand started for his hip but it stopped waist-high and dangled on a loose wrist like something forgotten.

Pap Fossler sounded breathlessly weary. 'He's got him a gun!'

The gun was low on Rocklin's thigh in a greasy black holster, and buckskin thongs from the holster's tip were knotted below the new pants-leg knee.

Sam Haynes, last in line at the bar, started forward to get between the men, but Gene's cane bore his weight in a long step and he caught Sam's shoulder. 'Don't be crazy!'

Rocklin walked in with his hands down, stopped some ten feet before Clint, and hooked his thumbs at his belt; he waited as if words were not going to be needed. His shoulders were high and straight, and he had the same look in coming back armed that he had had in going away under Clint's gun. When he saw that nothing was to be said, Rocklin spoke. 'I've come for my pot.' His voice was almost, but not quite, mild; and the smoldering blue eyes were not mild. They were hard-spoken; they said, 'Give it up or shoot it out!' He meant what his eyes said.

Clint choked up, angered and unnerved. He had a temper that could flare into furious recklessness, but Rocklin's unspoken warning was dampening, so that though anger reddened Clint's face it set nothing inside of him on fire. The vanity that caused him to wear fancy fixin's made him seek for a way out that would not be crawling, so he jerked his thumb backward across his shoulder and told Rocklin, 'Cap there – Cap is an old gambler – he says you were right. I didn't know, b-but I thought – and I was mad as hell and haven't any sense when I'm mad!' A vain little smile implied that the frank admission ought to make everything all right, have even a pardoning commendation.

Rocklin didn't see it that way, and he did not like the woman-faced softness of this man, the womanish way of half begging to be admired for faults, so he just went on waiting. Clint's eyes roved to men's faces, but nobody spoke up for him, then with

51

sulky slowness he drew money from his pocket and put it down on the bar.

He was dry-throated and rubbed his lips with his tongue before he could say, 'There it is!'

He moved away as Rocklin stepped up and gathered the money, dropping it into his pocket; then Rocklin said, 'I'm sorry it had to be in a friendly game.' He seemed mostly speaking to Pap Fossler. 'Night.'

As their eyes followed his back they saw that it was no longer night; the beginning of daylight whitened the doorway. Then they straggled out, leaving Clint at the bar, staring sullenly down his nose.

He rapped the bar with his knuckles. 'Whiskey, Cap.'

Cap put down the glass and bottle then ran the bar cloth back and forth.

Clint, pouring his drink, said, 'I wonder who that fellow is?'

Cap was walking down the bar, rubbing as he went. 'Tag on the valise said "Ken Rocklin."'

Clint's hand gave a startled twitch that splattered whisky, and he put the bottle down and took hold of the bar like a man getting his breath back; then he gulped the whisky and went out, hurrying.

CHAPTER FOUR

Clint crossed the street as if about to break into a run. A freighter with a dry axle dragged through the morning coolness, heading for the Emporium's alleyway, and the screech of the axle cut whiplike on Clint's ears. A couple of drowsy-eyed nesters, already in from the Flats with truck to sell and trade, lounged toward the Honeycomb for breakfast, and they clumped aside to let Clint pass and both grinned, thinking Old Man Harolday's boy was drunk. He went by the stage-company stables without looking aside. The night lantern still hung there, burning with a faded-out flame.

A Chinaman was swabbing the hotel entrance with a mop that was too big for his bucket, but nobody else saw Clint go by and up the stairs. He turned to the right in the dim upstairs-hall and knocked on the last door, front. He knocked furtively at first, then louder, and a voice grumbled, 'Who is it?'

When the door opened to a peek width Clint blurtingly whispered, 'Judge, that Rocklin – he's here! In town! I just had to tell you!'

Garley, called 'Judge,' did not say anything right then but opened the door, letting Clint in as if he didn't want him to come. The room was dark because the curtains were drawn to keep the sun out of a late sleeper's eyes.

Clint's voice was nervous, low, hurried, as if he didn't have much time and was afraid he might be overheard. 'The Caldwell girl come last night, but you expected her. He was on the same stage, and if that girl talked to him—'

Garley had a worried frown as he pulled a curtain aside. 'She don't know anything to talk about.' He sounded as if that were something favorable but not enough, then asked, 'Where's your father?'

'Over to the west ranch, but he's coming in this morning early.'

Garley was a big man, now in a long scallop-bottomed nightgown and sleep-frowzy, and his deep voice was deeper with morning huskiness. Men called him 'Judge' because he had the manner, wore a long black coat, had an air of amiable pomposity, drank and gambled in the way of manly good-fellowship, and was a good poker player. Politicians had stolen the county seat from Santa Inez and taken it over to Garden City when Garden City was a boom town, so there wasn't a great deal of legal business here; but Garley had made a living, though not quite

54

so good a living as since Red Caldwell's death. The Caldwell will named him executor and administrator.

Clint told how it was, dropping his words uneasily, and his fingers wandered about his chin, moved to the calfskin vest, plucked at buttons. 'Last night... Sun-Up ... poker ... tag on the valise...'

Garley scowled as he listened, and after a time he said stolidly, 'Well, set down, Clint. Have a drink?'

Garley poured a stiff eye opener, and Clint took a small one, and they drank in silence. Garley crossed to the rumpled bed and sat down on the edge. The tumbler was empty, but he held it and looked into it as if trying to read something that was not quite legible. He continued to hold the glass while he ran a hand around the back of his full neck, working at a slight headache. He had gone to bed late.

Clint sat on the edge of the chair and wiped at his face with the handkerchief about his neck, and the scratchy rasp of the silk on his overnight whiskers stirred shivers. He watched Garley with intent anxiousness, and the silence was something that hurt. Then Clint ventured, 'Judge, do you think Brotherton will – will talk?'

Garley lifted his head with a listening look, as if he had heard a sound that alarmed him, and a sly hardness lurked in his eyes.

55

'I'm afraid so.' He replaced the tumbler on the bedside stand. 'I thought I'd talked Brotherton out of damn foolishness.'

Clint's lips were dead dry and the words were a husky whisper. 'What can be done, Judge?'

Garley took up the tumbler, drained out the last drop, replaced it on the stand. 'Rocklin, you mean?' Clint nodded jerkily, and Garley said, 'All we can do is hope.'

Clint guessed at what kind of hope was meant, and he dropped forward with knees to elbows, fumbled his fingers together, looked at his fingers, and with a mumble said, 'He's quarrelsome.'

Garley scratched below his knee through the nightgown but watched Clint with the look of a man peering from ambush. 'Meaning?' He knew what Clint meant, but there was a satisfaction in getting it out into words, as if something spoken of plainly was that much nearer accomplishment.

Clint dodged around plain speaking with: 'There's Wally and the Clews boys – Jager, I mean. He's out of prison and is coming back. I was just thinking mebbe this Rocklin might have a run-in with them.' Clint fidgeted. 'You've been awful lucky. Mebbe you'll have some more luck like when somebody waylaid Red Caldwell.'

Garley staringly considered that, not quite sure of just how much Clint knew or guessed; then Garley nodded a little and said, 'Yes. Red had so many enemies there's no telling which one laid for him.' After that Garley rubbed at the back of his neck and pondered, then said, 'Right now it's Brotherton more than anybody that can make trouble. This Rocklin don't know who he is – yet. There's nobody that'll tell him but Brotherton. And if he's never told he'll be just another cowboy looking for a job.'

Clint started to say something but stopped with a startled look, listening.

Boot heels had thumped rapidly down the hall and came to a stop before the door, and knuckles now beat a lively drumming. The voice was quick and merry.

'Hi, Judge! Judge, wake up there! I hear the Caldwell girl's come, so I rode in! Open up!'

That was Jim Brotherton.

Garley opened the door with hand extended. 'Come right along in, Jim. I already have a caller!'

Small, wizened, lively Jim Brotherton stamped in and eyed Clint with surprise and long-nurtured disdain. His 'Mornin', Clint' was cool and abrupt. Brotherton detested Old Man Harolday, and for the past couple of years Harolday had morosely sneered at 'Judge' Garley, who had beat him in a few small lawsuits, though the loss of a dollar was never small to Harolday. Brotherton wondered what Clint was doing here and gave Garley a look that said so; then he turned to the whisky, helping himself.

Garley cleared his throat and seemed rather amused. 'Clint here has had a misunderstanding with a friend of mine, Jim. Funny to have a Harolday come to me for help, ain't it?'

Brotherton said, 'Good likker, Judge.'

Garley said to Clint in a tone that was unpromising, 'You go along now, and I'll see what I can do to smooth things for you.' He opened the door, and Clint went out, weary, unnerved, frightened. Garley closed the door and looked at it and shook his head and sounded regretful. 'From what I hear, Clint is mixing up with the wrong kind of fellows, Jim.'

'Hell, he's rotten spoiled. You seen the girl, Judge?' Brotherton spoke quickly and eagerly. 'That Dep' Sheriff Jackson run into Lee Frank over at Injun Wells, and Lee come hoppin' in all the way back to the ranch to tell me. What's she like, Judge? Purty? My boys'd like to have as purty a boss as the Santee, only' – Brotherton's lined old face curled into laughter wrinkles – 'we don't want one with such a temper! You've seen her?'

'Yes; take a chair, Jim. Yes, I was playing poker in the bar when she arrived last night. She and a companion. Aunt. They were too tired to talk. She appears to be an attractive young lady.'

Brotherton tossed his hat down beside a chair but did not sit. He was a talkative, frank, honest little old man, not very smart – so Garley thought – but meddlesome, damn meddlesome. He rattled on. 'Judge, you sure are right about her not bein' one to run a ranch!' He chuckled but was vexed, too. 'From how Jackson told it to Lee Frank, she wouldn't let him arrest that God-blasted worse'n worthless Stan after they found a K C hide. Said it was one of her cows! Folks from the East don't know much! Why, Arly Harolday would've put a rope on Stan's shypoke neck her own self and drug him to the nearest cottonwood! At least, nobody be surprised if she done it! Get into your long-tailed coat and let's get some breakfast. I rode off before the boys were up and ain't et.'

Garley got into undershirt and trousers and let the suspenders dangle as he stood before the washbowl, then bunched thick lather over his face and stropped the razor.

Brotherton turned about restively, talking of this and that, now and then looking out of the window and down the street where the town people had begun to sift about, all of whom he knew by their first names.

Brotherton pointed from the window with one of the judge's cigars that he had taken

59

from a box and lit. 'There's old Juan, so Miss Arly is in town. I thought she was stayin' out to Santee. Clint's no good, an' the Old Man is worse, but I allus more than halfway liked that girl.'

Garley brought the razor with gentle scrapes down his full jaw, leaned close to the mirror, spoke into the mirror. 'By the way, Jim, what did you ever do about that – what was his name? The man from Tahzo. Rock something.'

'He'll come.' Brotherton walked over near Garley and pitched the fresh-lit cigar into the washbowl, then began a cigarette in his nimble brown fingers. 'I sent money, care of Mel Milton.'

Garley turned from the mirror reproachfully. 'You never told me, Jim.'

'Told you I was goin' to. What I say, I do.' A match flared before the cigarette. 'Mel Milton wrote me back that Rocklin had a tough job to do and would come as soon as he got through.' Brotherton's voice hardened quietly and his small, quick eyes drove at Garley's large face. 'Don't you do any law-doodlin' till I've had my chance. That all clear, Judge?'

Garley wiped the razor on a strip of newspaper, stropped back and forth, spoke gravely. 'What you are up to is the next thing to illegal, Jim.'

'Law be damned. What's right is all I care

60

about. I told you once that Red never forgive himself for the fallin'-out he had with his sister when she married that ex-army man, Rocklin, and settled in Tahzo. She died quick, and Red allus grieved, stubborn. She named the boy Kenneth, which was her way of tellin' Red she wanted to be friends. And he hungered for the boy and talked about havin' him come out and work – just to see if he was a proper Caldwell. Tahzo's a long way off, but Red heard things that pleased him.'

Garley expostulated, 'But, Jim, due process of law and respect for the dead and–'

Brotherton said, 'Don't argy! I know what Red wanted in his heart. So you got to give me a chance to get Ken Rocklin out here, put him to work, look him over, try him out. From what I hear, he don't bounce in the saddle. If he measures up to what I know old Red would want – law or no law! – he's goin' to have him a share of the ranch. In that case, he can run 'er, and there'll be no call for you to sell it. And if you try to stop me, I'll go over to the district court with him and lay my cards on the table for a showdown, and I'll win and you know it.'

'But, Jim, listen to reason, please.'

'But if it happens he don't stack up like he ought, I'll just fire him and he'll never so much as know Old Red was his uncle. Nobody as I know of knows that but you an' me!'

61

'How the devil can you be so sure of that?'

'His father never told him; he hated Old Red, grim. And who else knew? Now listen, Judge. You're smarter'n I am, and that's fine and dandy, but I'm goin' to have it my way. That all clear?'

Garley's hand grew so unsteady at the shaving that he nicked his cheek.

After breakfast Brotherton walked with Garley down the street. 'Mornin', Jim. Mornin', Judge,' was called from doorways and sidewalks across the street. The judge, in a long black coat, raised his hand with amiable dignity, but Brotherton briskly asked after men's wives, children, rheumatism.

They met Harolday – tall, gauntly broad-shouldered, with a forward droop as if always peering ahead with a glassy stare, always walking with his hands behind his back,. Moneymaker and moneylender, secretive and friendless, coldly shrewd, and patiently far-thoughtful; and, so far as was known, if he took chances they had the risk calculated into a margin of safety, for he was thorough and methodical. He said, 'Mornin', Jim,' indifferently, and looked hard at Garley as they passed.

Garley looked straight ahead, avoiding the flint-gray eyes.

Brotherton gestured backhandedly. 'What good's his money? The boy's no good, so all

62

he's got's the girl – and she ain't his! She's like her mother, and her mother was hell-fire in skirts. Fire is kinda purty at that if you don't get too close! Foreigner of some kind and would ride sidesaddle 'stead of clothes-pin style. Allus rode as if tryin' to break her neck and one day did. Wasn't afraid of the devil and used her quirt on some fellows, she did. Arly's the same.'

Garley said, 'Yes, yes,' absently, having heard of Mrs Harolday for years. Men re-membered her as they might have remem-bered an unusual storm, and some of the older residents still wondered at times why, as a well-fixed widow with a baby and good ranch, she married Harolday. 'See you at dinner, Jim. Miss Caldwell ought to be up by then.'

Garley left him at the stairway leading up to his office above Brunsig's clothing store. He went up the steep stairs slowly, thinking of Rocklin, hoping that Brotherton wouldn't learn he was in town. He was afraid of Brotherton's meddlesomeness, and he sighed heavily on the stairs, for he was a big man and short of breath and had worry on his shoulders.

He reached his office, dropped into a padded chair, and slowly fanned his face with his wide black hat; then he put the hat down, got up sluggishly, and reached as high as he could to the top of the bookcase.

The pint bottle was nearly empty. He drank, scrouged up his face, wiped his mouth with a wadded handkerchief, and put the bottle into his pocket for refilling; then he returned to his chair and mopped his face and breathed heavily.

The memory of how Red Caldwell had stormed up these stairs and into the office was over seven months old, but it could still make Garley's knees weaken and shake.

Caldwell had been high-shouldered with a face of bronze and eyes that blazed when he was mad; but he was good company when he liked a man, and he had liked Garley after Garley had a falling out with Harolday and beat him in some lawsuits over collateral. So when the lawyer Caldwell had used for many years drank himself to death Caldwell turned to Garley, and Garley, being the new broom, put Caldwell's affairs into shape and had drawn up a new will. Three thousand dollars went to Jim Brotherton, and the residue to Miss Clara Caldwell, of Danvers, Massachusetts, a distant and orphaned relative whom Caldwell never forgot because her grandfather had been good to him as a boy. Old Red was like that; he never forgot and he never forgave.

That day, over seven months ago, when Caldwell came through the door Garley unsuspectingly got up to welcome him; but without a word Caldwell shoved him aside and jerked at a small drawer. It was locked.

Caldwell turned on him. 'Garley, I've just found something at the post office that makes me want to see the inside of this drawer! Open it!'

Garley trembled in sickened protest, for he knew then what Caldwell expected to find and would find, but under the staring fury of Caldwell's eyes he moved in the helplessness of dread, fitted the key, opened the drawer.

It was a drawer from which Caldwell had at times seen Garley take a sealed pack of playing-cards when a friendly game was played here in the office. Packs of sealed playing-cards still lay there. Each pack had a playing-card glued to the outside to show the design of the backs inside. Caldwell studied the designs for a long minute, then ripped open a pack and examined the new cards. He straightened up and with full swing of arm splattered the cards against Garley's face.

'You blackleg! Get out of this country! I'm going to Garden City, and if you are here when I come back–' He did not say what he would do, did not need to say, but turned on his heel, and the clatter of heels and spurs on the stairs, descending, came back like echoes of the warning, leaving Garley crushed and bewildered.

He had never been able to imagine what Caldwell could have learned through the post office, for he had never shared the secret of his marked cards with any man. They were fine glazed cards from a sporting-goods house in Chicago, and in various ways he had introduced them into games, but he was too clever to win always, and never felt in the least suspected. Now this!

Garley had gathered up his cards and brooded. He was no longer young and had had to tear his roots violently out of communities before because of certain unpleasant happenings; but now, at his age, and when everything was so snug and easy, he felt that he simply could not begin all over again among strangers.

Now there was no peace; that Caldwell girl had come in spite of his persuasions, and the meddlesome Brotherton had brought that Rocklin, and Brotheron's story, if he made up his mind to tell it, would win in any cattle-country court. Moreover, Garley knew that the old federal judge, in the district court over at Garden City, didn't look upon him with any great amount of favor.

So now Garley sat and sighed with an empty bottle in his pocket, and he rubbed and rubbed at the back of his neck, for the headache persisted.

Jim Brotherton zigzagged across the street for half the morning, saying 'Hello' and 'Howdy.' He went to the Emporium post

66

office, but there was no letter from Rocklin; and he went back to the warehouse to say 'Howdy' to Sam Haynes, whose family had once owned a ranch alongside the Caldwell – Harolday owned it now. Haynes told about the poker game in the Sun-Up, but Haynes didn't have any idea who the stranger was.

Brotherton was eager to meet the Caldwell girl and get back to the ranch, so before noon he tramped back to the hotel, and he learned that the women had come down for breakfast then returned to their room.

The hotel proprietor took Brotherton up, saying at the door, 'Miz Martin, this is Jim Brotherton, manager of your ranch.'

'The name is *Miss* Martin and it is not my ranch!' said the old lady, standing tall and straight with her elbows pressed to her sides.

'Yes'm,' the hotel man agreed nervously. 'I'll just leave you, Jim.'

Clara smiled at Brotherton shyly and took his hand, and her voice was low and sweet, and his kindliness brought a happy look to her face. He liked her right off and said so, just that. 'I like you fine!' He was an undersized man, tough in the saddle and frank with honesty.

Old Miss Martin's pernickety snappishness didn't bother him, and he sat on the edge of a rocking chair with his hat on his knees, his toes pigeoning in, and answered

67

questions. Miss Martin sat stiffly before him with her hands clasped in her lap, her elbows squeezing her sides, and the way she talked made him think of somebody using a rifle; she was that quick and direct. Certainly, she said, they were going to the ranch, to live there! Accommodations couldn't be more uncomfortable than here, could they?

Brotherton thought of the old log-built, mud-stuffed, dirt-floor ex-bunkhouse and said, 'Yes'm!'

Miss Martin made stabbing gestures about the room – stuffy room with cracked and faded wallpaper, and a person across the hall that snored, and they hadn't come all this distance to sit down in a dingy hotel and wait – wait – wait– How long would they have to wait before the property came to Clara's hands?

She said, 'Clara's,' but Brotherton had a feeling that she meant 'my'; and he told her, 'You'll have to talk to the judge about all that. The judge has more say-so than me. He's even cut my payroll.'

Then she wanted to know if Clara should prefer to have the ranch sold or keep it. Brotherton squirmed and gazed at Clara. 'I dunno. I'd like to stay on an' run it for you, but I dunno. With nesters crowdin' in and all, about the only man that'd make an offer would be Harolday, and I know he wants it, but he could cheat the devil in a dice game

– and would! I c'd run it. I run it for Old Red for purt-near twenty years, but you're just a girl and from what I hear about you last night at Stan's Place–' He smiled reprovingly. Face to face with the sweet girl, he was a little disquieted by his plan to bring in that fellow Rocklin. One thing was now sure – Rocklin would have to be quite a bit more than merely all right! He said, 'You talk things over with the judge. He'll be up to see you at dinnertime, but I'm going home. The judge lives down the hall about two doors from you.'

Brotherton stood up, looked from the window, and pointed abruptly. 'There is a girl that could run the ranch – any ranch! She does run one; raises horses, mostly. Best horses in the country, too.'

Clara pressed near him and gazed enviously at the back of a girl on a high-headed horse that walked slowly. The girl was astride in divided skirts and she was straight-backed and her head was up; and even at a walk it seemed that girl, horse, and saddle were of the same stuff; proud stuff, too.

Clara exclaimed softly, 'I wish I were like that!'

'Pooh!' said Miss Martin.

Brotherton said, 'She rides the best horses in the country but won't kill 'em like her mother did. She's Arlette Harolday. Folks call her "Arly." Mother was a foreigner of some kind. She never acted happy, and Arly don't, either, but *proud* don't tell the half of it; and if she's scairt of anything it ain't showed up in our part of the country – yet.'

CHAPTER FIVE

Rocklin was awakened by a knocking on the door, and he slid from the bed and opened the door a little, peering around the edge, for he was in underwear.

Mrs Bruce stolidly asked, 'Is your name Rocklin?' and he said yes, and she told him, 'Man here to see you.'

The man was the skinny Bob Clews who had been at Stan's Place, and he moved from behind the landlady, grinning. Rocklin's face stiffened with dislike, but Bob asked, 'Can I come in?' Mrs Bruce shuffled off down the hall in loose slippers, and Bob came in with clatter of spurs. Rocklin closed the door, and Bob grinned and said, 'High-ee?' brightly.

Rocklin, remembering things, wasn't friendly. 'What is it?'

Bob had a pleased, congratulatory air. 'Was it you stirred up the natives in a poker game last night?'

Rocklin was thinking of Dave's blood-smeared head and said coolly, 'I played some

70

poker; why?'

'Guns wasn't dealt but they was drawed; you won!' Bob sounded gleeful. Rocklin's look was tightened to a gleam, but Bob didn't mind even if he noticed, and he said, 'What I come for is Judge Garley wants to see you.' Then Bob laughed. 'Oh, not about the game. He's only called "Judge," anyhow. I don't know what he wants, but he asked me to come and tell you. All-right feller, the judge is; you bet! Exe-cutor, or whatever you call it, for the Caldwell ranch, and mebbe wants to give you a job. Mebbe,' Bob guessed, leering, 'that purty Caldwell girl asked him that you be hired!'

'Where is the judge?' Rocklin's voice was hard and low-sounding.

'You go down to the corner and turn right, and his office is up over Brunsig's store.'

'I'll come.' Rocklin opened the door.

Bob said, 'What the hell you act mad about?' But Rocklin only flapped his hand, and Bob went, looking puzzled.

Rocklin turned to the wavy, cracked mirror, rasped his palm against his cheek, and decided against shaving. He had not concealed his name and had no wonder as to how it was known, and it was an easy guess that this Judge Garley had heard of him from Brotherton and wanted to talk. *Not under that old woman's high nose, I won't!* he told himself. He had brought in a pitcherful of

71

water from the barrel at the rear before going to bed and now scrubbed with gritty soap, dampening his hair, then took a comb from his valise.

Gun and belt hung on the bed headpost, and he thought of buckling them on but decided against that, as it would look a little too much like hunting trouble. He rolled the cartridge-studded belt around the revolver in its holster and snugged it down in the valise with underwear, spurs, shirts, razor, and other traps.

He had counted his money last night and still didn't have enough to pay off Brotherton; not even, he figured, with the chips that had been left unbet when Clint Harolday's gun lifted him out of the chair. He ought to have asked Gene Dyer about them when he went back, but hadn't thought.

As he stamped into his tight handmade boots and drew the pants legs down over the tops he thought, *I'll write Mel Milton to send me some money so I can pay off and come home.*

He stepped out into the midday sunlight and trailed his hand on the railing as he went down the outside stairs, then he started along the side of the Sun-Up for the corner.

A woman on a horse turned the corner slowly. Beautiful horse. The girl's horse stood high on slim legs, was small-headed, deep-chested, and carried the neck in a proud arch with ears forward in lively interest. When he

72

saw that the girl was looking steadily at him he pulled his eyes away and set them straight before him.

Suddenly the girl jumped the horse across the street and, with restive beat of forefeet on the boardwalk, she angled her horse's head and shoulder before him, barring the way.

He stopped, scowled up, not knowing what to think and not liking it, especially not liking the way three or four men near the corner had stopped and were watching.

Her eyes examined him from boots to white hat, and her mouth had the look of tasting something she didn't like. 'You are that man Rocklin?'

Her right side was toward him. She was straight in the saddle, and a skirt of brown corduroy flowed over her leg. The boot was plain, high, and soft black leather, and the small spur looked like silver. He saw it all and more, with the gathering look of one who could read earmarks and fading brands on the run. A plain wide dark belt was about her waist, and the brown shirt was full and would flutter when she loped. She wore gloves without cuffs, a quirt hung from her wrist, and there was a flap holster over the saddle horn. Under her wide hat that had chin thongs her face was thin and very brown, but not a burned brown, for it had a gold color. She looked mad in an icy, disdainful way, and he wondered what the hell? The dark eyes were at once sharp and insolent, and hair that had been poked up under her hat crept out and curled.

He looked right at her, not replying except to put up his hand with no force and push the horse's head aside, meaning to pass. The horse was nervous but she held him steady.

'Are you?' she repeated, making it a demand; and her voice had a strong sound like the kind of music that gives a thrill without being loud, suggesting fierceness. Men were looking on and some were gathering in the side door of the Sun-Up not twenty feet away, and he wouldn't tell her that he was or was not Rocklin.

She asked again, 'Is your name Rocklin?' and men could overhear that her voice had an insulting sound. Her arm was straight down with the quirt dangling, and he sensed that it wouldn't take much to make her swing it. *Crazy or what?* He couldn't even begin to guess and he would not ask, but he knew that he was in a tight place and helpless, for no man could live down the laughter and jeers of other men if a woman used her weakness to bully him before onlookers. When a woman wanted to horsewhip you there was nothing for it but to run, knock her down, or stand and take it; each about equally humiliating. He gazed back steadily but would not answer.

Then she said, quietly fierce, 'Rocklin, I want that money you took from my brother!'

He knew then who she was, remembering the bartender's remark that it was bad luck to quarrel with her; and he could see why. But that gave him something to say and he said it, staringly. 'You can go to hell!'

'You took it at the point of a gun and–'

She stripped the glove off her right hand and moved the hand toward the flap of the saddle holster. She did it unhurriedly, letting him see what she was about, and he did not know whether or not she would pull the gun, but he would not grab at her hand. Her deliberateness looked like a bluff that was being played slowly to give him time to think it over, weaken, knuckle under, but he wasn't sure, and there was a dogged hardness in him that tightened down. His look was as mean as hers and he was mad, too, and he would not be bluffed, not by a girl, not on a street with men watching. She raised the flap and drew the revolver; it was a small dark gun that fitted her hand, and she leveled it within two feet of his head.

'–and I am taking it back at the point of a gun!' Her lip curled in faint scorn, and certainty was on her face, and contempt, too.

He would not duck and he would not grab, so he looked at the gun, looked at her, and looked away as he reached out slowly and gathered the bridle reins close up to the bit under the horse's jaw, and he did not jerk but pulled with upward reach of arm, raising the horse's head. Then he passed under and by.

Something bewildered flickered across her eyes, and she looked quickly at the gun, as if to see what was wrong with it; then her eyes flashed as she reined the horse back from the sidewalk and she rode up alongside of him and cried, 'Stop! You! Stop or I'll kill you!'

He turned his head, not stopping, and told her, 'Go ahead!'

'You think because I'm a woman that I won't shoot!'

He was looking at her over his shoulder and moving on as he said, 'I think because you are a woman that you will – in the back!'

Then his back and the back of his head, too, were toward her, and he walked on with unhurrying teeter of toes and clack-clack of high heels. Rage blazed on her face. Her small jaw tightened and she seemed trying to pull the trigger and couldn't, not at a man's back, not after he had said she would – in the back.

She pulled the horse about and rode off at a canter. Her tight-set face was flaming red and her teeth were locked, and her eyes were blurred with a film like the beginning of tears. Suddenly she drove in the spurs and cut down with the whip, and the horse lunged as if thrown into the air, and she rode wildly.

Rocklin roughly shouldered through the men grouped at the Sun-Up's side door. His back muscles ached from the strain of being braced against the impact of a bullet; he hadn't known whether or not she would fire and had not been guessing about it – he had merely been stubborn, but a command given from behind a gun was hard to ignore.

He went to the bar. Cap, changing shifts, was on duty again this noon. Rocklin said, 'Whisky,' and Cap merely nodded. There was no mirror behind the bar, and Rocklin looked straight into the bottles on the shelf.

Then a hand slapped Rocklin's shoulder familiarly and a loose, loud voice chuckled. 'You sure are some lucky, Rock! You bet!'

Rocklin faced about, knowing who it was before he looked, and as he looked he stepped back, measuringly, and let drive. Not a word, but everything he had of anger and weight was behind his knuckles, for his thought was, *You tricked me out on the street where the girl waited!* And there was also memory of the false friendliness toward old Dave. That was why his long arm straightened out with the snap of a bullwhacker's whip and cracked his fist into Bob Clews's face where nose and cheek met. Bob saw it coming and went bug-eyed as he threw back his head and tried to dodge and couldn't,

77

and he spilled off his legs. He hit the floor back down, and blood started out of his nose. For a moment he lay as if trying to sleep, then he began to scramble, crazy-mad, and his spurred feet kicked the floor, clawing to roll over and face about, and he was still on the floor when his hand fumbled for the gun's wooden butt. As he dragged it from the holster Rocklin jumped, and a pointed heel stamped down on Bob's wrist as on a snake's head, and Rocklin put his weight into the heel, grinding.

Rocklin stepped back, and Bob clutched the wrist. The hurt was like fire and burned clear up to his shoulder and splashed pain all through him, and he sat up and rocked back and forth with writhing weave. 'You broke it! You broke it, you—' Malignant fear gleamed through the pain.

Men looked on in the kind of silence that comes from being uneasy and not knowing why a suddenly violent thing has happened. The long-barreled revolver had spilled from Bob's holster and lay by him. Rocklin swung back his foot and kicked, and the gun skittered half across the saloon floor, hit a chair's leg, spun about.

Rocklin looked down at Bob, and the words dropped hard and clear. 'Try another trick like that on me and it'll be worse!'

Bob rocked forward with head down, hugging his wrist, and he groaned. 'I never played no trick! You broke my wrist, you–'

Men looked on, not pityingly, for they knew the Clews boys. The tall Cap rose on his toes to lean above the bar and stare at Bob, but he did not say anything. Bob got off the floor in hunched-over pain and stumbled to a chair and pressed his wrist against his stomach as he rocked back and forth.

Rocklin turned to the bar, took his drink, and went out; and as he passed, men studied his face and wondered that wrath could be so cold. He went back down the sidewalk toward the stairs, returning to his room.

Gene Dyer hesitated, then lurched forward with reach of cane, following through the door; and Rocklin heard him on the walk but would not look back. When the thump of the cane came along on the stairs he did stop and faced about inquiringly.

Gene said, 'There's some money comin' to you.' More than the look of a poker banker's meticulous repayment was in Gene's eyes, and he asked, 'Can I come with you? There's something you orta know.'

Rocklin tossed his hat to the unmade bed and pulled a chair about. 'Take a seat.' Gene sat down, favoring the leg. Rocklin drew tobacco and papers from his vest and held them forgetfully as he frowned with a vacant stare at the wall.

Gene said, 'The chips were mixed up on the table last night after the shindy, but I figger you had about ten dollars more'n Clint called. Does that fit in somewhere with your guess?'

Rocklin's glance crossed Gene's face and went on to the window. 'Less would be all right, too. Is that Harolday girl crazy or what?' He began the cigarette. Gene drew a pouch, plucked out a gold eagle, offering it. Rocklin didn't notice, but asked, 'Did she make it up or did somebody tell her that?'

Gene said, 'Tell her what?'

Rocklin put a match to the cigarette, shook it out, pitched the broken match away. 'She sent him up here to get me to come down on the street!'

Gene replied guardedly, as if not wanting an argument, 'Bob Clews? I don't think so.' Rocklin's eyes told him to go on. 'Here,' said Gene, offering the eagle again. Rocklin said, 'Thanks,' and took it. Gene put the cane upright between his knees and hung both hands on the curve. 'The Clewses – at least Jager, who's Bob's brother– are horse thieves, and she raises horses. She's mad because Jager's just been let out of the pen. So I bet Clint made up something, and she found you on the street, chance-like.'

'Mebbe so.'

'You've got some temper your own self,' said Gene mildly.

Rocklin shook his head. 'Only at women. And she's crazy.'

Gene said, 'She is queer. She won't let people like her. It's purt-near as if she didn't want people to like her. But she's purty. Everybody thinks she's purty.'

'I don't!' But Rocklin remembered her proudness, and the way she sat a horse, and the gold color on her face, and the hair that wouldn't stay under the hat, and the tawny eyes that looked right at you.

Gene cleared his throat. 'What I felt somebody orta tell you is that the Clews boys have got worse'n a bad name. So I'd be careful, awful careful!'

Rocklin turned from the window, not quite smiling. 'I am careful – that's why I hit him! I didn't want him to think he could get close to me by sneaky friendliness!'

While Rocklin was shaving, Mrs Bruce came in to do the room. She was dull of face, heavy, and her feet hurt, and that was why she shuffled about in loose slippers. Two or three times she appeared about to say something and changed her mind, for he had a brooding look that discouraged talk. She took up the slop pail and started out, then turned at the door. The pail was in one hand the other went to the knot on the top of her head, feeling for hairpins, and she said, 'Mr Dyer told me a little while ago what happened down there on the street this mornin' and why. The Harolday girl, poor thing, is proud and stuck-up and hot-headed, but once when old Harolday was sick I hired out to nurse him and she wasn't mean at all to me. All Haroldays are the unhappiest people in the country. There's that Clint, and if he's not quarrelin' with somebody he's sulkin' like a spoilt child or braggin' like a worse-spoilt un. But I thought mebbe I orta tell you to watch out or sure as shootin' she'll get even with you somehow. She sure will! Nobody ever got the best of her!'

Then Mrs Bruce hurried out and closed the door sharply.

Rocklin shook his head at the door. *They can't hurt you if you don't like them!* Then he buckled on his gun, tying the holster tip low down with buckskin thongs; he was not bothered by anything the girl could do to get even, but he was thinking of friends that Bob Clews might have. The deputy sheriff had seemed to be a friend, and that looked not so good; he knew from work in Tahzo that sometimes peace officers had dirty hands. And slow anger glowed in his mind over the way this Deputy Jackson had treated Dave. Rocklin liked the earthy solidness of old Dave and felt the kinship of the same breed, understandingly.

He went to the Honeycomb for dinner,

which was also his breakfast, and a scurrying waitress balanced rows of side dishes on her bare arm and scattered them before men at tables. Most of the men were earth-stained nesters with big, slow hands, and they stared at Rocklin but constrainedly avoided his eyes because he was a cowman and cowmen did not like them, but they liked what he had done to Bob Clews.

At the stage-company office Rocklin asked about his saddle. A flat-faced man in shirt sleeves with pink sleeve holders, and a pencil behind his ear, told him that it was all right and asked, 'Your name is Rocklin, I hear? Judge Garley and the Old Man, too, told me – oh, quite some time ago now – to be sure to let him know if your name was ever on the passenger list, but–'

'Old Man?'

'Harolday. But Dave had the list in his pocket, and I didn't know till I heard about you being in town.'

The agent began to grin with a look of over-friendliness, and Rocklin said matter-of-factly, 'At Garden City a man asked me to say for you to tell Miss Harolday that her saddle hadn't come.'

'Oh, and I hear you've already had a run-in with Clint and her, too!' The flat face grinned, inviting talk, but all at once the grin fled, for a shadow fell in the open door-way.

Old Man Harolday came in with a gaunt, broad-shouldered stoop and his hands behind his back. His trousers fitted loosely, as if he didn't have much flesh on his legs, and he had a kind of noiseless way of walking, with a calm air of trying to slip up on help and see what they were doing. He stood in the door and stared with flint-gray eyes at Rocklin.

'Mr Harolday, this is Rocklin,' said the agent, adjusting a sleeve holder.

Harolday said quietly, 'I judged so.' His eyes had the cold, appraising stare that a moneylender might give somebody who had asked for a loan, and there was no guessing at the thoughts behind their flinty glaze. Calmly and to the point he asked, 'Why did you and my boy have some trouble last night?'

Rocklin hesitated about telling him all the facts – that would have had a talkative sound – so he said, 'Poker,' and stopped.

As Harolday listened for something more he took one hand from behind him and twiddled the charm dangling on the watch chain across his vest, but even the twiddling was slow, nerveless, methodical; and when he saw that Rocklin was not going to say anything more he nodded as if satisfied and went to a ledger behind the high, sloping desk. But he looked up in peering scrutiny as Rocklin went out.

The agent, always eager to rub the Old Man's fur the right way, edged his tone with dislike and exclaimed, 'Acts like a purty bad fellow, Mr Harolday, don't he?'

Harolday, with no interest, inquired, 'Does he? I hadn't noticed.'

That was old Harolday's way; the agent knew you could never tell what he was thinking by what he said.

As Rocklin came before the barbershop a round-bellied man with *Marshal* on his vest rose slowly from the edge of the sidewalk where he was sitting and stepped on the walk to stop Rocklin. The marshal wasn't a bad fellow but a bit of a town joke because his roundness gave him a strut and he had a popeyed way of staring at people as if trying to scare them. 'Is your name Rocklin?'

Rocklin's look suspiciously took in the marshal's companion who also stood up, then he examined the marshal's face. It had the tight fatness of mumps. 'Are you looking for me specially?'

'Oh, no, not *specially* atall, only I like to meet ever'body. My name is Ager.' He ran a stubby finger along up to the star, making sure it would be noticed. 'They say Bob Clews's wrist is broke!'

'I'm not sorry,' Rocklin told him, as if to settle any doubts, then he went on.

The marshal's companion laughed, but the marshal said, 'I was goin' to tell him

Jager Clews has come to town and would be on his tail a-whoopin' for what he done to Bob!'

CHAPTER SIX

Rocklin paused at Brunsig's clothing store, thinking of a coat, but went on up the steep stairs, and a man at the top, who was starting down, told him, 'Garley? Right there up front. The door's open, and if the judge is out, go in and set.'

The judge was not in. Rocklin sat down and looked about. A black horsehair sofa was in a corner, and the end of the sofa was so close to the door that the open door would not swing back against the wall. A roll-top desk was littered with papers, and there was a table in the center of the room, and three or four chairs, one of them a rocker with high arms.

Rocklin heard old Miss Martin's sharp voice coming through the open door, but it was too late to avoid her; he was boxed in. She and Clara entered the office with Garley puffing behind them from the climb on the stairs. The old lady said stiffly, 'Well, how do you do, young man?' Clara looked at him pleasantly at first but, remembering yester-

86

day's rudeness, her eyes chilled and she turned away, for her hungering loneliness had pride.

Garley regarded the tall stranger amiably and asked, 'Your name, sir?'

'Rocklin. You sent for me.'

'Yes, oh, yes, Rocklin.' An uneasy shadow fell on his face and he mopped at the sweat to wipe off the uneasiness, and he looked keenly at Rocklin but smiled in a way that showed his big teeth.

When Miss Martin heard the name her neck stiffened with a backward jerk and she said, 'Ah!' sharply, then she tightened her lips as she looked Rocklin over, up and down, and her eyes brightened with cunning severity as she peered at Garley.

Rocklin said, 'I'll come another time, Judge.'

'Too bad I didn't know earlier that you were in town; Jim Brotherton was here. Set down a few minutes. You've come all the way from Tahzo. I believe you have met these ladies.'

Miss Martin raised the sights on her high-arched nose and shot a glance at him as if aiming at a vital spot, then she gave Garley a glaring look that disquieted him with its accusing directness. He had already learned that she could be difficult, but he dodged her eyes by moving the rocker. 'This,' he rumbled soothingly, 'will be comfortable.'

87

Miss Martin's thin mouth was set as tight as a healed knife slash, but her lips flashed, 'No, thank you! I prefer not to be comfortable! I find this is not a time and place for relaxation!'

Garley wadded his handkerchief against his forehead and peered askance as Miss Martin plumped herself down on a straight chair. Clara took the rocker and watched her aunt with a worried look that seemed begging to know, 'Now what on earth is the matter?'

Rocklin crossed the room and sat on the foot of the slick horsehair sofa that the open door touched. He rested his elbows on his knees and looked at Clara without really thinking about her. She was wearing a dark-blue dress that was ruffled at the hem, snug about the breast, with white lace at the collar and round cloth buttons down the front. Then he caught the old woman eyeing him from behind her web of wrinkles, and he met her stare unyieldingly.

Miss Martin said, 'How very clever!'

He hadn't the faintest idea of what she meant, but he said, 'Yes,' and could see that it made her furious.

Garley turned from his desk with a folded paper and tried a wide, urbane smile that did not spread very far. 'My dear Miss Martin, here—'

'I am not your dear-miss-anything, if you

please!' She ended the statement on a rising inflection that had the twang of a too-tight wire just before it breaks and backlashes dangerously. Then by a swift turn of eyes she caught Rocklin watching her from under lowered lids. 'You find it very interesting, don't you, Mr Rocklin?' The 'mister' was mostly a hiss.

He said, 'Yes,' dragging the word a little, and nodded, too, and was sure that she was wishing a look could kill.

Garley pulled his padded chair about and sat down, and his voice oozed persuasiveness as he offered the paper with stretch of arm. 'If you will look over this–'

'And is our private business to be discussed in the presence of this man?' Miss Martin asked angrily.

Clara exclaimed, 'Aunty, please!'

Miss Martin pushed Clara's protesting hand away and retorted, 'Be quiet! You don't know what is going on under your very nose!' Her words then whipped out at Garley. 'You wrote everything you could to prevent my niece from coming out here, and now I see why! Just who is this Rocklin, if you please?'

Garley deepened his voice, spoke slowly, and his staring look contained the thought that she was at least slightly out of her mind. 'He is an employee of your ranch, and I wish to have a word or two with him before–'

Miss Martin almost rose from her chair.

'That man on Clara's ranch? Never!' She smacked down her hand on the table and glared at Rocklin.

And Rocklin nodded, saying, 'My idea exactly!'

'What is your idea?'

'That I wouldn't ride for you, lady – not if I had to walk for somebody else! I made up my mind last night at Stan's, but this morning the judge sent for me and–'

'Oh, *sent* for you, did he?' She turned on Garley. 'Oh, so you *sent* for him! And to work on Clara's ranch? Ho, ho!'

Clara could not sit quietly. She had grown up under Aunt Elizabeth's thumb, was now of age, and had the rebelliousness that ached for a right to her rights; and she was made increasingly miserable by the way her aunt deliberately provoked people, enjoying their discomfiture and anger. 'I don't see anything so wrong; I just don't!' Even now there was a gentleness in her voice, but it was as if she must be fair and just. 'I don't see why you talk as you do to the judge, or to him.' She gestured toward Rocklin. 'I just don't, Aunt Liz!'

'Oh, you don't?' Miss Martin intoned sarcastically. With that, the old lady twisted her face into a grimace that looked like pain; but it wasn't pain at all, for the expression settled into a smile with a preparatory gleam of triumph in her black eyes. 'Then I shall tell you!' She paused, listening to rapid steps in the hallway that came hurriedly nearer, and the Harolday girl flashed into the open doorway.

Arly saw the women, but Rocklin was out of sight on the end of the sofa behind the door. She had not expected to see them and stopped short, for a surprised moment looking at Clara, who was near her own age, and in a city dress, and pretty, too. Garley arose politely in a heavy bow, not quite at ease, for Arly was breathless, the quirt dangled on her wrist, he knew how she disliked him, and she was unpredictable. Then Arly turned to him and said quickly, 'Jager Clews is back in town, and Jim Brotherton ought to know, for the Jager's said what he'd do because Jim testified against him, so you ought to get out word to him right away!'

'Thank you, Miss Arly. Thank you, and I'll—'

Arly was not listening; she had given the neighborly warning and was now again looking toward Clara. 'You are Miss Caldwell?' Arly said friendlily.

Clara got up from the rocking chair and exclaimed with impulsive eagerness, 'And you are Miss Harolday! I saw you this morning, and Mr Brotherton told me what a wonderful girl you are!'

Arly took the hand that Clara held out, and as they touched hands the quirt swung for a moment between them like a pendulum. Arly's thin face was tense almost to sullenness, but Clara was all eagerness, for she had seen this girl in the saddle, heard Brotheron's praise, and so much feeling gushed up within Clara that it overflowed into: 'And, oh, how I wish I were like you!'

A startled flicker crossed Arly's eyes. 'Like me?' Suspicion glinted and passed away. This Eastern girl was gentle and frank and sweet, and her very city manner, and even pretty helplessness, and the way she wore her clothes, was like something that Arly Harolday unappeasably craved and could never have. For a moment she held her tongue, then fiercely: 'Don't ever wish that, no! I'm the meanest little bitch in this country – and proud of it!'

Arly whirled about and started for the door, but she stopped, gasped, and took one step back. Rocklin was standing there. Arly at once deliberately planted the foot she had drawn back to where it had been. Her hand was waist-high and the quirt jiggled on her wrist, for she seemed to tremble and her eyes blazed. He was tall and she had to look up, and she eyed him as if trying to speak but found her jaws locked.

Garley was startled, for he knew this girl and her temper, and he sat down, wanting to be out of the way. Miss Martin hovered forward, looking from Rocklin to Arly, for there was anger between them that had to flash. Clara's hands tightened on the table's edge before her.

For a long minute it seemed that Arly couldn't find the words she wanted, but the words came. 'I was looking for you! *I*' – the pronoun was underscored with all the feeling of her slim, tense body– *'I* don't want you on the ranch or anywhere around, but Harolday has just said to find and hire you! To hire you at foreman wages. That's sixty dollars! So come on and start! We need somebody just as mean as you are!'

Rocklin looked back at her with a coolness that he didn't feel, for the surprise flurried his thoughts; but something stirred inside of him and made laughter break on his mouth, and an impulse hit him so hard that he told her, 'All right, damned if I don't do it! Lead the way!'

She marched by him and out, stiff-backed, angry, and hurrying, and he followed.

Miss Martin leveled a finger at Garley and spoke rapidly.

'So you "sent" for this Rocklin! I remember the letters old Ken Caldwell's sister wrote Clara's people when she married a Rocklin and went to live in a place called Tahzo. We heard there was a baby and then she died, and there was never another word until here, now, today! "Rocklin" is a name you remember, and "Tahzo" has an ugly sound you never forget! I suppose he will divide with you whatever you help him *legally* steal from my niece, is that it?'

Garley rose out of his chair, confused, very astounded, also shaken, and hoarsely implored her to believe. 'I've had nothing to do with this Rocklin!'

'You sent for him!'

'Only to come to my office after I learned he was in town. That's Brotherton's plan. But he doesn't yet even know that Caldwell was his uncle!'

'Preposterous!'

'It is preposterous!' he admitted, and sat down and wiped his forehead with the wadded handkerchief. 'Ladies, I feel as outraged as you do! Brotherton–' He told what had happened. Garley talked well; he had a deep, grave voice and used it with persuasive slyness to say, 'The fact that Brotherton is preparing to oppose and thwart the wishes of his dead friend and benefactor, and to deprive this lovely young maiden of her rightful inheritance, must compel the suspicion that he anticipates personal advantage and profit!'

Miss Martin nodded jerkily. 'Of course he is! And we must get rid of this old Brotherton. Expose and dismiss him! I want the pleasure of doing that! I did not like him, not at all! I distrusted him instantly!'

Clara spoke with astonishment. 'But you

94

did like him! You said you liked him!'

'That isn't the way of it at all! You said you liked him! I agreed merely to please you, child!' Her bony hand lived in the gestural command that Clara sit back and be quiet. To Garley: 'He must at once be removed from the ranch!'

Garley nodded and pondered, then murmured, 'Let us consider what is best.' Miss Martin sat stiffly suspicious, but Garley leaned toward her confidentially and rumbled, 'We dare not have any kind of falling out with Brotherton, not at present. He would at once take sides with Rocklin and urge his claims. Therefore it is advisable that you conceal from even Brotherton your knowledge of who this Rocklin is. Possibly we can arrange it so that Brotherton will form an unfavorable opinion of him. So I say most earnestly that you, Miss Clara, must do everything you can to win and hold Jim Brotherton's liking and sympathy! We must keep him on *our* side! I suggest that you even encourage him to believe and expect that you, Miss Clara, will reward him substantially because of his long friendship with Caldwell! By doing so you can remove the threat that this Rocklin now makes against your welfare!'

The old lady beamed approvingly, but Clara's voice trembled with: 'I think that is horrible – just horrible!'

'It is for your own good!' Miss Martin snapped.

Clara jumped up and gave the rocker a push that set it sidewise. 'And how can it be for my own good when it is just as much lying and cheating as anything can be? And I do like Mr Brotherton; and I never thought it in you, Aunt Elizabeth, to be a hypocrite!' She hurried on, a little dazed by her own anger. 'And you, Judge Garley, how can you be an honest man and talk like that? And anyhow, I don't want anything that isn't rightfully mine, and if Mr Rocklin is entitled to what we are trying to keep him from having, I think it is wicked, just foully wicked!'

She could not go on, for she was beginning to feel blinded by the tears that came. Her hand fumbled out for the rocker, then she sat down with a handkerchief to her face, and her shoulders shook.

Garley watched Miss Martin with bland and submissive inquiry, and Miss Martin sat rigidly, tightening her elbows at her sides, tightening the handclasp in her lap, tightening her thin lips. She smiled coldly, then: 'Young and inexperienced persons must be guided!'

Garley bowed his approval and gently rubbed the tips of his fingers together.

Arly marched up Main Street, her eyes unseeingly straight ahead; her cheeks were flushed, and her boot heels went click-click-click. Rocklin followed at her heels as if led by an invisible rope. Marshal Ager, smelling of bay rum, lifted his hat, showing the fresh haircut, and was ignored. Rocklin could tell that men's eyes were on his face, trying to understand what was happening, and he felt like a fool tagging at the skirts of the straight-backed Harolday girl.

She went under the arch of the stage-company stables and, without looking at him, said, 'Wait here.' Three or four men were standing there in the hot shade, and one that lounged silent and motionless, with his back to a stall post, was an old Mexican, long-legged and dark as an Indian, and his eyes met every man with a look of smoldering distrust.

Arly asked, 'Where's Harolday, Juan?'

Juan Romeras looked carefully at Rocklin as he pointed backhandedly and said in Spanish, 'I will tell him, señorita,' but she walked by him and went on. Juan's eyes lingered on Rocklin, then he turned and followed her.

Harolday was in the vacant lot out back of the stables before a horse that was being offered by an owner who used many oaths in affirming the animal's fine points; but Harolday, with hands behind him as if to keep them from meddling with the coins in his pocket, listened uninterestedly. He saw his girl swing the door wide and stop with Juan close by her. 'Thirty dollars,' said Harolday, and the owner said he would be double-damned first, so Harolday shuffled off in stoop-shouldered peering.

An angered sound was in Arly's voice, but she kept it down so that it would not carry out to where the horse trade still waited, and she met Harolday's look and told him, 'I've just hired that Rocklin and said you made me do it! Sixty dollars, and he'll earn it while he lasts! So you go talk to him. Send him out to Santee with me and Pete tonight!'

Harolday pondered inscrutably and looked at Juan, but Juan said nothing; he seldom said anything to anybody except Arly, for he was like her shadow, as he had been her mother's. Harolday's tone was flat. 'Why'd you do it, Arly?'

'I met him and all of a sudden just did it! I hate the man, but we can use him. Pete saw him in the Sun-Up this morning, and he gave Bob Clews the thrashing nobody has dared give him before. Jager is in town and will probably kill him for it, but while he lasts I want to use him!'

'But sixty dollars?' said Harolday.

'I was afraid he would refuse, so I made it big. You can see by the way he looks and acts that he thinks he is better than anybody else, but I'll take that out of him – then fire him! That's why I did it – so I can fire him!'

Harolday could never tell which way Arly's temper would jump, but her angered look broke into an exasperated laugh. 'I'll fix him!' she said.

Juan had the patience of a shadow, and he rested a shoulder, without slumping, against a doorpost and studied her face; he had known her since she was a baby, had nursed her as a baby, and no one understood her as well as he did.

Harolday's glassy eyes also studied her face. Arly did as she pleased, and there was not much that he could do about it, not often that he wanted to do anything. The Santee had been her mother's ranch, and Arly ran it as if it were her own, making money but not caring about the money. 'I hear he's come to work for the Caldwell, Arly.'

'I've hired him!'

Harolday nodded, then: 'You want to get even because you overplayed your hand this morning?'

'I feel like using a quirt on Clint!'

'Clint?'

'When he came home this morning he looked like a ghost, or had seen one. "What's the matter with you?" I said. So he told me he had been in an all-night poker game and after he won a big pot this man Rocklin went for his gun and made him give it up. "Went for his gun"! What else was I to think? I asked some more about this Rocklin.

'Then I saw him on the street. Knew him, for who else in this part of the country wears a white hat? He was coming down the Sun-Up stairs. I put my horse on the sidewalk and stopped him – and he went on! With a gun at his head, he went on!

'I rode back to the house and woke Clint up and said, "Why did you lie to me?"

'You know how Clint does in a corner! Oh, no, he hadn't lied! I just misunderstood! "Went for his gun"? Rocklin had gone upstairs for his gun. No, he hadn't drawn it, but – but – but! You know how Clint's tongue squirms! And now you go talk to this Rocklin!'

Harolday beckoned and Rocklin followed him into the office. The flat-faced agent snapped his sleeve holders higher on his arms and pretended to study the ledger. Three or four loafers outside in the dusty driveway scuffled their feet, looked through the door, and wondered. Arly rode by them and to the street. They could see that she still looked mad. There was mystery here that the small town must talk about and never quite understand. Old Harolday was morosely aloof, Miss Arly proud and willful, so what was going on between them and this Rocklin? Juan came up, rolled a thin cigarette, and put a shoulder against a post; and when a man spoke, inquisitively, with jerk of thumb toward the office door, Juan shrugged a shoulder and that was all.

Harolday pushed back his hat and rested an elbow on the high side of the tall, sloping desk. Flies buzzed in the stale heat. Harolday had a way of staring long and hard at a man before he spoke, but Rocklin asked at once, 'Why are you hiring me?'

Harolday slowly twiddled the watch charm, and the glassy look was impersonal as he inquired with the faint surprise of having been asked a needless question, 'Why does a man usually hire somebody?'

'But your boy's got a grudge and your girl hates me.'

'I pay the wages. We are havin' trouble and may have more. You don't appear to mind trouble.'

Rocklin told him, 'One thing, though. Jim Brotherton hired me, sight unseen, and sent money. That's why I'm here. Before I got here I made up my mind I wouldn't work for Brotherton. There's a hundred and fifty dollars to be paid back. I've got just better'n a hundred. Will you make up the rest so I can give it to Brotherton? I can't go to work till I pay him back and tell him I'm riding for you.'

Harolday stopped twiddling the charm, and his eyes were far away. 'Sixty dollars is big wages. I can get good men at thirty.'

'If you've changed your mind, say so.'

'Why don't you want to work for Brother-ton?'

Rocklin took his time. 'For one thing, he was offering only forty.' Harolday went on staring at Rocklin with silent insistence, asking for something more, and Rocklin added, 'But I can't work for you or anybody else till I've told him.' Harolday's eyes were unresponsive. 'Nothing else would be fair.'

'Fair?' Harolday repeated, as if wondering what the word meant. 'So you want fifty dollars advance?' He seemed doubtful that the risk was good; that was his way, and he always seemed doubtful. Harolday took his hand from the watch charm and put it to his chin. 'And if I don't let you have it?'

'I'll just have to assign him my wages. But I'll feel better to pay him back right off.'

'You can assign it,' said Harolday.

Rocklin's back was to the door, and he turned when a clattering stamp of running boots passed on the sidewalk and through the dusty window, barely saw a man running by; but Harolday, facing the street, had seen more clearly, and he looked in an expectant way toward the side door that opened out on the driveway.

A wiry young cowboy whom loafers out in the drive had told where to find Rocklin came through the side door breathlessly, and the loafers crowded up close to the door.

Harolday asked, 'What is it, Pete?'

Pete's bright eyes were on Rocklin, and even if excited he drawled a little. 'Jager Clews heard what you done to Bob an' says he'll kill you on sight! He's down at the Sun-Up, likkerin'!'

Eyes studied Rocklin, and the tall Juan stood back and looked over other men's shoulders as if it were important that he watch this man and judge him Rocklin took out tobacco and papers but held them idly as he sized Pete up, found him young, with a keen twinkle of impudence in eyes that were as blue as lupine, and he suspected that this Pete was quite a hand at playing jokes. It was for Rocklin to judge whether they were giving him an honest warning or trying to see if he would scare. So he spilled tobacco into the brown paper, closed the sack with pull of teeth on the string, stuffed it into his vest pocket, and rolled the cigarette, all the while listening to the men behind Pete, who were making a ragged and anxious chorus of warning.

'Jager's shore a bad un!' 'Been in pen'tent'ary twict!' Dead quick shot!'

Rocklin put a match to the cigarette, shook out the match, broke it between thumb and fingers. 'The town's sure all excited!' Pete told Harolday, then looked quizzically at Rocklin, who thought that all this had the sound of something that hadn't been very well rehearsed.

Harolday looped his hands behind his back and walked to the street door, stepped through, peered down the street toward the Sun-Up, and when he came back he said to Rocklin: 'Street's cleared, all right. Men have got their heads out of doorways, watchin'.'

Rocklin still was not sure; in spite of Harolday's taking part it looked like something made up to see how he would play his hand, and he was cautiously more afraid of a joke than he was of a gun fight. He looked at Pete, and Pete said, 'I'm tellin' you what's so, mister! And Jager is as bad as they've ever come in this part of the country!'

Rocklin asked, 'Looking for me, hm? Does he know where to find me?'

'He'll look all over but mebbe thinks you won't be around if you know he's lookin'!'

Rocklin nodded, then: 'Go down and tell him I'm here – waitin' out in front!'

Pete gave his head a perky lift and looked at Harolday, but Harolday was watching Rocklin; then he caught Pete's look and nodded almost imperceptibly.

Pete said, 'All right, mister. But I'll stand a long way off when I do it!'

CHAPTER SEVEN

The hot street was as deserted as if men had hurried to shelter from a storm, and from sheltered doorways they thrust out faces, now looking toward the Sun-Up's street door, behind which Jager Clews and some fellows were drinking, now looking toward where Rocklin waited at the edge of the sidewalk before the stage-company office. The afternoon sun poured its heat through the east-and-west street, and the glare would be in Rocklin's eyes when Jager came out and he would come. A bad man, when called, had to face the showdown; and Pete, having taken the message which he delivered through the Sun-Up door without going in, had come back to say, 'He's still likkerin' up.'

Every minute or so some man stuck his head out of the saloon door and looked up the street, and each time the watchers thought that it was Jager coming out; but it would only be some one of the men there, seeing if Rocklin still waited.

Across the street, about halfway between the stage-company office and the saloon, people stood in the Honeycomb entrance, the bare-armed waitress among them with a dish towel and plate in her hand. Somebody asked about Marshal Ager, and there were grins; the fat marshal got out of the way when gunmen walked abroad, and Deputy Sheriff Jackson was also keeping out of sight if, as some said, he was in town.

The long-legged Juan stood at one side of the archway and watched out for more than the duel, because he knew Arly was coming back from the Harolday house and bullets might be flying with her in the street.

Rocklin didn't like standing out there with half the town peering at him; he was, and felt, conspicuous. Now he knew it wasn't a joke, for apprehension hummed along the street and there was the morbidly quieting curiosity that men have when other men may be killed. Pete was squatting in the office doorway tossing away half-smoked cigarettes, rolling others, and keeping an eye toward the Sun-Up. Rocklin half turned. 'Go back and tell that fellow to get out here on the street or I'll come down after him!'

Pete pitched his fresh cigarette over the sidewalk and stood up slowly. 'Yeah?' he drawled 'If I say that, he'll take a shot at me, Jager will!'

Rocklin told him, 'In a saloon more than one may get hurt.'

Pete's impudence crept through his uneasy grin. 'Breakin' their legs gettin' under tables! You want that I go say that?'

106

After word had whipped up and down that a fight was coming business stopped and men waited, tensely. Shooting scrapes that broke out suddenly were one thing, but a set duel right in the center of town was new; and men wanted to see, but it gave them time to think that bullets sometimes went wild and hit bystanders. And nobody was stopping it. Fat marshal Ager would as soon have put his hand in among hot coals and grabbed a fistful as to meddle with Jager Clews.

Pap Fossler, out of bed late, pulled his long beard and told Gene Dyer, as they waited before Brunsig's store, 'That Rocklin'll kill him sure!' Little bald Brunsig was unhappily rubbing his hands as if washing them.

'Let's hope!' said Gene, answering Pap and feeling the sweat of his palm make the cane's handle slippery.

Two women came out of the stairway entrance beside the store, and Garley was with them. Brunsig gasped and fluttered his hands, urging, 'Gid pack! Gid pack, Shudge!' Word of Jager Clews being on the warpath had not reached to Garley's office, and now he was returning to the hotel with the women. Garley had come down the stairs with the pleased expression of one who has seen some troubling matters straighten out. Miss Martin had her head up and Clara had her eyes down, for they had been binding her with advice and instructions, and she now helplessly felt that one of the most hateful things she had ever seen on a man's face was Garley's smile. Moreover, now she knew that there was a hypocritical dishonestly in her aunt Elizabeth. Wretchedness made the unlucky girl desperately want to snatch out for what was honest, but her hands seemed tired, and Garley and her aunt complacently assumed that she must do as they wished.

A flurry of voices followed Brunsig's in giving warning. 'Look out, Judge! A fight's comin'!'

'Get the ladies off the street!'

'Jager Clews, and Rocklin waitin'!'

'Bullets may come this way—'

Then they heard Pete's voice sing out. He had pulled the swinging door wide and yelled as loud as he could 'Hi, you, Jager! Rocklin says if you don't come out he'll come down here after you!' Pete let the door swing to and dodged away, for it would be like Jager to rush out and take a shot at him.

Silence came down on the barroom talk like a lid clapped on noise, and Cap paused in wiping the bar and gazed with masklike disinterest at Jager. He was as tall as the rail-thin Bob but older, much heavier, with the same squint-narrow hatchet face and a smelly, unwashed sweatiness, and he had been overdrinking.

Bob stood by him, his arm in a sling; it had not been broken but so badly crushed that a clean break would have been better. Much whiskey had helped him forget his pain but increased his hatred for Rocklin. The Clewses always got even; that was a threat the nesters remembered when a barn burned and haystacks went up luridly in darkness.

The half-dozen men about the Clewses had shut up suddenly with necks twisted toward the doorway. Insults were new to Jager; he was used to having his way with a scowl, and the sudden silence hurt him. He turned slowly, looking at men, and none of them spoke up, flatteringly, so for a moment or two it was about the same as being among strangers.

Baffled fuddlement was in Jager's squinty eyes as he slapped the bar and told Cap, "Nother whisky!'

Bob, not sober, had the good sense to say, 'Don't drink no more, Jager. Not till after'ards!'

Jager reached out and spread his hand on his brother's face, then pushed. 'Shut up!'

Cap watched him spill whisky, overfilling his glass; then Jager threw back his head, poured the whisky down his throat, grunted, 'Er-aa!' and wiped at his mouth with his forearm. He straightened up, jerked down his hat, hitched at his belt which was heavy with two guns, and lurched toward the door. 'I'll go git his ears!'

Cap stopped Bob with: 'Somebody pays for that drink!' The Jager was halfway to the door, but the Cap's lean finger called Bob's attention to the empty glass, and Bob hurried his left hand into a pocket and splashed down change angrily. Cap had a sawed-off shotgun under the bar and was known to have used it when bartending over at Garden City.

Jager hit the door with a bull-like rush, knocking it wide, and stamped out unsteadily, blinked at the sunlight, then scowled hazily up the street. He knew he was drunk but was drunk enough not to care, and he roared, 'Where is that—' The foul name rolled out with wrathy bluster. He didn't have to ask; Rocklin stood on the sidewalk's edge before the stage-company office, alone.

Jager stopped at the edge of the sidewalk and peered up and across the street at the solitary figure, not quite a block away, under the stage-office porch; then suddenly he clapped both hands to his guns, and all along the street men fell back farther into doorways, but he didn't draw. Jager ran his hands down along his holsters, settling them the way he wanted, making sure they would hang just right. He knew people were watching and he liked that; and he announced to the street again, 'I'm goin' up and git his ears!'

'Drunk!' said Garley. 'Hasn't a chance!'

Jager was drunk; anybody could see that, and Garley set his heavy jaws, breathing hard. *Too bad!* he thought. *Too damn bad!* Just when there was a beautiful chance for some helpful luck the Jager had to be drunk.

Gene Dyer swore prayerfully into Pap Fossler's ears and thrust out the cane, pointing. 'Look at him, cool and waitin', Pap! He'll get 'im sure!'

Rocklin was out on the edge of the sidewalk, not even near a porch post. He pulled his hat forward and low, shading his eyes, but his hands hung with the thumbs hooked over the front of his belt; tall, lean-hipped, not moving, he peered with studying intentness.

Jager stepped with uneasy jolt from the sidewalk into the cross street and plowed through the dust, still keeping to the opposite side of Main Street. His hands swung loosely, never far from his guns. When he had crossed the street he stamped his boots on the walk, clearing the dust as if it weighted his boots; then for a long moment he stood still, watching Rocklin. Men nearest could see that he was glowering, and it made their insides quiver, but Rocklin was too far off to feel as they did about it.

Jager suddenly yelled, 'I'm comin' and you better run, you–' He lurched unsteadily, stamping hard on the boards.

Drunk or pretending, Rocklin didn't know; but he thoughtfully made his guess, then stepped off the sidewalk, angling through the dusty street straight for Jager with his thumbs still in his belt, and his eyes had the steadiness of bright nailheads.

Jager, seeing him coming, stopped, and his hands trailed about his holsters as he stared, loosemouthed, more than half drunk and fuzzy with wonder. The man's coming at him silently with thumbs in the belt was something new, and Jager watched, fuddled and uncertain.

Rocklin reached the sidewalk some twenty feet from where Jager stood and kept coming with an unwavering look on Jager's face that caught his eyes and held them; then Rocklin spoke. The waitress heard and dropped her plate; it clattered behind Rocklin, not breaking. Two men by her sucked in their breath for they had heard him say, 'You touch a gun and I'll kill you!' There was the implied promise of life if Jager wanted to live and the certainty of what would happen otherwise; and what he said, and more than what he said, his look, got far enough through the whisky to make Jager feel his helplessness; and Rocklin kept coming with the same short, stiff-legged steps, high heels thumping the boards. When he was an arm's reach away he whipped up his gun and crashed it alongside of Jager's head. The barrel struck though the crown of the hat, and Jager went down like a hammer-struck steer, lying with his head lolling off the edge of the sidewalk.

Rocklin gave Jager a glance, scarcely more, and put his gun away as he stepped from the walk, again crossing the street and not looking back as men clattered up to have a look at Jager. Cap, a half-block away, slowly rubbed his palms down along his apron and said with enigmatic approval, 'Buffaloed him, by God!'

Harolday met Rocklin at the edge of the sidewalk and drooped his head far forward to ask harshly, 'Why didn't you shoot?'

'He was drunk!'

'Drunk or not,' Harolday began, 'he's a horse thief an'–'

Rocklin eyed him and cut in. 'You might as well say, "In the back or not!"'

Arly, returning from home, had stopped her horse up the street just as Rocklin started across the street to meet Jager, and now she came up on the lope. Juan took the reins as she dropped them and swung off. 'What happened and why?' It was in Spanish, and her eyes brightened excitedly.

Juan told her swiftly, saying what was true without belittling Rocklin but also without an intimation of praise, being as factual as a tally keeper.

Arly listened and frowned toward where

113

men were clustering up before the office, and her eyes were very bright, but she snapped, *'Qué me importa eso?'* Then, hurrying the words and even adding a stamp of foot, she told Juan, 'I hate that man! I have never hated anybody as I hate that man!' She watched fiercely to see if he doubted, and Juan did not smile.

Arly came up among the men there and ignored Rocklin but looked at Harolday, and he told her how it was. 'He won't go to work, Arly, till he's seen Jim Brotherton.'

She merely said, 'We can ride by the Caldwell tonight. It won't be much out of the way, and I want to see Jim, anyhow. Since Jager is loose we'd better help each other, and not be like the last time when Caldwell said he'd rather lose cows than be friendly with you.' She turned on Rocklin. 'How soon can you be ready?'

'I am ready.'

She was about to say something more, but Garley and the women were there on the way back to the hotel, and Rocklin moved aside. Arly's quick look saw that Clara's eyes were red and swollen and that she gazed from under lowered lids at Rocklin steadily, as if wishing he would look at her.

Garley lifted his hat to Arly, not speaking. He had a wadded handkerchief in the other hand; the collar about his thick neck was moist as a dishrag, and when he set the hat

114

back on his head he again took Miss Martin's arm, but she had an idea and pulled away. She lifted her high nose and walked directly to Rocklin, pointed a finger at his face. 'I saw you hit that poor drunk man!'

'Yes'm. Hard as I could.'

Jager had been lugged down the street and into the Sun-Up.

Garley's full face showed distress; he knew the erratic old woman was beginning her plan to blacken Rocklin, but 'poor drunk man' would not get any favoring response in the town. It was silly, and he took her arm again to urge her on, but she moved straight to Arly.

'Miss Harolday, I warn you, you can't trust this person, not in the least, not in any way!' Her wrinkled face was tight with malice.

Arly didn't seem to hear; she was watching Clara, whose saddened face pleaded with Rocklin not to think that she shared her aunt's feelings, but Rocklin wasn't noticing.

The wiry Pete drawled, 'Pore drunk man. Let's all weep some!'

No one smiled, and Arly felt suddenly furious. She was not so tall as the Martin woman but had as direct a look, and the sun-gold color of her face flared as she demanded, 'We are glad to know, for why else do you think Dad hired him? That's just the kind of a man we want!'

Miss Martin was unused to having people snap back, and the best she could do was to sniff and glare, then she stalked on, holding her long skirt with a stiff arm straight down by her side.

Garley avoided the glassy inquiry of Harolday's eyes and turned to Clara, offering his arm, but she took no notice and hurried on.

Harolday fingered the watch charm. 'What's she got so against you, Rocklin?'

'I never saw her till yesterday. If she's not loco, I can't guess.'

But a look of understanding had come into Arly's face; she knew, or thought she did, that there had been a flare of romance between him and this Clara. Things happened like that sometimes, so Arly had heard; but she couldn't see how! *Men? The best of them were just good cowboys* – so Arly had thought and said. But the old lady had caught them making eyes, or something more, and put her foot down and was still stamping. Clara's sadness and Rocklin's sullenness made the guess fit in every way. *He loves her!* Arly thought, and she gave Rocklin a look that had the glitter of a scalping-knife as it strikes.

Deputy Sheriff Jackson loped up the street, splattering dust, stopped with hard yank of reins before the stage-office sidewalk, and

116

shifted in the saddle. He needed a shave, and the straggling mustache overflowed his mouth. He said, 'I just rode in and–' But Rocklin felt that he had been keeping out of sight, knowing what Jager Clews was up to. So good a friend of Jager's brother must have a certain understanding with Jager, and the star glinted on the deputy's vest. It was this glint that touched off Rocklin's anger when the deputy's roving look singled him out and he demanded, 'You? What you been up to?'

Rocklin gave him an answer in plain, un-hurried words. 'I laid a gun barrel over the head of a drunk friend of yours. Like one of your men did to a friend of mine!'

It was a word-slap as straight in the face as words could go, and the surprised deputy demanded, 'What's that? What's that? What you talkin' about?'

Rocklin told him, 'You or Bob Clews broke old drunk Dave's head last night.'

The deputy straightened in the saddle, blurted, 'I don't know nuthin' about what you're sayin'!'

Rocklin said, 'You're a liar!'

Everybody heard and stiffened; that was all and enough, and the talk had swirled so swiftly into its climax that people were caught by surprise, not quite understanding what was meant – except that Rocklin was asking for more trouble. Deputy Jackson was caught flat-footed, for there was a hardness about Rocklin that pressed in from all sides and did not leave a man any graceful way of backing up and getting out of his corner.

Arly's lips parted tensely in a strained, listening look, for she had never seen any man so deliberate in his anger; and now she understood why Clint had believed that Rocklin could and would have killed him. In a way, Clint had not really lied to her.

Jackson, red-faced and choked, began, 'Now you looky here, young feller!'

Rocklin said, '"Don't hurt him!" you said last night. You said, "We're his friends!" Then you took Dave out and beat him over the head. That makes you a liar and a sneak, and that badge ain't big enough to cover you up! Do something besides talk!'

Arly's hand went up as if slapping her own mouth, and Pete grinned, nervously gleeful; it was for Jackson to swallow or spit! Harolday's hard look slid toward Arly, showing the thought, *You're going to have your hands full with this man!* Juan moved up with a shadowlike glide to be nearer Arly and thrust her aside and stand before her if guns were drawn. Three or four yokel-mouthed nesters gazed dully, some with wonder as to how Harolday felt about it, for this deputy sheriff did mortgage foreclosing and seized collateral for Harolday. Hot blood was scalding Jackson's face, and Rocklin waited, thumbs hooked in his belt; and the words, 'Do some-

118

thing besides talk!' seemed to linger audibly in the silence.

Jackson merely jerked the reins, backing his horse a little, making ready to ride off. 'Harolday, I hear you're hirin' this feller.'

'We've made a sort of dicker.' Harolday's voice was toneless.

'I wouldn't do it, Harolday!' The deputy lifted his voice in a weak bluster. 'He's come a stranger – nobody knows anything about him! And I got reasons for thinkin' mebbe he's on the dodge!' Jackson swung his horse about, stabbed with spurs, and loped down the street; but he reined up at the Sun-Up, piled off, and rushed into the saloon.

A nester or two grinned, and the wiry Pete laughed, but Harolday was solemn. 'Rocklin, what's this about Dave?'

Arly, not waiting to hear, spun about; and, going into the office, she ran through the side door and on back to where Juan had put her horse in a stall. She went to the horse's head and hugged it.

'Belle,' she said, 'Belle, what's the matter with me? Oh, honey-girl, I hate that man, but I can't help myself – I just can't! And she can't have him, Belle; she just can't! No other woman in the world can have him! He's mine – *mine!* – and I don't care what else happens, I am going to have him!'

CHAPTER EIGHT

It was dark when a Chinaman came shuffling along and paused at the stage-company office. A lamp was burning, and Arly, alone, brooded. Aimlessly she flipped the quirt's tip at a drawer knob. The Chinaman came in, bobbing and bowing. She knew him but at first could not make out for whom he was asking; then the Chinaman showed her a letter addressed to *Mr Kenneth Rocklin.*

'Who sent this, Sammy?'

'Lung lady at 'otel, missy.'

'I'll give it to him.'

When Sammy backed out Arly turned the letter over and over slowly. It had a faint smell of lavender, as if the paper had been in a tray with sachet. The handwriting of the address was straight, the letters finely formed. Arly resented the neatness of the writing; also the scent of lavender.

She had believed they were in love and was now sure. Why else this letter? *Love?* Her thought of it had always been scornful; the married women she knew were unhappy, and her mother had been, too.

Arly found writing a tedious chore. She flung the letter on the desk as if throwing it away and had the bewildering impulse to open it, read it, and not give it to Rocklin. She felt that she must know what Clara had written; and she would know, somehow.

She found Rocklin squatting with haunch to heels in the twilight gleam of the lantern at the grain-room door, and there was an aspect of loneliness about him that made her believe he was thinking sadly of the Caldwell girl. The horse he had been given was saddled and ready and stood with head down and reins trailing. She said, 'Rocklin,' sharply.

He gathered the reins and stood up, ready to mount.

'Is your name Kenneth?' she asked, as if the sound of 'Kenneth' was unpleasant.

'I've never been called that much. Why?'

'Somebody seems to know it very well! Here, a letter!'

'Letter?' He reached out slowly.

Arly walked off as if with no interest at all, but she waited in the shadows up near the office and saw him stand close to the lantern, tear the envelope. He read slowly; she saw that he reread, too, then he stood in trancelike thoughtfulness. After a time he folded the letter carefully into the inside pocket of his vest.

They rode from town, Arly and Juan jogging on ahead, and Pete kept by Rocklin but soon quit trying to talk. After some miles over the Flats they crossed the Hesico that it came down from the mountains and ran its water underground into the Flats where any well digger could have luck; then they took a short-cut trail over the hogback and got into the darkness of timber. The air was chilly.

Pete asked, 'Ain't you cold?' Rocklin said he wasn't but buttoned his vest, and Pete thought, *You're a liar!* and told him, 'It gets cold as hell nights.' He laughed, adding, 'Silly thing to say unless you don't believe the Bible!'

Rocklin was unresponsive. Clara Caldwell had written: *I should be very unhappy if anything I did, even by silence, prevented you from obtaining what is rightfully yours, so I shall tell you…* The language was unfamiliar but clear. *Your uncle was Kenneth Caldwell, and Mr Brotherton sent for you because you are a nearer relative to him than I am…* Rocklin never in his life had heard of Caldwell as an uncle. *My aunt Elizabeth will do anything she can to make Mr Brotherton dislike you… I cannot put into words how much I dislike and distrust Judge Garley… Please destroy this letter.* He would, of course, destroy it after another reading or two.

When they crossed the steep hogback and came down into the slow, rolling hills that flattened out in a way to please nesters, he stared through starlight at the shadow-

122

blurred figure of the Harolday girl and wondered that he was riding behind her. Sudden impulse had tripped and thrown him again. He did not like her and she hated him, but her unfriendliness was a kind of honesty. Women that didn't like you could be trusted more than the others.

As for that letter in his vest, and the *rightfully yours?* It didn't stir up any belief of rights. What the law might say didn't make things right. He had seen Mel Milton lose thousands of dollars by keeping his word, though there hadn't been the scratch of a pen to bind him, and nobody had been surprised or expected anything else. Rocklin couldn't see that he had any claim on the property of a man he had never heard of, uncle or not; especially as the man had done what he wanted with the property.

He puzzled over Brotherton's motive, believed he saw Garley's connivance, and anger grew in Rocklin's mind. *Bring me out here to help them seal what they can by a law trick and expect me to divide!* His thoughts boiled. Expect him, did they, to help try to cheat a helpless girl like that? They'd learn something before he was through!

Juan hailed the house, and Jim Brotherton bounced to the door, a small, unalarmed figure, grayish in underwear. When he knew Arly was out there he shouted, 'Wait till I get my pants on!' and scurried back into darkness. He returned to the door again with a lighted lamp above his head and sang out, 'Come right along in, Miss Arly.'

Arly went toward him. 'Jim, Jager Clews showed up in town today!'

Brotherton peered at the figures that were leaving their horses. 'Jager, eh?' He called, 'Come on in, boys.' Then, matter-of-factly: 'Sure a waste of time to send a hoss thief to prison ain't it?'

Inside the house Brotherton's hand flew up in greeting to Juan and he said, ''Lo, Pete,' with liking. He told Rocklin, 'Howdy,' with offhand friendliness, then jerked a pair of old chaps out of the big chair, urging, 'Set down, Miss Arly.' She sat down, side-glancing at Rocklin, and guessed from the way he looked that he was still thinking of Clara Caldwell, and that stirred her malice. Brotherton swept his arm about the room, indicating its rude barrenness, and he said worriedly, 'I don't know what to do! The Caldwell girl is comin' out here to stay, and her aunt!' The coming of the women troubled him more than Jager Clews. He looked at Juan and told Arly, 'You've got Mexicans that make things homey at your place, but what can I do?' Again he swept his arm about and followed his gesture with a bleak look.

The old house had mud packed in between rough-hewn logs, and it had a dirt floor. No woman had ever lived here; few had ever entered. It was a strong house with high narrow windows that had been used for loopholes when the Caldwell riders bunked here years before and Indians came more boldly than now, when they sometimes jumped the Reservation and went raiding. The floor, rammed and pounded by trampling feet, was as hard as shale and of the same color. Two beds were nailed to the wall; the table's legs were driven into the floor. A round, rust-red stove stood at one end of the room.

'I can go down with the boys, but women up here alone – how'd they even eat? Still, it's her ranch. Have you seen her?'

Arly unbuttoned her jacket, loosened the chin thongs, and pushed back her hat. Her voice was indifferent. 'Yes, in Garley's office. I went up to tell him to send you word about Jager. He didn't, of course.'

'As f'r Jager and *me*–'Brotherton snapped finger and thumb, showing how little he cared. 'But as f'r rustlers – the judge whittles my payroll. I got only six men working now. I tell 'im that's losin' money. Red kept eight to ten the year round, and he was good as any two or three himself!'

Arly turned in the chair and pointed. 'Jim, that new man over there Harolday just hired wants to see you. His name is Rocklin.' She was curious about him and wanted to get behind the hard set of his face.

125

'Rocklin?' Brotherton pushed Pete aside and jumped close to where Rocklin stood just inside the door, and out went Brotherton's small brown hand welcomingly. Then what Arly had said followed through his thoughts, and he dropped his hand, turning toward her. 'Your dad hired 'im?'

Arly said, 'He speaks English!'

'Why,' Brotherton exclaimed, facing about, 'I hired you, Rocklin!' He had a perplexed frown and was hopeful that what he thought wasn't so.

'Changed my mind.' Rocklin held a buckskin pouch, offering it. 'Here's some of your money back. I'm riding for the Haroldays, and they'll pay you the rest.'

Brotherton took the pouch without thinking about it. 'You can't do that, Rocklin.' He was looking the tall man up and down. 'What'd you mean, "changed your mind"?'

Arly spoke up wickedly, and truthfully – so she thought. 'We're paying him sixty! Big money for a saddle tramp!' The 'saddle tramp' part wasn't truthful.

Brotherton's perplexity grew to anger. 'I send you money and you promise, then you hire out before you even see me! If that's the kind you are, I don't want you! Go ahead, ride for the Haroldays! I've found out all I wanta know!'

Arly smiled at her hands. 'I don't think he'll last long with us, either, Jim.' Then she

126

looked up and smiled queerly at Rocklin. Arley's quick little brain was guessing that old Miss Martin had put her foot down to keep him from working for the Caldwell. She felt that Rocklin was boxed in and couldn't explain.

For the moment Rocklin forgot all about Brotherton in taking her stare, and his look tightened stubbornly. Her smile was puzzling, and he had not imagined that she would be boss when he hired on, but if she wanted to make it a fight between them, all right.

Brotherton said wearily, 'You just ain't no good, Rocklin!'

Rocklin's voice was slow and cold. 'Not to you, no! It just happens that I know why you sent for me, Brotherton. You wanted to look me over. All right, *look!*'

There was no mistaking that he knew what he was talking about, and Brotherton's voice got away from him. 'The judge told you!'

Rocklin shook his head, but Brotherton shouted, 'He had to! Nobody else knows! But you – you, knowin' what I want and why, you still won't work for me?'

Arly's eyes were shining, excited, and mystified; and Pete, too, could tell that there was much here that was being played out like a game you could watch and not understand. Juan twisted a thin cigarette, not glancing at his hands, for he didn't take his eyes off Rocklin except to flick his look at Arly and back again.

Rocklin's suspicions of why he had been sent for were hardened now. Bringing in Garley's name seemed to make it certain. 'No, I won't ride for you!' Then he looked across the room. The lamplight was near enough to Arly's face to bring out her features against a background of shadow. He knew she wasn't pretty, for her face was thin and wickedly tense, but she *looked* pretty now, and he resented thinking so. He stared straight at her as he said, 'when the Haroldays fire me I'll ride for the Caldwell girl!' Arly could have killed him for that, but there was something going on here that wouldn't fit in with her guesses. She saw how he eyed Brotherton and added, 'Help her hold what's hers! From how I figger, she'll need help!'

It seemed to Arly that her guesses were crumbling. Rocklin had meant it insultingly, but Brotherton, who had been good and mad, now scratched rapidly at the back of his head and began to look happy. 'Boy,' he said anxiously, and pleased, too, 'it's not like you think!' He turned to her with jocular pleading. 'Fire 'im, Miss Arly! Right now. He's mine by rights!'

Rocklin turned on his heel and swung through the doorway, going into the darkness, and Brotherton stood at the door and

128

his eyes followed as far as they could. High-shouldered, lean of waist, with the drive in his look and the bony hardness of face, and the unbreakable hardness of will that was like Old Red's. *Aye, and honest!*

Brotherton faced the room, rubbed his hands gleefully, and laughed; and there was no understanding why. Arly had known Brotherton since she was a little girl and had never disliked him as she did Caldwell, and she asked, 'Jim, what's the matter with you – and him?'

Brotherton shook his head. 'Can't tell you, not yet.' He took up the pouch from the table, jiggled it, told the pouch, 'He's all right, he is! Better'n I thought. Makes me feel I was tryin' to do wrong; damn if he don't'. He looked up eagerly, laughed. 'Hurry an' fire him, Arly!'

Rocklin was squatting under the horse's head with a cigarette in his fingers, the reins trailing through the other hand, when they came out. Pete had something in his arms. Brotherton's spidery silhouette was framed by the door with the lamplight behind him, legs apart and an arm up high on each side of the doorway.

Pete held out his arms, saying, 'Here,' to Rocklin.

'Here, what?'

'Coat and slicker.'

'Why? Whose?'

'Yours now. I told Jim you didn't have a coat. When he said you had about the same build as Old Red, I said you could use a coat. You'll need it. But if you want to get mad about it, go ahead. I'll watch!'

There was too much friendliness in Pete's impudent drawl for Rocklin to get mad, but he folded the coat into the slicker and made a saddle roll and tied it on. He had said he wasn't cold and he wasn't going to wear the coat, not this night.

The Santee was hard-rock country and good for the horses that were raised there, making them sure-footed, hard-hoofed, strong. The army liked Harolday horses; so did the Indians and other horse thieves. A plateau rose almost sheer from the valley edge and was called the Table, and it was thickly covered with grain-colored, sun-cured grama grass, and mountain water came down through the wide valley where Harolday cows fed.

Arly said to Pete, 'Tell Abner I want to see him,' and took the right of a Y turn in the road, Juan keeping by her.

Rocklin turned in the saddle, his gaze following, and Arly looked around; their eyes met and lingered as if wrestling. All night in the saddle, yet still straight with a lift to her head. The slanting sun brightened her face. He was irritated by thinking that she was

130

pretty, and he thought, *She knows it!* and added, *I'll never let her think I think so!* She rode on toward the hillside clump of great cottonwoods that were fluffing their lint like a light snowfall.

'Juan's people live over there. She stays with them. Juan has a lot to say about what goes on, but he says it only to her.' Pete flung out an arm. 'There she is, your new home!'

Rocklin studied the layout in the long valley below, mentioning the greenness, and Pete drawled, 'Springs all over the place. Even the cook has spring water in the kitchen, and that makes him lazier. Across over yonder on the Table is where we run horses. All the watchin' they need is so they won't come down on the range, overeat water grass, and get bloated fat.'

They rode into the stable shed. Rocklin lifted off the saddlebags that held his traps, but left the slicker roll tied on. He swung the saddle over a horizontal pole under the shed, spread the blankets over the saddle, hung up the bridle, and with a hackamore took the horse to a log trough that had been hollowed from a big log. Water overflowed wastefully and ran off in a trickle with tall grass and fat weeds hugging the wetness. *Some day,* he guessed, *nesters will get all this!*

Pete left word with the cook for Abner to see Miss Arly; then, in the dim bunkhouse, he pointed to a bed. 'You can roll in there.'

131

He pulled his boots in the long-forked jack which would grip up beyond spur shanks and sent the jack skittering across the floor to Rocklin. 'I'll be dead in two minutes,' said Pete, and gave his pants a fling, then he fell forward face down on the blanket with an arm curved above his head.

Tiredness dragged at Rocklin, but his thoughts were astir as he undresssed. With a foot across his knee and a sock in his hand he looked up toward the peg where he had hung his vest, thinking of the letter. Rocklin slowly draped the sock over the edge of the boot as if doing something important. *Could Garley and Brotherton have wanted Caldwell out of the way?* There was no conviction in the thought, but murder did not seem totally worse than robbing a girl.

Rocklin rolled over on his back and laid a forearm across his face. A warmth of liking for Clara had slowly been gathering inside of him; she was unlike other women, and their tricky deceit was not in her. Also, she was some kind of a relative; so, after all, he was not entirely alone in the world, and kinship, even distant, colored his feeling and memory of her pretty sadness. Then his thoughts drowsed aimlessly into the haze of half-sleep.

Something too soft for sound moved in the dead and sultry silence of the dim bunkhouse, and it made enough of a blur in Rocklin's drowsiness to quicken his atten-

132

tion, almost incuriously. He had one eye barely open under the shelter of his forearm and lay quietly, and he could see that Pete was getting off his bunk with stealthy intentness and looking toward him; then Pete began to come toward him with long steps and hovering balance of hands, as if trying noiselessly to walk a crack. There was no guessing what he was up to, but Rocklin lay motionless until Pete had passed close by him and stopped. Rocklin stiffened his neck backward on the pillow, moved the arm, looked up, and then he left the bunk.

Pete swung about with the letter he had drawn from the vest in his hand. He was small and frightened and said, 'God!' as he flashed the letter behind him with a childish impulse at concealment. Rocklin, not speaking, hit him. It was as easy as punching a sack of grain. Pete's knees gave way with a look of being broken and he thumped face forward.

Rocklin reached down slowly and took the letter from the floor and sat on the edge of the bunk. He held the letter by a corner and tapped his thumb and stared at the boy who moved as if afraid. When Pete got to his knees he had a hand cupped to his eye, and Rocklin quit tapping his thumb and told him in a dull voice, 'I'm sorry.'

A hurt look burned in Pete's face, but he wasn't angry; he had had it coming to him and he had got it. He arose as if afraid his bones were brittle and sat on a stool, bent over, and rubbed gently at the eye.

Rocklin quietly tore the letter in two, retore the halves, tore the small pieces into smaller. 'When did she tell you to get it?'

'Before we left town. Said she wanted it the first time you went to sleep. I was scairt to try, but if you work for her you do what she tells you.'

Rocklin scrambled and bunched the torn pieces into a huddle on the blanket beside him, then ran his fingers in and out as if not paying attention to what he was doing, but any piece that turned up much larger than a postage stamp was retorn. At last he said, 'All right, there it is, all of it. Take it to her! I oughtn't have hit you, but I didn't think.'

Pete kept feeling of his eye as he rode past the giant cottonwoods. Below, in a pocket valley were four or five 'dobe houses with stake fences about small gardens to keep out deer and rabbits from the melons, corn, beans, and red peppers that were already beginning to festoon the southern side of the low, dark-walled houses.

He swung off before the only house that had an upstairs and told the fat, pleasant young woman, with brown babies clutching her skirts, that he had to see Miss Arly. Señora Romeras gazed anxiously at the swollen eye but gave him a soft refusal. 'The señorita sleeps, Pedro.'

Arly was awake and she called down, 'Come on, Pete! Come on up!'

The señora was shocked, and Arly knew it and did not care. The señora would tell her husband's grandfather, but Juan would not be shocked. Long, long ago Arly's mother had taken him from the hands of drunken men that had a rope about his neck. No doubt about it, Arly could do things that he possibly thought were wrong, but if so, all right – as long as she didn't get hurt.

Arly stood at the head of the steep, narrow, unlighted stairs as Pete clumped up. He paused awkwardly on the landing. 'Come on in here,' she said, and, closing the heavy door, she stood close to him expectantly. Her hair was down and she had been combing it and held the comb in her hand. The robe she wore was an ox-blood red; but the room, with only two narrow windows cut in the thick walls, was dim, so dim that after exclaiming, 'What's the matter with your eye?' she had to stand Pete, with quick pull and push, up beside a window to see just how bruised and swollen it was. Her voice fell disappointedly. 'You didn't get it?'

Pete was uneasy; he said. 'Yes'm – in a way.'

'In a way?'

'He sent it – the pieces, that is.' No drawl now; Rocklin had shaken him up and Miss

135

Arly made him miserable.

'You told him!' Arly accused, and was about to strike with the comb but he stood in his tracks and shook his head.

'No'm!' Pete swallowed. 'He woke up and seen me. He knocked me down and he didn't ask why I done it. He somehow knew.'

Arly said, 'Oh,' as if stumbling suddenly. 'But how could he?'

'I don't know. He tore it up and said for me to bring the pieces to you.' Pete drew a handful of torn paper from his trousers pocket, and some of the pieces fell with wavering drift to the floor. He held out his fist, showing her.

There was no table in the room, only a wide bed with stretched strips of hide for springs and a big chest with a huge lock that was never locked. Arly pointed toward the bed, and Pete laid the fragments there; then he turned his pocket inside out, picked off a few small scraps that had adhered to the rough seam, and laid them carefully on the bed.

Shame was running hot fingers along her cheeks and she could feel the flush clear into her hair; she was mad at Pete for failing, mad at Rocklin for guessing; more mad because he had sent the letter in a hundred pieces, contemptuously.

'He said he'd break my neck if I didn't bring 'em, Miss Arly. He does what he says, that fellow!'

Arly told him to get out, and Pete hurried, glad to go. Then she tossed the comb at the bracket on the wall under the small mirror and stared at the handful of litter on the bed. Arly swore in Spanish, slowly, deliberately, with feeling. She flung off the robe with a backward toss toward the chest and bent down, carefully gathering up the bits of paper about the floor. *I'll put this together if it takes a year! I'll put it together if I have to go without sleep for a year!* She would have to have a table; Juan could find it. She would need flour paste and paper. She must have a good lamp to work by. *Other people also do what they say!*

CHAPTER NINE

Late in the afternoon Abner came back from seeing Arly and eyed Rocklin curiously. His hair was partly gray and his face had the color of an old saddle; a quiet, tired man with rumpled clothes on his spare form, he seemed unforcefully patient. Abner looked a bit puzzled as he told Rocklin, 'You're goin' to the cabin on the Table Top. Bowles'll go along for a day or two. Not much ridin' up there. You'll have to cut trees and heave rocks.' He waited, expecting a protest.

Rocklin said nothing. She was out to give him hell, and he wouldn't let her have the satisfaction of making him quit. She could fire him any time but would have to lie if she said it was for work not properly done.

Abner moved a bony hand around his jaw as if thinking about a shave, then he took off his hat and peered aimlessly into the crown; after that he set the hat far back on his head. 'Rocklin?' Rocklin listened. 'I've got to tell you the last time Injuns were out – two year ago – they come this way. Over the mountains. They come down and swept 'cross Table Top. Killed the man at Cabin Camp. They had guns but used arrers on him. Filled 'im full! Some bucks've jumped the Reservation again. You'll be alone up there.'

Rocklin thought it over, then asked, 'Did she say for you to tell me that?'

'Well, now,' Abner began evasively, unsure of how to reply. Then he admitted, 'yes, yes, she did.' And Rocklin could see that Abner was wondering why.

After breakfast Rocklin began making ready to load the pack horse behind the kitchen storeroom. The cook, with Abner's list in his hand, gave grudgingly of flour, potatoes, onions, bacon, coffee, canned stuff, and foretold, 'You won't stay up there long enough to eat all that'; then, sounding pleased: "Pachies comin'! They'll git you!' Rocklin tantalized him with indifference and no answer. He put a blind on the mare, set the aparejo, estimated the load, and divided it with wrappings of canvas.

Bowles scratched under his tattered hat and offered his help, but felt unneeded and didn't mind. He was a tall, slow, lazy man; half the time his half-smoked cigarette was unlit, but he had a gentling way with horses, and Arly allowed him to fool away the summer breaking breed horses in his own way. Sometimes he would turn over a horse as broken that had never so much as bucked off an un-cinched saddle, and his horses came when he whistled, followed like dogs. Harolday could sell such gentled horses at a high price. The rough-heeled busters were scornful and envious. Bowles would tell them, 'You fellers ain't lazy enough!'

When Rocklin took in the slack of the pack's rear rope by standing up close to the mare's heels and heaved back as if falling, Bowles asked admiringly, 'Who the hell taught you to pack?'

Abner had walked his horse up, paused to watch Rocklin take the fifty-foot rope and throw the diamond hitch expertly, then go from side to side, snugging up all the slack. When Rocklin undid the blind Abner lifted his hand, said, 'Luck!' and rode off slowly. He liked Rocklin and wondered that Miss

139

Arly didn't; wondered the more as to why she was having him around if she didn't like him.

The second mare carried the tarped bedroll with the sheepskin coat that had been furnished him, and the slicker and Caldwell coat were still in a saddle roll.

Rocklin jerked his head at Bowles.

'All ready.'

They went out of the valley and up over the barrenness of broken rock, climbing steeply for the uplands. The whole side of the Table seemed to be a devil's slide. When they paused for breath Bowles relit his cigarette and guessed that something big in the way of an earthquake had quite some time ago jolted things, and he asked serenely, 'Do you reckon God figgered that far ahead on makin' it a hoss pasture for the Haroldays?'

Rocklin said, 'Likely so,' as if he believed and wasn't sure that he disbelieved.

'In the which case, he must've figgered, too, that I'd break jail as a kid back in Missoury and hike West. Know what I was in for? Hoss-stealin'! Yes'ir. Man back home owned a big stallion and clubbed him. To do it over again, I'd kill the man. Bein' a kid, I stole the horse.'

The Table wasn't a table but a great narrow shelf with one layer of rock brokenly overlapping another and slanting away smoothly with a gradual fall toward the west, and the

140

mountainside was buttressed by cliffs and box canyons.

Bowles pointed toward the mountains. 'Only birds can get out that-a-way. Horses won't drift over the slide, but they mosey west. West, they come down out on the range where rustlers grab 'em, so line riders shoo 'em back. But over yonder east, where the cabin is, there's canyons we fenced across. Why they are sendin' you up here I don't know. We was up this spring and overhauled the canyons. Water comes snortin' down in winter, washes things out. Two years ago the 'Paches got in here and run off horses. They killed and et some!'

'And the man that was up here?'

'What man?' Bowles asked.

'Staying at the cabin?'

'No man up here. What anybody be up here for? Abner sends somebody up ever' now and then to look around, like ridin' fence. I can't figger why he's sendin' you.'

'Two years ago the Indians didn't kill anybody?'

'Hell, no. They come an' was gone before we had time to git scairt. Harolday went down to the Reservation, but didn't git no hosses back. What you find so all-fired funny to grin at?'

'I was thinking of a joke I heard. It had to do with arrows, a man filled with arrows. The Indians had guns but used arrows on him!'

141

The horse-gentling and gentle-hearted Bowles said, 'I don't see how a joke like that can be funny.' Rocklin didn't tell him.

They moved into the darkness of the pines about midafternoon. Two deer that hadn't minded the horses got a sniff of the man smell, bounced up, and whipped off. Bowles watched them go like wind-blown shadows, then said, 'The only hankerin' I ever have to kill anything is some man I don't like!'

The cabin stood in a small, sunless clearing, and second growth was pointing its needled fingers skyward among the stumps left when the cabin had been built. Fifty yards back was a log corral with trees in it from which the lower branches had been cut. That beat trying to rip out stumps. A solidly built shed crossed the corral gate, giving the horses protection from rain on one side, gear and traps shelter on the other.

'The shed's her idea,' said Bowles. He never referred to Miss Arly by name; it was always 'she' and 'her,' as if no other woman mattered. He asked, 'Are you good with an ax?'

Rocklin said, 'No.'

'Then why the hell did they send you up here?'

The long one-room cabin was dank and musty, from being closed, and very dark. The windows were without glass and had heavy shutters that Bowles now opened and swung out. Four bunks in tiers of two, end to end, were against the east wall. An old kitchen stove stood at the other end of the room, and the woodbin was empty.

'How they got that stove up here I never could figger,' said Bowles. He lit a couple of candles and stuck them into beer bottles from which the bottoms had been broken, then he put the neck of one bottle into a knothole on the table, the other into an auger hole in the shelf by the stove.

Rough-hewn beams crossed the room, and wire with hooks at the ends dangled from the beams over the kitchen part of the cabin. Food that was hung there could not be reached by rats and mice.

Rocklin was unpacking, and Bowles took up the ax. 'I'll fetch wood. You can cook.'

The next day they rode up toward the fenced canyons. The barriers at canyon mouths were largely brush, piled up and overlaid with logs, sometimes with rocks at the base. 'All in good shape. She orta know. She rode up to see, her and Juan. It ain't rained much since. You're goin' to have yourself a lot of nuthin' much to do. I'd like to stay around and help.'

'Rustlers?'

Bowles hooted quietly. 'How'd they get up this way and why'd they wanta come? They'd have to haze the hosses back down along the Table. They try to catch 'em down in the valley. One of our hosses'll fetch a rustler purt-near a hundred dollars. Fishin's good up here. Mebbe they's gold back up yonder in the mountains – if you can find it.' Bowles's lazy voice discouraged the search. 'And it gits cold; all summer long it gits cold up here, nights.'

Rocklin was in a brooding muddlement as to why he had been sent so uselessly. She had guessed wrong if she thought that loneliness was punishment, but the man-filled-with-arrows was perhaps her idea of torment. Indians could come like shadows through darkness, but Bowles had made it a joke.

Bowles stayed on for three days – one longer than he was supposed to remain; and he would leave in the morning, reluctantly. 'You're a good cook!'

Rocklin was busy with supper and had stirred up a double batch of biscuits. A panful of trout that Bowles, with no need of artfulness, had twitched out of the icy canyon water lay in the skillet, ready to sizzle.

Bowles sat bareheaded by the table with the bench cocked back, as if trying to see how near he could come to falling over backward without falling. Pine snapped in the stove; otherwise there was silence and the whispering *shuash* of the pines in the darkness.

Rocklin's fingers were gummy with dough

and he walked to Bowles, lowered his head. 'Take off my hat, will you?' Bowles lifted it off, and Rocklin went back to the shelf table by the stove. Bowles studied the inside of the hat, then tried it on.

'Just fits. Let's trade?' He set the hat far back on his head. 'Not many fellows hereabouts wear white hats. Shows dirt too much, I reckon.'

Rocklin rubbed his hands until the sticky dough crumbled and, partially cleaning his fingers, he put flour on the dough and patted it out. He took up an empty baking-powder can for a cutter and set row after row into the greased pan. The fish were beginning to hum in the bacon grease, and the coffee foamed over with steamy and fragrant hiss. Rocklin pushed the pot to the back of the stove and was reaching out with a dipper of cold water to settle the grounds when the rifle was fired.

Rocklin jerked his head up and around, flinging the dipper away. For a long strained moment silence, the slightly deafened silence of numbed ears, and a whirl of powdersmoke, like a devil's halo, spread out in lazy drift above the candle on the table. He struck backhandedly at the candle on the shelf close to him and nicked his hand, without noticing, on the broken glass. When the candle was out he was in deep shadow, for the glow of the stove hearth was before him and the flame of the other candle was on the table before Bowles.

Bowles had his head down as if he hadn't heard a thing and was falling backward. He had been sitting with the bench off balance; the shock of the bullet into his body had given an impetus forward but not enough to overcome the teeter of the bench, and, with a delayed motion, he toppled backward. As his face passed backward through the candlelight it seemed strangely placid. Bench and body thumped down.

Rocklin reached behind him for the damp flour sack on a nail and scrubbed at his gummy hands. His revolver and belt were on a bunk near the other end of the room. The murderer might or might not know that, but undoubtedly knew there were two men here and perhaps waited. The outside darkness was as black as the blackness before the sun was created, and he could watch through the open window; perhaps was watching.

Rocklin worked the gumminess off his hands as well as he could, then rubbed his palms down against his legs. He wanted his hands clean when he got to his revolver, and he could feel the moisture of blood but no pain, and at first did not know that he had nicked his hand. He had to have darkness; as long as there was candlelight in the room the watcher at the window – if still there – would have it all his way. Rocklin wadded the damp flour sack loosely, bent forward, and tossed it; the sack spread out a little and fell across the candle on the table, whiffing it out.

Rocklin clumped on the run along the room. It would take more luck than an assassin had a right to to hit him. He tried to run lightly, but his footsteps sounded as loud as the beat of a club, and he jolted against the end of the bunk sooner than he expected; then he groped over the blanket, found the belt, moved his hand to the holster, and drew the gun. The blood trickle bothered him with its wetness on the handle, but things were more even now, and he waited in the hope of a revealing sound. The acrid odor of burned powder had spread like a stench through the room, and he could hear the trout sizzling in the greasy splutter of fast frying. From outdoors was only the gentle *shuash* of soft wind in the pine tops. The murderer had run cowardly, or waited patiently with an even greater cowardice.

Rocklin waited and nothing happened. It was too much like a cat at a mousehole, and he decided, *The hell with it!* He went to the front door, swung it open, jumped out and to one side. His feet were nearly noiseless in the matted needles. He couldn't have seen his hand a foot before his nose but felt security in being outdoors rather than cooped up in a room. He couldn't afterward recall just when he began to realize that the intention had not been to kill Bowles but him. The hat, and Bowles's back to the window, had given the fellow a wrong guess. The rifle had not been ten feet from Bowles's back.

He shifted the revolver to his left hand and wiped the blood on his leg. The air was chilly, and this waiting was too much with the strain of listening for any stir of movement. There was nothing to face, only the blank darkness and silence and sound of the wind in the trees.

He became sure that the man had shot and run, unaware of whom he had killed. Believing Rocklin dead, he would have no wish to shoot Bowles; that is, if it were Rocklin he had been after, and the white hat in the cabin's dimness made it look that way.

Rocklin tried to add up what facts seemed sure; the first was that Bowles had been killed mistakenly. Next, it must have been somebody who knew the lay of the land hereabouts; perhaps knew what to expect and was surprised to find that Rocklin wasn't alone. Bowles had stayed one day longer than he was supposed to stay. But the fellow had come to kill, and did, guided to his assurance by the hat. All that slowly added up to something, and he didn't like the answer.

He felt his way around the cabin, cautiously listening, and when he went back into the cabin it was with an awareness that the crafty murderer might have slipped inside and be waiting. He judged the chance and decided that a back shooter didn't have that much nerve, and struck a match and put it to the candle on the table, holding the revolver waist-high and ready. No one was in the room. He closed the door and went to each of the heavy shutters, drawing them to and hooking them. The trout was burning smokily. Rocklin picked up the skillet, opened the back door, flung it out.

He took the candle from its bottle and got down on a knee beside Bowles, staringly. This, then, was why he – Rocklin – had been sent up to the cabin to be alone. He frowned with the bitterness of thinking, *I'll take Bowles in across his saddle and tell her to have somebody try again!*

He went to the corral with a candle lantern. It was cold, the more cold because of an inner chill, and he raised the sheepskin about his neck. His glass-cut hand was stiffening slightly. He found the corral gate wide open; the horses were gone. He swung his lantern clear around the corral, making sure that none were snugged down in the needle warmth under a tree, but the corral was empty. The pack mares and saddle horses had been turned out.

There were many things to guess at, but Rocklin settled on the belief that the man

149

with the rifle had expected to find him here alone, and when he was dead there would be no one to feed the horses, so they had been turned out. Either that, or, having discovered Bowles was still here, the man had run the horses off and meant to leave Bowles afoot so that he couldn't get back to the ranch and tell the news.

He returned to the cabin, built up the fire, reheated the stale coffee. Whoever came up would find Bowles dead with a bullet in his back, and only Rocklin's story for how it happened. *She'll say I did it, that Bowles and me quarreled! Be like her; like a woman!* He looked across to where he had laid Bowles on the bunk under a blanket and felt the man's loss from the world, for there had been warmth in him and gentleness.

He heated water and soaked his hand, wanting the stiffness out of it; and after that he cleaned the fish skillet, threw out the coffee, threw away the biscuit dough, and methodically straightened things about the stove.

Dawn was late, and when he went out he saw why. The air was damply like rain. He began his search for some trace of the killer but could find no signs that he was sure of, not even the empty shell outside the window. He and Bowles had tramped all about the cabin, and he couldn't tell which were their boot-heel marks and which were some other man's. Of course the man had come on horseback, so Rocklin began a slow, plodding search, going around in an ever-widening circle. It was tiring to march on the slippery needles and he was unused to marching. At noon he stopped for more coffee, then returned to the search; and when he found where a horse had been tied he found merely a blurred trample that proved nothing, but it did make Rocklin suspect that the man had not ridden up to this spot until after dark. It was within two hundred yards of the cabin. *Of course,* he said, *anybody she sent would know the lay of the land!*

Nobody came that day, and Rocklin studied about trying to walk to the ranch. It could be done but would be hell. There was no chance at all to catch a horse, not loose on the Table, not on foot.

That night he sat sullenly by the fire with the shutters hooked and hated himself for a feeling that seemed cowardly. He couldn't believe that the man would come back, most certainly not until it was known that Bowles had been shot; but he felt something that was like uneasiness, and unceasingly he thought of the Harolday girl. *At least,* he thought, *she never made out that she liked me!*

Pete rode in the following afternoon with two saddle horses that had returned to the ranch. Rocklin heard his halloo and waited in front of the cabin. Pete began to drawl good-natured insults about a fine pair of cowmen that didn't know enough to keep a corral shut and so were set down on foot. It had been sweat-and-swear to lead the horses up the narrow rocky trail to the Table, and Pete wanted to rub in the salt; but Rocklin didn't speak or lift a hand, and Pete was still in the saddle when he sensed something wrong. 'What?' he asked. 'What?' Pete's eyes had much the color of bruised blackberries.

Rocklin said, 'You'll see,' and took the lead ropes, and Pete dropped out of the saddle and followed. Rocklin put the horses into the corral and stood by while Pete unsaddled under the shed. When Pete's horse was in, Rocklin closed the gate. It was made of poles from which the bark had begun to fall and sagged so that it had to be lifted to close or open. Then Rocklin said, 'Come on,' and they went in the back way.

Pete was young and had liked Bowles, and he had no thought of not believing it was just as Rocklin said. He sat down and put a hand to his stomach and said, 'God!' His mouth was so dry that his lips stuck, and he went to the bucket and drank, then came back and asked, 'Who could've done it?'

Rocklin shook his head. What he had figured out was his own secret, though he did say, 'It was meant for me.'

Pete studied. 'If Jager Clews hadn't gone

South, I'd say it was him! Or Bob; only Bob's cripple from how you tromped his arm. They make their brag that they allus get even. Just can't be anybody else that has it in for you – is there?'

'Who could it be?' Rocklin asked. Then: 'Somebody that knew his way around up here.' The old Mexican was in Rocklin's mind. Then: 'From what I hear, a rifle in the back is the way it's done over in this country. And how is the Harolday girl?'

Pete grinned solemnly. 'She raised billy-hell before she went back to town. She cornered me and wanted to know if I wasn't mad on account of my eye, and I told her no, and she said that showed I didn't have spunk. She looked mad as the devil, then all of a sudden laughed, real happy-like. Ever'body is goin' to feel bad over Bowles. Abner may want you to go on in an' tell how it was to the sheriff.'

'I'm staying here.'

'Whatever for?'

'I was sent here. If I'd had horses I'd have taken Bowles in; but you can, and I'll stay on till I'm told to leave. I'm not quitting.' Rocklin was quietly hard about it.

'But, man alive! if the feller finds out he didn't get you, and you're still here, he may come back!'

'Hope so!'

'You'd have no chance!'

'There are ways of evening chances. I'll try.'

153

'But you in here and him out there in the dark – you're crazy, man!'

Rocklin let it go at that, not explaining what he had in mind; he didn't feel it anything to be proud of.

The next morning there was a drizzle seeping down from the mountains, with the clouds in a low, foglike sag and seemingly caught in the treetops. They put the tarp from the bedroll about Bowles and lashed him over his saddle.

Rocklin rode out with Pete well beyond the timber, then turned back. He was wearing Caldwell's slicker over the sheepskin and had hung up the coat on a peg by the door.

One thing he recalled continuously – Mrs Bruce's warning about Arly. 'She'll get even with you somehow. She sure will! Nobody ever got the best of her!'

He soaked his hand again in salt water. The soreness bothered him even at making cigarettes, would be worse if he had to use a rifle. He had buckled his revolver on the left, not liking to do it, but his other hand was swelling.

That afternoon he set about making his tell-tales. From the toolbox under the shed he got the tools to draw the lead from rifle shells, then shook out the powder and filed the heads off. On each side of the cabin he worked a shell through a chink in the logs,

154

about four feet from the floor. He had a large spool of black packthread in his kit for sewing on buttons and mending rips, and he led a piece of the thread out through a shell and staked the end about fifty feet from the house. He took four empty tin cans, punched a hole near the top edge of each, and tied the other end of the thread to a can and set the can on the floor, leaving the thread not quite taut. He did that four times. Whoever approached the cabin in the dark would almost certainly disturb a thread, and if a can clinked over he would hear it; awake or asleep, he would hear it. The feel of the thread might alarm whoever was trying to sneak up, but if so, all right.

CHAPTER TEN

The next day a sopping rain fell with monotonous drip, drip, drip, and the bleakness of twilight darkened the cabin at noon. He fed the horse, chopped wood – not easily, for his hand had swollen – and that afternoon he inspected his thread lines and found them sagging, but when they were tightened the cans fell over. He weighted the cans with bolts from the toolbox, fixed dinner, cleaned up, and thought about shaving, but his hand was stiff and painful. He sat down over an old Gallup saddle catalogue that he had found on a shelf. The sob of the rain droned through the window that was unshuttered to admit air.

Full darkness came. He turned the catalogue pages slowly. A can clinked over. It fell as if without meaning. At first he didn't move except to look toward the can and wonder if a pine cone's fall or increased wetness on the thread had pulled it over, but he couldn't ignore the signal even if he had to feel a fool later for using stealth to match an enemy that was not there. He swung his legs around the bench and crouched low to keep below the open window as he moved to the back door.

He had not paused for hat or slicker, and the wet blackness momentarily blinded him. It was the can that stood as a telltale for the open-windowed side of the cabin that had fallen, and he stepped softly to the corner and looked along the side.

A figure was there, a small figure, peering through the dim candlelight and leaning the closer because no one could be seen inside, and in the window's light he could see the rifle that slanted down across Arly's forearm. He called harshly, 'Safer to sing out, don't you think?'

She cried back at him, 'Oh, Rocklin!' with the sound of calling his first name eagerly, and her face left the windows and was lost in the darkness as he answered.

'No chance for a mistake this time!'

She came toward him with uneven swish of feet among the wet needles, and she paused lingeringly close to him in the darkness, and there was a lavenderish smell about her that vaguely reminded him of something; but he didn't know what and didn't care. He had seen the rifle balanced muzzle down in the crook of her left elbow, and at that moment the protesting voices of angels could not have persuaded him that it was otherwise than he thought.

The back door was ajar, and he opened it wide and she went in ahead of him. Water dripped from her and spilled down the barrel of the rifle. She was wearing a heavy wool jacket but no slicker, and the divided skirt clung as if loosely glued to her legs. She stood the rifle quickly against the wall, flung off the jacket, let it fall to the floor, loosened the chin thongs of the flat-brimmed hat and tossed it away, and lifted her head, looking up at him. Her tawny eyes were bright, and she stood on her toes and her lips were parted, and the glow on her wet face was a promise and an invitation; but it made him mad. He had been kissed before in the way of deceit and betrayal, and he was sure that she hated him, so this could mean nothing except that she thought him a complete fool.

He said, 'Don't you know better than to set a rifle against its sight?'

That was something to show how little he cared, and he took up the rifle and laid it on the table, noting the half-cock. 'Where's your horse?' First, the proper care of the rifle; now the proper care of the horse, while she held up her face inviting him to kiss her.

A shocked look came into her face, and sudden pale anger, and shame whipped little tongues of fire all over her body; but she turned quickly, keeping a stiff back, and would have sworn her soul away in denying there had been any such offer or weakness. She went near the stove and held her un-gloved hands to the heat. She did not look at him and her voice was carefully cool; she was refusing to admit even anger now. 'Out there. I'd just got off.'

He came near her when he took a splinter from a piece of pine, dripped it into the fire through the hearth, and touched the candle. He was set, too, but now he set down the lantern and took his hat, slipped into the sheepskin, and pulled the slicker on over it, bulkily. Caldwell had been a big man.

When he was at the door, leaving, she asked, 'What do you mean to do?'

'Put up your horse.'

'Put up my horse!' Now she was looking at him and looked astounded, too. 'You don't suppose I am staying here, do you? Put my

158

saddle on one of yours.' Then: 'I came to tell you Jim Brotherton is dead and you are to–'

Rocklin said glumly, 'In the back?'

'How could you know?'

He held his words, then: 'It's the way men die in this country!' He stared for a moment at her rifle on the table, looked up at her, gestured toward the open window, then nodded. 'I have reason to know!' he added, brutally careful to pack his tone with what he meant, 'I was told you'd get even with me. You will, I reckon!' Amazement swirled over her face and she caught her breath; and his calmness mocked her, and with deliberate fall of words, as if he meant them unadmiringly, 'Not many have got your kind of grit. "Try, try again," hm?' Then he went out.

For a long time Arly stood rigidly, as if still listening to what he had said, then she began to shiver and sat down on the bench, hating him but hating herself more, for shame went down into the marrow of her bones and ached. She wanted to bawl, but her eyes were dry and her fingers were clenched together and her nails marked her palms.

She knew what had happened to Jim Brotherton, for she had just returned from town when Pete came down from the Table with Bowles across the saddle; and Pete told her that Rocklin was still up at the cabin and would stay, stubbornly. 'Whoever wants to kill him that bad can do it easy and will come

159

back sure!' said Pete.

It was then that Arly remembered what had been in her mind in the first place when she had sent him to the cabin to be alone, and she had no shame about, for she loved him. She had never before loved anything but horses and brown Mexican babies and her own self. She had never in her life resisted an upsurging impulse, and she made up her mind to go at once to Rocklin, and go alone, without even Juan knowing; and what Juan might think afterward she didn't care. Of all the men she had known, Rocklin stood tall and unyielding and unboastful, with a quiet hardness that made her furious, but it had made her love him. Jealousy of Clara Caldwell had gone out of her as though it had never been, and in town she had even bought a sachet from the druggist and pinned it inside of her waist.

So Arly had slipped away without anyone knowing. She had no fear for herself, but as she rode into the wet darkness of the timber she could anxiously imagine that a man, or men, were again prowling about the cabin. The Clews boys, or at least Jager, she thought; so she had taken the rifle from its scabbard and had retained it when she dismounted and came to peer through the window to see how he looked and exultantly imagine the surprise he would feel when she snuggled close to him for warmth from the wet cold and for warmth from the world that gave her a restless and bad-tempered loneliness.

Now not even pride nor anger nor the heat of the stove could keep the chill out of her, and she locked her jaws because her teeth chattered; it was like a weakness that she despised in herself.

Rocklin took a gunny sack and rubbed down the horse that Arly had ridden in; it was his way with horses and gave him time to think, and the thinking hurt. He knew now that he didn't want to believe, and didn't believe, what he had first thought when he had found her at the window with the rifle. He put her saddle on another horse, and with a sore hand it was slow work.

He went back into the cabin and stopped beside the door and eyed her, but she would not look at him. When he began to take off his slicker she said, with face averted, 'Keep it on. You are staying out of here till I dry my clothes. Then I am leaving.' Her hurt had too much ache for mere temper, and she was concealing the hurt as best she could.

He picked her thick woolen jacket from the floor; it was heavy with wetness and would not dry for hours. Arly faced about and said, 'Let me have that.' She took it from him and ran a hand into the side pocket and brought out a folded paper on which the pieces of Clara's letter had been pasted. Slowly, persistently, with throb of eyestrain from such unfamiliar, tedious labor, she had fitted the torn bits of paper. Moisture tonight had loosened many of the pieces, but there were enough in place to prove that she had put the letter together. She did not offer the reconstructed letter but merely laid it on the table, showing him, and she did it without petulance. 'You will want to work for the Caldwell now, anyhow.' It was said unbitterly, but she would not look at him.

He crumpled it slowly, lifted a pothole cover from the stove, dropped it in. The fire had burned down, and he took up pieces of pine left-handedly and laid them among the coals. He asked, 'Why did you send me up here? Nobody stays here. Nobody is needed. And that story about the man filled with arrows?'

Arly wouldn't look at him. She slowly pushed at her damp hair, getting it off her face. She would have let her tongue wither before she would have told the truth, which would have been something like: *I hated you for making me love you, but I was without shame; and I wanted you to be alone and far off, so that I could come to you!*

Rocklin added, 'I was hired at top wages. Sent here with nothing to do and no sense in being here. Why?'

Then Arly did look at him. 'I am sorry

Jager Clews mistook Bowles for you! We'll miss Bowles.'

He told her, 'It couldn't have been Jager. He was out of the country. Went South.'

Her face had frozen tightness and she kept her voice down. 'Jager always leaves the country when he means to burn a barn, steal a horse, shoot somebody.' Her hand moved toward the door. 'Please go out.' She was icy about it: She could see how he was looking at her and read his mind. 'Don't apologize!' That was icy, too.

He ignored it and walked along the room to reach out and bring the shutter to and hook it, giving her privacy for drying her clothes. In returning, his foot struck against a can, overturning it with rattle of iron in tin. In a quick moment her puzzled peering at the cans on the floor changed to understanding. 'Oh, coward, too!' she said. 'I hadn't thought *that!*'

Rocklin faced her from across the table. *Coward* left a bruise, but he wouldn't quarrel. Putting up signals was no more cowardly than setting men to guard. He wouldn't say so. He did ask grimly, 'Why are you so sure it was Jager Clews?'

Arly hated the steadiness of his look; it was like something that took hold of her and held on and made her helpless. She drew a long breath, then said, 'I sent him! That's why!'

163

Rocklin waited beneath the shed with the candle lantern on the ground beside him. He was wet under the sheepskin and slicker, and the chill ate on him gnawingly, and his hand hurt. He could see now what a fool he had been to suspect a thing like that of this girl, but nothing could be done about it. He tried to think of Jim Brotherton – in the back, too. Like Caldwell; like Bowles. He couldn't argue with her about it having been Jager Clews that shot Bowles, but he wasn't convinced and would like to ask, 'How does it happen Jager knows the Table so well?'

The back door opened, and Arly called, pitching her voice against the plash of rain, 'Bring my horse here!'

He didn't answer and went to the house, bringing the lantern but no horse. She faced him at the door with: 'Where's my horse?'

'I unsaddled,' he said, and pushed by her. That was definite; then he added, 'No night for a horse to be out.' He wouldn't admit, 'Or a girl.' He stripped off the slicker, shed the sheepskin, and his shirt clung clammily. He held his hat by the brim and swung it down, shaking off the water, then hung it on a peg.

She had her head up watching him. 'What do you mean?'

'You can go at daylight.'

The steamy smell of wet wool filled the room; the jacket was across the drying-line at the back of the stove and still dripped. Arly had put on her hat, but the chin thongs were loose, and by way of a wrap she had taken Caldwell's coat from a wall peg and rolled back the sleeves that overlapped her hands, and the skirt of the coat hung below her hips. He sensed a change in her, as if some new thought had come alarmingly, and she was bracing herself against his presence; not fear, exactly, but rather as if she had decided that he was despicable. It was in her eyes; maybe she put it there to make him feel bad; maybe she really felt uneasy because he had refused to bring her horse. He wasn't going to let her ride off in the dark and try to go down the rocky Table trail in the wet night.

He unlatched the stove door with the end of a piece of stovewood and poked the wood in.

Arly said, 'You ought to be killed!'

He stepped back and closed the stove door with his foot, then flipped up the top of the coffeepot. She had spoken as if she meant it, not merely out of bad temper. He reached for the bucket dipper, poured water into the pot, and moved the pot out onto the stove to boil. She watched him spread the jacket on the drying-line, and when he turned she said, 'So you cheat at cards!'

She tried to make a whiplash out of her tongue, but what she said didn't mean anything to him. It wasn't worth an answer and he wouldn't quarrel, not over something her malice had made up.

He said, 'I'm going to change my shirt. You can look the other way.' He started by her toward his bunk for the dry shirt, but Arly stepped before him, barring the way.

Her head was scarcely above his high shoulders, but she meant for him to stand and he did. He was calmly puzzled as she reached deep into the inside coat pocket of the big coat and drew out a small folder. With the folder came three playing-cards that slipped with slick newness from her fingers and fluttered in zigzag fall. His glance followed them and returned to her face.

She thrust the folder at him. 'Read it!' she said. 'Then lie out of it – if you can!'

He took it and read: *To Cardplayers. These cards are by far the finest ever printed … marked on all four corners alike … almost impossible to find the marks without the key which, when learned, makes out cards as easily read from the back as from the face…* This offer is open only to our regular customers, such as you… *Samples of Nos. 1, 3, and 6 enclosed… Price per pack $2.* There was a Chicago address.

He turned the folder over and back and shook his head. *This offer is open only to our regular customers, such as you* was heavily underscored with a pencil mark. He said,

166

'Nothing to do with me. That's Caldwell's coat.'

'Red Caldwell cheat at cards!' She seemed about to whip up her hand into his face. 'I never liked him, but he wasn't a blackleg!'

'You saw me get the coat that night. Brotherton gave it to Pete. I've never had it on.' He studied rememberingly, added, 'Never once.'

'That's easy said, Rocklin. And you would lie about it – wouldn't you?'

'Anything else in the pockets?'

'I think it enough, don't you?' She wouldn't back up, but she had to remember how he had got the coat, and at the moment of finding the folder she had wanted to believe the worst she could; now she couldn't quite, but she could keep on pretending. She pointed toward the sample cards that had fallen. 'I suppose you never saw them before?'

He stooped to pick up one of the cards, but it was new and glazed and the fingers of his right hand would not take hold, so he used his left. He took up the three cards and turned close to the candle and looked at their backs. Two were blue and one was red, and they all had an intricate design of curlicues about like other playing-cards except that the basic figures were rosettes and trefoils, though he didn't know the names of such things; and very good-looking, too.

167

He held out the folder and cards, offering them to her, and said, 'Go ahead; say so to folks, if you want. But you'll want to show these when you tell your lie!'

Arly's hand went up as hard as she could swing it; the smack sound was like the bursting of a small paper bag, but it didn't move his face and she might as well have slapped a board. He looked at her steadily, without smile or frown, and he didn't seem angered. She stood defiantly, as if daring him to strike back, but he walked around her and went to change his shirt.

Arly said no, when he offered coffee, but he poured a tin cup full and put it before her anyhow, and she wouldn't touch it but longed for it. She pretended not to notice while he soaked his hand in hot water, but her look drifted again and again to the basin he was using. She had seen how swollen his hand was.

He told her, 'You'd better go lay down; have some sleep.' She said no, but the night dragged and she was weary, tired from the long ride, and tired from the tug and strain of anger, the bitterness of having been a fool. At last she got up and went to a bunk and was glad in a way that he hadn't let her have a horse; she could have saddled for herself if she had really wanted to go, but she was worn out and knew it. Now she didn't believe that he was a blackleg, but she didn't believe it of Red Caldwell, either. The bunk mattress was pine needles overlaid with canvas. She spread the coat over her legs and faced the wall, and through the night, when she stirred and raised herself up, she saw him sitting at the table with his back to her, and much of the time his hand was in the basin of hot water.

In the morning they ate breakfast in silence. She refused more coffee by putting her hand over the top of the cup and not looking at him. He could use his hand only with difficulty, and when he began washing up she took a flour sack and wiped, not saying a word.

Her heavy wool jacket had dried by the fire all night, and she got into it. He tossed the slicker toward her, saying, 'You can use that, too,' but she paid no attention and let the slicker lie where it fell, and he didn't pick it up.

He opened the door, and she said, 'Rocklin?' and he turned and waited and his face was blank. He was carrying her rifle, taking it out to the saddle scabbard, and she pointed toward it. 'You really thought that last night?'

'For a minute.'

'You thought that's why I sent you up here?'

If she knew about Judith she might understand, but he couldn't say anything about her; but he did say, 'I still don't think Jager

169

Clews would've got here so quick or known his way so well!'

'Still meaning I had something to do with it?'

There was temper in her voice now and a readiness to say fierce things, but he answered gravely, 'No, not a bit. Not now. But for all I knew, you had it in for me bad. Some women'll do anything. I don't know 'em well enough to tell what they'll do. A man's easy fooled if a woman wants him that way. The best thing is to be careful.'

Arly's lips curled with studied scorn. 'If I ever shoot you, it won't be in the back! I'll want you to know who's doing it!' She flipped her hand, telling him to go on. He went and she followed.

The rain had lessened, but there was a drizzling drip through the pines. He lifted on the saddles, but without a word she put the latigo through each cinch ring because the suppleness had gone from his right hand. They rode off, leaving the corral gate wide, and he held back, letting her lead.

She could ride, that girl; saddle, woman, and horse were of a piece. He didn't know that she had been cradled on horseback in the arms of a woman that rode sidesaddle and headlong.

When they reached the foot of the trail coming down from the Table, Juan was there. He hadn't known when Arly left or where she was going, but he had a telescope and had seen her returning. He could read her face, and his distrustful eyes seemed to expect a quarrel with Rocklin, for he said to her in Spanish, 'This man has angered you.' But Arly snapped, *'No puede ser tal cosa!'*

Then she turned, suspicious that Rocklin understood, but he was readjusting the sheepskin before him on the saddle. The day had turned warm, hot even. He pretended a disinterest in what he didn't seem to understand, and he knew that he didn't in the least understand her.

Juan said quietly, *'Eso si que no me gusta!'* and looked hard at Rocklin, but Arly spoke rapidly.

'I am tired, and do not question me; you have no right to question me!' Juan's narrowed eyes did question her, and she continued swiftly and in Spanish. 'He must go at once to the Caldwells, for he is the girl's cousin, and I rode to where he was merely to tell him that. He would not have believed anyone else! Let him have a fresh horse.'

Then Arly twisted her body in the saddle and called, 'Rocklin!' When he looked up she said furiously, 'I have just told Juan that you are a liar, a cheat, and a coward and are never to set foot on this ranch again!' She loped off.

Rocklin sat and watched her go, and when he quit trying to puzzle that one out he saw

171

how Juan was watching him. He looked into the Mexican's steady eyes and said evenly, 'You understand English?'

Juan nodded. 'Yes, señor.'

'Then what about it, now?'

Juan spoke gravely. 'Also I understand the señorita.'

'Damned if I do!' Then: 'Since that didn't make you mad at me, what else would she need to say?'

Juan shrugged a shoulder and was unsmiling. 'Her words say any wild thing!'

Abner's hand moved with no nervousness around his jaw, pulling at the wrinkled flesh. 'We hear you're the girl's cousin. I hear she told Lee Frank so herself and wants you to run things. She'll need somebody, now that Jim's dead. Somebody honest.'

'Brotherton was?'

'Caldwell's manager for near twenty years!'

Rocklin wondered, still suspicious of why he had been sent for. That didn't have an honest feel. He asked, 'And Garley?'

Abner thought it over. 'Personal, I don't know. About Jim, I do. Jim had gone to town with Lee Frank and hired a rig, and Lee was drivin' the women out to the ranch and Jim was on ahead to get home first. They come on him in the road, not more'n a mile from the ranch house. Shot in the back like Red Caldwell had been.'

'Same man, you think?'

Abner shook his head. 'Don't know, but off-hand it looks that way. Only why? Men that couldn't get on with Red got on fine with Jim.' Abner pointed. 'Your hand is bad swole. Soak it in Epsom salts and put on an onion plaster. You'll need two good hands!'

'And Bowles,' Rocklin said 'He got a bullet in the back that was meant for me. Looks like somebody might want to wipe out all that has anything to do with the Caldwell ranch.'

Abner considered that but said, 'Don't think so. We are purt-near sure it was Jager Clews killed Bowles. The Old Man went up yonder, and he said Jager was makin' his brag that he'd foller an' git you.' Abner bobbed his head emphatically. 'He's mean; both Clewses are mean.'

'Then he didn't go South?'

'He's got friends to say he did if he wants.'

'How did he know his way around so well up there?' Rocklin asked, still doubtful. 'And as a horse thief, why did he turn the horses loose?'

'He turned 'em loose so the man he thought was Bowles would be afoot. Been a big risk to try to lead 'em down off the Table. And as for knowin' his way around – don't ask me how horse thieves know the country so well!' When Rocklin started off Abner slowly raised his hand and said, 'Luck!'

Rocklin thought, *I'll need it. Maybe the women have gone back to town. I hope so. If that old lady is still there when I ride in, the roof will fly off!*

CHAPTER ELEVEN

He went out over the wagon road, and when he came to the Y he looked toward the cottonwoods. Her lies, Juan had as much as said, were unimportant; but how to know the truth? He put Arly out of his mind, for there were murders to think of, and the Caldwell girl, and old Miss Martin, the fat Garley, too; and had he misjudged Brotherton's honesty? He thought of the folder and marked cards in Caldwell's coat, which he was now wearing; they definitely meant some kind of dishonesty. That brought back Arly's 'So you cheat at cards!' She had momentarily believed that. He was glad that he knew Spanish, but he wasn't sure whether she had lied to Juan to shelter him or herself from the old Mexican's reproach. He said, 'Damn her!' wishing now that he had taken Arly, as bad as he thought her, into his arms when she came to him offering her lips. He thought grimly, *When you don't make a fool of yourself you wish you had!*

174

He left the road at the trail turn-off and for a time went downhill with his gaze searching. He had been this way only once, in darkness, and couldn't be sure if other trails came in; it would be dark again before he reached the Caldwell ranch. Rain splatter had reached out just far enough to obliterate old tracks, and there were no new ones on the trail. His hand hurt as if the devil had his teeth in it, and he thought of town and a doctor, for he knew what blood poisoning could do. He ached for a cigarette but couldn't roll one; the fingers had stiffened; the palm was swollen and boil-red.

As he rode he saw that it was mostly good grazing, though high, stony outcroppings and tall thickets were good for rustlers and would make men swear on the roundup; but water seeped down from the mountains, and a lush green in the dips showed where there were pools, or would be, if men dug. *Nesters go to water like flies to a carcass.*

Luck and a sense of direction helped, and when he came over a hill and looked across to the far thrust of the hogback they had short-cut when coming out from town, he knew he wasn't far from the Caldwell: It was near nightfall, and he lifted his horse into an easy lope.

Rocklin rode up and hailed the house. It was dark but scarcely bedtime for chickens, yet there was no light and no reply, but he could smell wood smoke. Even that didn't make him sure anybody was here, but he got off and went to the door and knocked. 'Anybody home?' He heard a vague stir inside but no reply, and he knocked again.

Old Miss Martin's high voice came through the door. 'Who are you?'

'Rocklin!'

She cried, 'Go away! Go away from here! We don't want you here!' Then she screeched, 'We have a gun!'

He thought, *The hell with you!* and almost said it, but he heard Clara call, 'Mr Rocklin! Don't – don't go away!' Her voice had a plea like desperation.

The old lady began scolding shrilly, but there was the sliding scrape of the door bar, and the door opened, swinging inward from the pull of Clara's hands.

The lamp was burning, but it had been turned low and boxed in to hide the light, and torn strips of tarp hung before the closed windows, and the big room had a smothering staleness, rank with coal oil; and there was a smell of coffee that had been heated on the rusty round stove. Loneliness and fear had made these Eastern women try to cover themselves with darkness, as if pretending that the house was uninhabited would give them protection; but nevertheless they had used a fire.

Rocklin was ready to think they were all a little crazy. Old Miss Martin backed off and held a rifle with the awkwardness of one who didn't know a thing about rifles. The butt was far back under her armpit and the muzzle stuck up and to one side. 'Don't you dare set foot in here!' she warned.

He walked in as if he hadn't heard, and as he went by, Clara clutched at his arm with no force, timidly wanting to hold him back from danger. He went straight to the table and slapped the cardboard away from the lamp and turned up the wick. The lifted flame ran shadows back like frightened things into corners. He turned to Miss Martin and, not speaking, took hold of the rifle and pulled it from her hands. She didn't let go readily but did not try to resist; she was afraid, for he looked as if he might strike her. He saw that she hadn't known enough to cock the hammer, and when he threw open the breechblock he also saw that the gun was unloaded, but he doubted if she knew that.

He turned away from her, and she put on her severest manner, lifting her head and demanding; 'What are you doing here?'

His back was toward her and he was close to Clara, and he answered the old lady by saying to Clara, 'To do whatever *you* want!' He had thought of her letter and its honesty, and there was a kinship, too, and he wanted her to know how he felt.

Clara looked as sadly weary and haggard as if she had endured torment, and he knew it must be torment to live in the shadow of the Martin woman. Clara stared up at him and said, 'Oh!' The unexpected and greatly desired had come to her, and her fingers touched his breast as if afraid to touch it; but he reached an arm about her and she pressed yieldingly against him, overpowered by tiredness.

Miss Martin rushed up and gave him a push. 'Take your arm from around my niece!' She was almost hysterical, but Rocklin looked at her and said matter-of-factly, 'We are cousins!' That gave her a jolt that shut her up for a moment, for it meant that Rocklin knew who he was.

He led Clara to a chair, and she sat down with a stare in her big wide eyes that thanked him and seemed begging for more reasons to thank him; but Miss Martin was not speechless now, and she came at the girl, trying to stab her with staccato shrieks. He wasn't a cousin, she said, not even a tenth cousin, not even from the same branch of the family, and all he wanted was to delude and cheat Clara; that was why he had come into the country. '–and you won't listen to me! After all these years that I have protected and looked after you like a mother.' Rocklin eyed her and thought of an angry blue jay's squawky petulance. 'Clara Caldwell, you *are* going back to town if I have to drag you!' That was hysteria.

Clara left the chair to get away from her, and as she passed Rocklin she told him in a weary, beaten voice, 'It has been like this for days! Just like this! And I am not going back to that horrible Judge Garley!' Clara's strength seemed all passive, but it was strength; she would not give in. She moved tiredly to the end of the room and sat on a bunk and closed her eyes.

Miss Martin gathered herself into the tightness of pressed elbows, stiff shoulders, and started to follow, but Rocklin stood in her way, and she glared along her high-arched nose to defy him. The pain Rocklin felt in his hand brightened the anger in his look, and he had the coldly deliberate impulse to hit her. She saw it and exclaimed, 'I believe you would kill me!'

'Gladly!'

His reply and anger frightened her and she stepped back, backing so quickly against the chair Clara had just left that she tripped backward and sat down, dropping hard and out of breath.

Rocklin glowered. 'Let that girl alone. I mean stop your chatter and squawking. You heard me say I'd do whatever she wants done. I'd like for her to ask me to choke you!'

179

Lee Frank saw him riding up to the bunkhouse, and when Rocklin swung off, ground-hitching his horse with fall of reins, and introduced himself, the three or four men in the doorway shuffled aside, inviting him in, and silently sized him up.

The many days' growth of coarse, dark-red stubble concealed the outline of his face. Their own faces were shiny from the supper wash-up, and the marks of the comb teeth had dried in their wetted hair.

He showed his hand under the lamp, letting them see why he hadn't shaken hands. Lee Frank sent a man to unsaddle, and Rocklin said, 'I'd like a smoke.' Left-handedly he drew sack and papers and laid them on the table, but a sour-looking man named Joe rolled from his own and gave the cigarette to Rocklin, who rested his elbow on the table and kept the swollen hand raised on a straight forearm because that somewhat eased the throb.

Lee Frank said, 'We got no cook. He got mad over the women bein' here and having to lug grub.' Lee was short, had a roughly good-natured face, ugly, pleasant, hard, and he droned the words, not smiling, but not even with: 'He tried to scare 'em back to town by sayin' Indians was liable to come. He even fixed up a door bar and give 'em old tarp to hang on windows to keep Indians from peekin' in and a rifle that won't shoot.

But they wouldn't go, so he did. Said it was the only way for him not to kill that old woman. Now Joe here is cookin', and he's purposeful bad so somebody else'll want the job.'

The men didn't smile much and Joe not at all; they knew this palaver was a kind of warming up for more important talk.

Joe flipped a thumb at Lee. 'He told the girl there wasn't no Injuns.'

'We like the girl,' said Lee.

Rocklin slowly blew smoke across the lamp chimney and the heat spun it. Nothing more was said for a time. A man scratched a match he had been holding, relit his cigarette; another moved a chair and straddled it with his arms across the back, chin resting on his arms. Lee was eyeing Rocklin. 'That's the coat Red had tied on his saddle when he was killed.'

Rocklin told them, 'There was an advertisement for marked cards in a pocket of this coat and samples of the cards. I've wondered why.'

The quiet was solemn, and they looked from one to another and slowly shook their heads, denying that Red Caldwell would have anything to do with marked cards.

Lee said, 'Jim told me he give you the coat. And a slicker. Jim liked you. Liked you so much,' Lee went on, dropping his voice, 'he wanted that money you left with him give

181

back to you.'

'But we met only for a minute!'

'It was enough. Jim was killed down the road a piece. I was bringin' the women in Harolday's double-seated buggy. It's still here. We found him layin' in the road. Ther's rocks and scrub oak and a draw to ride off in there. The feller somehow knew Jim would be along ahead of us. Knew the country!'

'Jager Clews!' said Joe bitterly.

Rocklin dabbed out his cigarette and for a moment soothingly stroked his hand. 'Jim and Bowles the same way; and Red, too, I hear. Jager was in prison, so he didn't kill Red.'

Joe spoke up wrathfully. 'No, but he allus said he'd get Jim. I hear he said he'd kill you, too. It looks like mebbe he tried.'

Lee asked, 'And who else but the Clewses would have it in for you, Rocklin? Oh, you had a little run-in with Clint Harolday, but Clint's only a kid. He never done it.'

Joe in his half-angry way said, 'I wouldn't put it past him!'

Rocklin looked thoughtfully at his hand. 'Three times the same way – with a rifle in the back! That looks like one man's work.'

'Meanin' you don't suspicion Jager?' Joe asked, almost quarrelsome.

'Meaning he might know Jim would be riding home ahead of the buggy, but how would he know to find me in the cabin on the Table? Know to find the corral gate up there in the dark? Know even to find his way about up there?'

They pondered that but were not impressed, then Lee Frank said, 'The girl wants you to run the ranch. She told me so. Told who you are. I think Jim talked with her about you. Are you goin' to run it?'

'Can't say – yet. This man Garley may stop me. I don't know. We are going in tomorrow to see if he'll try. See if he can if he does try.'

Rocklin's hand ached through the night and his sleep was unrestful.

When Joe stumbled sleepily into the kitchen at 3 a.m. he found a fire going and Rocklin with his hand in a pan of hot water.

Later, but still early enough for lamplight, he talked with Lee Frank about driving the women into town. 'I can't drive with this hand like it is, and I want to go ahead and get to a doctor.'

'I'll send somebody in with 'em,' said Lee.

Rocklin rode off in the dawn and passed the low house a quarter of a mile down the road where the women had blinded the windows to keep Indians from peeking in.

Soon by a far look from the uplands he could make out the miles-away green patches of nester-fenced land over the Flats where the Hesico spread its water underground, betraying cattlemen by giving its moisture to the enemies of open range. Sooner or later the farmers would come creeping over the uplands, too, and there would be dams and ditches and fences, and there would be nothing much that cattlemen could do about it except hang on, refuse to sell out, and be licked in the end. They were always licked in the end, but there was something about not giving up that found a favoring response in Rocklin's understanding.

Doc Riding took his heels off the window sill, twisted his head toward the door, but did not get up. He saw a tall, stubble-bearded man in a white hat and a look of pain in his eyes. 'What's the matter with you?' the doc asked gruffly. He had lived in the West so long that a kind of sunburned, weather-beaten crust had formed on him.

'Cut my hand on a bottle five-six days back. Bothers me.'

'Come over here and let me see.'

Rocklin laid aside his hat and edged by worn chairs, squeezed between the desk and the wall, held out his swollen hand. 'Hm,' said Doc Riding, feeling high up on the forearm and squeezing to see if the pain went as far as the elbow. 'I've seen worse. No pus?'

'No.'

'Too bad. The trouble with you healthy fellows, you heal too quick.' He opened a cupboard and poured a double drink of whisky into a thin glass. 'Drink this and set

184

down. Mighty swollen but I'll gouge around and see what we can find. If you bellyache like the last fellow with a bad arm, I'll strap you down. Bob Clews. Know him?'

Rocklin finished off the whisky. 'Seen him a time or two.'

The doc put a leather bag on the desk and bent over it, looking inside. 'A man named Rocklin stepped on him.'

Rocklin thought it over. 'That's my name.'

'That's what I guessed, white hat and all.' He raised his glance, studied Rocklin, noted the way the revolver was slung. 'You left-handed?'

'No.'

'Bob Clews is in town. Him, Wally Russell, and another fellow – stranger. That's three. You're one and one-handed. Bob's hand is good enough to hold a gun. I'm a doctor – would treat a sick dog – or I'd never have dressed his arm. The kind of man I like to work on is old Dave Staller. He come in and I shaved his head and sewed it up. He didn't know whether he'd fell off the stage or tried to butt down a house.'

'Is Dave around?'

'He's freighting for the Fossler boys. Harolday'll soon want him back. Red Caldwell was your uncle?'

'That's what I hear. I don't know more than I hear.'

Doc Riding had his back to the window

185

and was whetting a razor-edged scalpel on the desk. He opened a drawer and took out a piece of lead for Rocklin to look at. 'That's what come out of Red.' He reached into the drawer again, offered another piece of lead that was less perfect in its bullet shape. 'This, Jim.'

'Same gun?'

Doc Riding shook his head. 'I don't know, but the same caliber – .38-.40.'

'What about Bowles?'

'Arly had him buried up at Santee because she liked him. As coroner I could go dig him up, I suppose. And get shot myself, depending on the mood she is in.'

Rocklin studied the two bullets and asked casually, 'Has she ever shot anybody?'

The doc put away his oilstone. 'No, but don't for a moment think she wouldn't!' he sounded serious, and the look he gave Rocklin added to his seriousness. 'Don't ever again walk away from her when she's holding a gun!'

'Over in my part of the country there aren't many .38-.40s. Men don't like them.' He returned the bullets to the doctor.

'No, not for anything much over a hundred yards or so,' Doc Riding agreed. 'This fellow probably shot from twenty yards – both men. I asked the Fossler boys. They sell shells. This kind mostly to nesters. I didn't learn anything helpful. All right, now hold out your hand and keep your mouth shut.' He picked up the scalpel.

A half hour later Rocklin left the office with his bandaged hand in a sling. It hurt, but with good, clean, honest pain, not a gnawing throb, and he reeked with the smell of carbolic acid. Doc Riding had shown him a chip of brown glass not half the size of a match head.

Rocklin was in the barber's chair when the flat-faced agent came in and smirked up close with: 'The Old Man wants to see you.' The barber twitched the razor from the half-shaven face as Rocklin took his hand from under the apron, wiped a knuckle across his mouth to clear off soap, and said, 'I'll come.'

Harolday stood behind the high, sloping desk and laid a finger on the ledger, holding his place when he looked up and said, 'Mornin',' tonelessly; then he told the agent to go to dinner. After the agent had gone Harolday closed the ledger, eyed Rocklin's bandaged hand, then he crossed his hands behind him and said, 'Tell me all about it.'

'You mean Bowles?'

'For a start.' His drooping gauntness gave him an air of peering forward with a cold and calculating stare. He had a right to know, and Rocklin told him but made no mention of Arly or of marked cards. Harolday listened with a pondering look and kept his eyes on Rocklin's face, except once or twice when he glanced toward the wide white hat; then he nodded as if satisfied and with no inflection said, 'Next time mebbe you won't let Jager Clews off so easy, like here in town.'

'He must be a cat-eyed Indian to find his way around up there on the Table in the dark!'

Harolday thought it over. 'You don't figger it was Jager, then?' He put the question as if he had no doubt about it at all and was a bit surprised that Rocklin didn't feel sure.

Rocklin said, 'I don't know who else to guess at. But just in case it wasn't Jager, who'd you say it might've been?' He stared at Harolday, wanting an answer.

But Harolday didn't say anything, not right away. Street sounds came through the open doors, and outside the stable entrance the sudden laughter of a finished joke. Harolday put a hand to the watch charm but didn't move it, and the glassiness in his eyes had a shimmer. 'Why think I could guess?'

'You're an old-timer, know the people. I figger I've been shot at, and I'd like some idea as to who did it. I don't believe it was Jager!'

Harolday looked off at nothing, moodily. 'Well, I'd say Jager. If 'twasn't him, it must mebbe have been somebody that didn't want

188

you to cut in and claim some of the Caldwell property.'

'I'm not claiming any!'

Harolday said, 'Huh?' and listened for something more, and when Rocklin didn't go on he asked, 'Why not?'

'I don't see I have any claim coming.'

Then Harolday looked aside, took up a pencil, tapped slowly. 'Do you mean you're not having anything to do with the Caldwell property?'

'Can't say yet. The girl wants me to run the ranch for a while, but Garley won't. I hear that you don't like Garley, so tell me about him.'

Harolday took lots of time before he said, 'Nothin' much to tell. It's all personal.' He studied for a while, then asked in a flat voice, with no emphasis and with no shade of an opinion in his tone, 'Do you and the girl aim to get Garley removed as executor and all, if you can?'

Rocklin said, 'Thanks,' and rested an elbow on the sloping desk. 'Good idea! I hadn't thought that far ahead! You don't like him, and you must think he's unfit for the job; so how could we go about getting him thrown out?'

Harolday gazed afar off consideringly and shook his head. 'Can't say. Far as I know ther's nothin' really against the judge – nothin' a court would listen to. It would have

189

to be argued before the district court over at Garden City.' He stopped reflectively, then added, 'We used to be friends, but he beat me in a couple of lawsuits. Naturally, since then I don't like him. Just what would you charge against him?'

'For one thing, Miss Caldwell don't like him.'

Harolday said, 'I see. I see.' Then with a cold humorless grimace that seemed intended as a smile he added, 'And she does like you, eh?'

CHAPTER TWELVE

Marshal Ager dogtrotted along the sidewalk with popeyed haste to overtake Rocklin on his way toward the hotel and blurted, 'Bob Clews and a couple of fellers are down to the Sun-Up and know you're in town! Cap sent a man on the quiet to find you, and the man told me! So you better have friends with you all the time, you with your hand hurt, too!'

Rocklin gazed broodingly at the round, fat face, but he was not in the least thinking of the face; then he said, 'Well, Marshal, you're a friend enough for me. There's something I want to know. Bob Clews can tell me. So come along. We're going down there for a talk!'

The marshal protested. 'You're jokin'!' Then he said, 'You won't stand a chance! They won't give you no time to talk!'

Rocklin told him, 'This is important. They'll talk. Bob, I mean. He ought to be glad to.'

So the marshal reluctantly marched back with Rocklin. When they came to the saloon entrance he wanted to pause and peek through the swinging door, size up the setup; but Rocklin shouldered the door wide and walked in, spotting men as he came on.

Bob Clews with two others idled at stud for drinks in chairs at the poker table. Rocklin heard his name spoken in a gust of soft alarm. By the way he came in men saw that he knew whom he would find. Gene Dyer and a well-dressed stranger were at the bar and Cap was behind it. Gene's cane was hooked on the bar's edge and the cane dropped when Gene groped for it, and the sharp clatter rang through the barnlike stillness of the barroom. The poker players shifted jumpily at the sound, whipping their eyes toward Gene then back at Rocklin, who was cutting toward them.

Marshal Ager followed Rocklin in, and his build gave him a strut as if he came bravely. Cap saw Rocklin's arm in a sling, saw the holster on the left, then he watched the poker table. The well-dressed stranger could smell trouble and asked shakily, 'What's up?' Nobody answered him and he turned toward the side door, which was nearer, but curiosity froze his feet in their tracks.

Rocklin's spurs rattled in the dragging stride and his heels clicked hard as he came up fast. His left thumb was hooked in his belt and he kept his eyes on Bob Clews, for he knew, or felt certain, that if he could hold Bob down nobody else would make the break. Bob didn't move from his chair; he was surprised and wasn't sure of what to think, and his own arm was still sore with black-and-blue traces of bruises, and a rag was wrapped about his wrist.

Rocklin walked up to him and stared down and saw the dread and wishful hate on the tight hatchet face. Caught flat-footed, Bob's safest play was not to start anything, yet the expectation of hell to pay made him deathly afraid and it showed through his skin. He had seen Rocklin do things, and fear stayed with him.

But Rocklin was up against something he hadn't expected. Bob didn't show fight, but a fellow jumped up from the table with muscular resilience and moved back, ready for trouble; more than ready, almost asking for it. His name was Wally Russell, and he was a squatty fellow, saddle-worn, roughly dressed, with lumpish cheekbones and suspicious eyes, and there was a scar on his left cheek. He stood with head lowered and shoulders hunched, and his hand was down below his waist and is palm was back and shadowed the gun butt. He had small, hot eyes.

Tricky and bad! Was Rocklin's guess, knowing he had to take the play away from this fellow or there'd be smoke. Rocklin felt that he was in here alone, or the same as alone. Gene Dyer was friendly, but unarmed; bartenders can stand neutral; the well-dressed stranger was an outsider, and Ager didn't count.

Right off he challenged Wally with: 'You looking for trouble?' But he remained close to Bob Clews and kept his thumb hooked in his belt. It was ticklish to count on Bob staying quiet, but right now Bob wasn't the man to watch.

The snapped-out question lingered in the silence. There was the offer, and it was for Wally to say what. He couldn't say no, for that would be crawling, and if he said yes, Rocklin would have to give it to him or be backing down himself. Wally glanced shiftily at Rocklin's arm in the sling, judging chances, but when he looked at Rocklin's face he wasn't so sure; then he flicked glances at his friends, wanting a sign; but Bob wasn't moving, not even an eyelid, and the third man had both hands on the table, showing that he wanted to be counted out.

In the meantime Marshal Ager was sidling close before the bar, carefully not intruding the least sound and getting well away from behind Rocklin, for he guessed that was the way bullets would go. Cap stood motionless with his hands down out of sight; as gambler and bartender in many places he had seen a lot of plays and knew the signs.

The silence made it Wally's turn to say something. With so many eyes on him he wanted to hold up his end, but he wasn't sure about wanting to make it a fight, so he came back with a snarl. 'You stomped in here like you was!'

'I am!' said Rocklin, and then there was some more silence.

Wally hesitated, but hedged with: 'I ain't ever seen you before! An' the way you come rampin' in here I thought it was mebbe me you was after.' Then Wally sullenly went back to his chair and glowered as he listened for what was going to be said.

Rocklin said it. 'Come along to the back of the saloon, Clews, for a talk!'

Whatever Bob had expected, it wasn't that; he darted an appeal toward his friends, but he wasn't having any help from Wally now. Wally had made his play, and Bob let him down. The other man still kept his hands on the table. He was sandy-complexioned with colorless eyebrows and turned-out, fishlike lips, and he looked mean but he didn't move. Then Rocklin tapped Bob's shoulder; the authority of an arrest was in the gesture. 'Come along!' he said.

Bob didn't want to stir but pushed back his chair a little, not rising. 'What the hell?' He was sullen about it and bracing himself to refuse, then something in Rocklin's look made him afraid that a gun barrel might come alongside of his head. He had seen how it could happen to Jager. Bob got up resentfully and went with Rocklin toward the back of the saloon, very like a prisoner being taken off by a sheriff. Men's wondering stares followed, and the sandy man leaned over and whispered to Wally.

A space at the back of the saloon had once been partitioned off for a poker game, with a small window, so dirty now it looked frosted, let in high off the ground. The doorless room was a catchall these days, with mops, buckets, old brooms, boxes of empty bottles; and cobwebs dangled grimly in corners; and there was the stale stench of not-clean beer bottles. They went in there.

Bob's mouth opened like a panting dog's and his eyes took on a questioning shine, suspiciously. Rocklin could see that he was queasily afraid and loathed him, but wanted to learn something. 'Everybody is saying Jager killed Bowles, thinking it was me.'

Bob squinted, shook his head, mumbled, 'He never done it!'

'I hear he talked big and loud of what he'd do to Jim Brotherton and me, too. Did he?' Bob listened, wary and morose, and wouldn't say. Rocklin went on. 'But no man is such a fool as to brag like that then make his brag good with a rifle in the back.'

Bob growled, 'He never done it, I tell you!'

'That's just what I'm trying to think,' said Rocklin.

Bob didn't understand. He couldn't; it just didn't make sense that Rocklin wouldn't want to believe the worst possible of Jager, and he insisted, 'He didn't, I tell you! Wasn't in the country, even!'

'That's his trick, I hear. Hides out and pretends he's gone.'

'He went, I tell you! What's all this talk about? You caught him drunk, and he wanted to get away from people that knowed about it! Jager ain't scairt of you or no damn man! You caught 'im drunk, that's all – an' gun-whipped him! He'll get even – you can bet on that! An' why are you tryin' to pump me? Anyhow, he never done it!'

Rocklin spoke patiently. 'I don't believe he did it. But I want to be sure. So give me some facts. You don't want that kind of crime pinned on him, do you?'

Bob's thin face was distorted in puzzlement. 'What you tryin' to get at?' he asked, unsure, suspecting trickery.

'If Jager isn't guilty, somebody else is –

and I can start looking! I don't believe he is. So give me something I can tie to.'

Bob sounded a little fuddled in guessing, 'Are you tryin' to make out you want to be friends?' His narrow eyes had a sneaky gleam; making out that you wanted to be friends was something that he did understand, a game he knew how to play.

'But that was too much, and Rocklin gave up, seeing the uselesssness of talk, but was almost convinced anyhow. Bob's denials didn't mean a thing, but there was a lack of glib alibis and detailed explanation that helped Rocklin continue to be halfway sure that Jager hadn't done the back-shooting. He said, 'Friends with you? No. I'm talking of murder. And want the man that did it. That's all.'

Rocklin stepped backward through the doorway and walked up toward the bar where Gene Dyer was waiting, and when he saw Rocklin coming he turned to Cap, thumped the bar, and said, 'Set out the drinks!'

Cap didn't pay any attention but stooped a little with hands out of sight, and his look was on the sandy-complexioned man who was lounging in the side door smoking a cigarette. Each time he puffed he would take the cigarette from his mouth and stare at it thoughtfully; then suddenly he threw it down.

It was Marshal Ager who let out a warning whoop at Rocklin, and the marshal was on his way belly down to the floor as Bob leaned out of the junk-room door and hurriedly fired at Rocklin's back. The bullet whanged by and smacked into the front wall. Wally was at the bar, drinking alone, and his vision toward the rear was obstructed by the well-dressed stranger. When the shot was fired Wally whirled and gave the stranger a shove that sent him tottering. Wally found himself in Bob's line of fire and bounced for the far side of the barroom. His head was turned toward the rear as he went, and he struck a chair that threw him into a staggering lurch so that he bumped up against the side wall before he got his balance.

In the meantime Rocklin had faced about and had drawn his gun. He thumbed the hammer when it was waist-high, but with his left hand that was awkward shooting. He straightened his arm shoulder-high, sighting, and Bob's second bullet whiffed wind alongside of his face. Bob's hurt arm wasn't strong and supple yet, but he was using it with a sheltered reach through the junk room's doorway, keeping his body out of sight. There wasn't much for Rocklin to aim at, and left-handed shooting was not instinctive.

Then it was that Gene Dyer yelled, 'Turn round! Turn round!'

Rocklin knew the warning was meant for him, and he swung his head in a half-turn and saw Gene gesturing fearfully toward the side door where the sandy-complexioned man had been purposely lounging while Wally waited at the bar. Now his gun was leveled at Rocklin. Too late Rocklin saw how he was trapped by cross fire; the fellow couldn't miss, not at that distance, but Rocklin swirled his back up against the bar, meaning to shoot as he went down. Then there was a blasting sound, as if something big had blown up behind him, and the echo reverberated thunderously through the bar-sized saloon and the sandy man swayed as if struck by a club and pitched headlong.

Rocklin looked behind him, wondering what the hell? He saw Cap break the double-barreled, sawed-off shotgun, and the ejector kicked the empty No. 10 shell over his shoulder and it fell among the bottles on the shelf behind. Cap was as cool as if breaking bottles. He took up another shell from the cigar box on the bar shelf, slipped it in, and all the while kept his eyes on Wally across the room. Wally had hugged the wall and his revolver was half drawn, but as soon as the shotgun fired he let go of his gun, settling it back into the holster, and he flung his hands out and down before him, showing their emptiness, and he yelled, 'I ain't in this!'

The shotgun had changed things so much that Bob Clews cut and ran, pounding for the alleyway door. He ran so fast that he bumped into it, then jerked and jerked, but the door wouldn't open. It was locked, but the key was in the lock, and Bob's feet hopped a frantic dance as he lost a second or two in turning the key. He lurched through, banging the door wildly behind him.

Marshal Ager, with no embarrassment at all, was getting up off the floor and slapping with his hat at the dusty front of his clothes, then he put on his hat and went across to look down at the sandy man.

Cap spoke as if trying to show excitement and not knowing how as he asked Rocklin, 'Why didn't you let him have it?' and pointed toward the alley door through which Bob had disappeared.

Rocklin said, 'I'm not much good left-handed. I hate to shoot and miss!'

'I seen what they was fixin' up for you,' said Cap. Then, with slow beckoning of finger, he called, 'You, Wally! Come back here and pay for that drink!'

Wally came, and Cap eyed him. 'You used to be a purty good boy, but now – the hell with you! Git out and don't ever come back!'

People were coming in from up and down the street. It was said that Bob Clews had been seen spraddling it out of town bareheaded and on a horse that wasn't his. And soon some man came in and said, 'Wally's just rode out, hell-for-leather!'

Gene Dyer said to Rocklin, 'Guess now you see how the Clewses shoot in the back.'

'Yeah,' he admitted.

He wasn't happy about how things had worked out here in the Sun-Up. There was no spontaneity to the left-handed shooting, though he knew that he could be accurate if slow enough, but Boot Hills were filled with slow men, and there wouldn't always be an imperturbable Cap with a shotgun standing by.

He learned that the women had come in from the ranch just a little while ago with one of the boys driving, and a saddled horse followed on a rope behind the buggy. That meant the boy would go right back to the ranch where they were short-handed.

The hotel man looked at Rocklin, pulled up the sleeve of his collarless white shirt, and said, 'Yeah, they're here. The old lady – she's a case, that woman! – is with Judge Garley. Up in his room. The girl she come down just a while ago and told me. Told me she wanted to see you as soon as you come. From how she acted I don't think she wants the old battle-ax to see you! You're a cousin, she said.'

'Something like it, so I hear.'

On his way up the stairs Rocklin thought

201

that he would rather be going toward Garley's room; thought, *They're in there stacking the cards on us!*

Clara opened the door the instant he tapped; she had been hovering there with her hand on the knob, and she was breathless. 'I thought you never would come!' Her voice was low and tense; she added, 'Aunt may be back any minute!' Then she looked at him strangely, and she backed from the door as if discovering that this wasn't the man she had waited for and now wanted to get away from him.

Rocklin asked in puzzled friendliness, 'What's all wrong?'

He could see that she had prettied up some after the long, jolting, dusty ride. The brush had left a glossy shine on her hair, and she wore a dark-blue dress that was new. She was very young, with an air of unworldly helplessness, and looked awfully tired, but she was watching him so queerly that he had a mild dread of tears.

'Do sit down,' she invited in a constrained, toneless way. She seemed to be trying to hold herself together, though there was a frantic something inside of her that she mustn't let get out, and he couldn't guess what her staring meant. She asked about his hand, and he explained that it would be all right in a few days, but she wasn't listening to what he said, and the frantic look beat in her eyes.

He sat down and put his hat on the floor beside the chair, and Clara took the rocker in front of him and gripped its arms. Again he asked as helpfully as he could, 'What is the matter?'

Clara's lips began to writhe, and he couldn't tell whether she was trying to make herself smile or trying not to cry. She gasped, 'Oh, you'll think I'm crazy – or worse than that!' It baffled him because he could see that she meant just that.

He said, 'Not you; no. Never. So tell me.'

Her hands were on the end of the chair's arms and gripped so tensely that the knuckles turned white, and she drew a slow, resolute breath. 'I don't know what you will think of me, b-but I am going to say it if – if – if I don't die first!' Her voice broke in the forced half-laugh of: 'I feel like I will!' She seemed to mean that, too. He sat motionless and was uncomprehending and wanted to be helpful, but there was nothing he could do except wait.

Breath quivered in her throat, gaspingly, when she tried to go on, and her lips went together in a tight squirm as though they just wouldn't let her speak; then she opened her lips and her teeth were edge to edge and there was a desperate look in her dark eyes as she forced out, 'Will you marry me?'

He didn't stir and seemed calm, but a flush was burning up around his ears and he was not calm inwardly, and if he had spoken at once he would have said, 'Hell, no!' But he looked at her steadily and saw the desperation on her face, and then he understood and half smiled slowly. 'You think that better than having to go on putting up with the old lady?'

Clara relaxed and nodded thankfully that he understood, but her eyes wavered down as she said, 'Yes.' They lifted as she added, 'Anything would be better.' Her voice was not bitter; it was simply that she had reluctantly decided and must follow her decision.

It was his turn to nod, understandingly; and though he murmured, 'I think you're purt-near right,' there was no acceptance.

Clara took her hands from the rocker and leaned forward, still embarrassed, but at least she had found sympathy; and she explained hurriedly, with an air of talking against time.

'Last night after you left us it was terrible! I thought she had lost her mind; I really thought just that! She cried – I have never seen my aunt cry before – and she said that you would kill her so you could marry me! It was disgustingly senseless, but it made me think, "Oh, I wish he would!" Marry me, I mean, for I would rather die than have her harmed! But I can't, just can't, and I won't go on living with her.

'And I can't run away from her, for I

wouldn't know how, and I haven't any money. I wouldn't know where to go or what to do – not in the least! I have lived with her all my life, but now I am grown. I am of age. I am nineteen! She still treats me as though I were nine, and a not very bright nine! And last night I couldn't sleep and I made up my mind that the next time I saw you I would – would ask you – so if – you – me – don't you see? In that way it will be your property, too!'

Rocklin peered at his palm, turned the hand over, examined the knuckles. 'Yes, sure. Yes, I see.'

Clara almost choked up, blushingly, and she blurred the words in trying to explain. 'It doesn't need to mean anything, really – except, you know – except – I'll be away from her!' Then Clara brightened her look. 'Besides, Mr Rocklin–'

He raised his eyes, murmured, 'The name is Ken!'

In the long silence they exchanged faint smiles, then her voice raced on with: 'You must honestly be entitled to some of the property, because if you weren't, that horrible Judge Garley and Aunt Elizabeth wouldn't be so afraid you might get some of it! People just can't go to court and get things they haven't the least right to, can they? They just can't, can they – Ken?'

He was gazing at her and gave his head a

sober shake. 'I don't know. Don't know much about courts.' With deliberate quietness he added, 'And I'm not doing anything to find out. It's all yourn, Miss Caldwell.'

Because now again he was looking at his palm with a studying air of reading the lines, he didn't see the warmth that overflowed her dark eyes. 'The name,' she said softly, 'is Clara!'

Then the door was opened by Miss Martin with the suddenness of intended surprise, but she hadn't suspected in the least that Rocklin was here. She stopped short, and the set look of satisfaction on her wrinkled face became an astounded grimace. 'You!' she snapped, and gave the door a swing to that jarred the wall.

Rocklin stood up, slowly straightened his high shoulders, and he said, 'Yes'm, me,' with maddening calm.

The old lady's eyes stabbed at Clara, but Clara wouldn't look at her, then she tried withering Rocklin. 'A nice thing, this! Here – alone! You and my niece!'

His face was hard, and her stare could not break up its hardness. 'Just havin' a little visit.' His slow voice was casual and disinterested, then he looked toward Clara. Her fingers were squirming in the cloth of her dress and she would not look at Rocklin, either; but her eyes could not rest, and their glance fled guiltily about the floor and into corners, as if looking for a wide crack.

Miss Martin drew herself up and spoke crushingly, grimly pleased to say to him, 'Judge Garley has just assured me that you will not be permitted to work on our ranch! And, moreover, my explicit request is that you never come near it – or us! – again!' She stepped stiffly aside and pointed. 'There, sir, is the door!' She liked this sort of scene, and this was a pleasing tableau as she saw it, and complete triumph.

But it didn't work. Rocklin shrugged a shoulder, looked around at Clara, then he walked over to her and put an arm about her waist. For a long moment she turned away from him and quivered resistingly. Then she gave way and swirled about and leaned against him with hands clutching at his breast. He told the aunt, 'Clara has just said she'd marry me!'

That brought a vacuous expression of dumfounderment on Miss Martin's face, and she opened her mouth wide but she was speechless, and for a long moment her black eyes had a rigid empty stare, something like idiocy.

'And it's to be right away, too!' he added.

The faint odor of Clara's lavender came up into his face, and into his memory, where it mingled with the piny wetness of the forest, and he tightened his arm about her involuntarily. Clara misunderstood, and she responded by pressing more tightly against him.

Miss Martin lost her head and shrieked, 'Clara!' Then: 'I won't permit it!' She was screaming, 'You don't even know him and he's only after your money!' She was standing close now. 'Judge Garley won't permit it! We won't let you do such a mad fool thing! Clara, look at me!'

Clara wouldn't look around and her voice was muffled because her face was against Rocklin's breast, but she cried, 'I am of age.'

There was finality in Rocklin's voice, 'Do you no good to yell or argy, lady!'

Then Miss Martin begged, 'Leave us alone, please, just for a minute! Oh, I must talk to this poor child! She is my niece. I have been like a mother! She is mine, my very life, Mr Rocklin!' She put a bony hand to Clara's shoulder and tugged, pleading; but Clara clung to him and shook her head, burrowing her face against his shoulder.

Rocklin tightened his arm, and this time he meant it protectively and said, 'No, you can't talk to her alone! You want to make her feel bad. From now on she's my wife. We're going out now to get married!'

CHAPTER THIRTEEN

The hotel man – his name was Carruthers – beamingly gave Rocklin and Clara directions toward the justice of the peace's office and promised, 'I'll have a nice room fixed up!' But he wondered at their sodden quietness.

Upstairs the stiff-backed Miss Martin sat for a time as if her back were broken, but she didn't weep. She was mad and resolute; she had been bested just when Judge Garley had given her assurances that seemed to mean triumph, and now she meant to do whatever must be done to defeat what she thoroughly believed was Rocklin's craftiness.

She jumped up and hurried out in the hall and on to Garley's rom. She bruised her knuckles by rapping, but he had gone; then she flew downstairs.

Carruthers saw her fury and lied blankly in saying he didn't know where the judge was but would have somebody right away try to find him. When she went back up the stairs he went into the bar and told Garley.

Garley groaned, 'Now what?' And swallowed his whisky, took his unlighted cigar, and started up. He didn't like the old lady but needed her good will, and he believed that he had learned how to get on with her.

Two words from Miss Martin and his fat face hardened into angered worry. Oaths burst in his mouth, and as he paced the floor he snapped the unlighted cigar between his fingers and flung it down and stared after it. Suddenly he turned on her gloweringly. 'Can't you swear she's not of age?'

Miss Martin squeezed her elbows to her sides, threw up her head, and said dramatically, 'I'd swear my life away to save Clara!'

There wasn't a continuous sidewalk on the street, and Clara held her long skirt from the dust; but dry weeds rustled against her, for she crowded the path in holding to his arm. Both were silent until he gazed toward her averted face and diffidently said, 'If you don't want to, it will be all right.'

She tightened her hand on his arm and replied softly, 'But I do, Ken.'

No one was in the unlocked office; it was dim and bare, with a few straight chairs in a disorderly row before a table, a spittoon near the table, and some benches along the walls. The loneliness seemed a forbidding omen.

Again Rocklin offered, 'Are you real sure?'

Doubt hurt Clara's eyes as she looked at him with timid steadiness. 'But if you aren't, Ken–'

'Me. Sure I'm sure. Of course.' He wasn't really lying. He liked this girl – she was sweet and pretty and honest – and he detested her aunt, and there was almost as much satisfaction in cheating the old woman out of her chance to be mean as there was in helping the girl escape from that meanness.

'It is not just feeling sorry for me, Ken?' she begged.

That was wholly unexpected and a bit of a shock. *Why the devil else was he marrying her?* Love hadn't been mentioned, and it wasn't her money – he had made that clear. He could eye any man and be coldly truthful, but the pleading in her eyes put a kind of weakness inside of him and he said, 'No, oh, no; I should say not!' He wanted to lie as he felt a man ought to, and it wasn't really lying to add, 'I like you fine!'

'Oh, Ken, honestly?'

There he was, clumsily swearing that it was honestly said when, in a way, he felt trapped; but he couldn't back out and wouldn't try because the beginning of happiness was so warmly aglow on her face and she clung to his hand with both hands. 'Ken!' was all she could say, and it was enough. Clara had often wondered how love came into a girl's heart and what did it do to her, and now she knew. It came like unexpected fire, bringing light and warmth to a place that had been cold.

They saw Pap Fossler going by on the other side of the street, and Rocklin called to him. He came across, and Rocklin told him that they wanted the justice and why. Pap pulled at his beard, and his eyes danced as he said, 'I'll fetch 'im! He's down behind the store, whittlin'.'

The justice of the peace came back with Pap, and Marshal Ager was among the half dozen who had heard the news and tagged along. Their feet clacked hollowly in the echoing bareness of the room. Rocklin stood up, having to shake hands left-handedly, and he looked glum for a man who was supposed to be happy.

Pap Fossler leaned to Clara. 'I seen a barrel o' kids grow up and git married!'

She thought that he looked like a bright-eyed little boy who had found long gray false whiskers. Other men stared at her with solemn gawkiness because she was young, pretty, different in her Easternness, and the girl to whom old Red Caldwell had left his ranch.

The small justice put on silver-rimmed spectacles and smiled peeringly at Clara. His pen was bound with string, and he dipped the point in gooey ink then looked about for something to clean the point with. After the pen was cleaned on a scrap of paper he wrote down their birth dates and so forth in a quick, sprawling hand. Ager and the others hovered close as if it were important that they hear the answer to all questions.

'You sign,' said the justice, giving the pen to Rocklin. 'Lady don't need to.' Rocklin signed the application. The justice said, 'That'll be a dollar.' As deputy county clerk he could issue licenses, as justice perform wedding ceremonies. Then the justice stood up and asked, 'You got a ring?'

Rocklin said, 'No, we were in such a hurry.'

Clara glanced down at her fingers, regretting a ringless marriage, and she asked uneasily, 'It isn't absolutely necessary, is it?'

'No 'am, but fittin',' said the justice. He knew the ring ritual like his ABCs, and any variation would be halting and contrary to rote. 'But if you folks want it without, I'll tie just as hard a knot as with. You can't join hands by his right un, so the left'll have to do. Do you, Kenneth Rocklin... Do you, Clara Isabella Caldwell... By power vested in me... I now pronounce you man and wife. Kiss the bride or I'll do it for you!' No ceremony was without that little tag.

Clara looked up shyly expectant, her cheeks on fire. Rocklin unsmilingly kissed her.

A shadow filled the doorway, pausing; then Garley came on into the room, hurrying bulkily. He had been running and was breathless and sweating as he strode up with plop of broad flat feet, and his big face was

213

hot and foreboding as he thundered at the justice, 'Have you married these people?'

The little justice didn't like Garley and said, 'Yep!' snapping his jaws to. Then he unlocked his jaws to clinch the 'Yep' with: 'All done! Just waitin' for witnesses to sign.' He dipped the pen, said, 'here, Marshal,' and gave the pen to Ager.

Garley raised a hand forbiddingly. 'I have something important to say!' He laid his hat on the table, drew himself up with a portentous air, and held the silence, making drama; then in a voice of announcement he proclaimed, 'Clara Caldwell is not of age!'

Excitement shivered across men's faces and stares swung at Clara. She caught her breath with the look of being guiltily astounded. Ager reached out and slowly laid down the pen without signing.

Garley continued in deep and rolling tones. 'On behalf of my poor heartbroken client, Miss Elizabeth Martin, who is this young lady's aunt and guardian, I now wish to assume the custody of Clara Caldwell, a minor. And to swear out a warrant for the arrest of this man, Kenneth Rocklin! He knew she wasn't of age! Miss Martin is prepared to swear that she so informed him less than an hour ago. She accuses him of marrying her niece because she is an heiress. He finds that easier than trying to break the Caldwell will!'

They all looked at Rocklin, and Rocklin looked at Garley, and Garley evasively mopped his face. Rocklin was set to say something, but Clara spoke first with out-surging impulse. Her voice was soft, as if she didn't know how to shout. 'Oh, that isn't true and you know it!' Her breath came quickly and so did the words. 'She is my aunt but was never my guardian, and you know that, too! She wrote you herself all about me, and the answer you wrote back is in the trunk at the hotel and we can get it and prove it!' They could tell that she wasn't through though she paused, then she took a deep breath and came a half-step closer and she told Garley, and all the world, too, 'And it was *I* who asked him to marry *me!*'

Clara was in love and looked proud and defiant; she was learning what love did to a girl, and she wouldn't have them thinking that Ken Rocklin had been after money, and she didn't care what they thought of her.

Rocklin put an arm about her quickly, drawing her back. He felt embarrassed, for it wasn't a thing that a girl ought to admit, however honestly. The little justice blinked through his spectacles, and Pap Fossler moved nearer, as if choosing sides, and patted her arm. Even the marshal stared with big-eyed surprise and approval, but she was a little flustered now and lowered her face.

Again men waited for Rocklin to say

something. He stepped close to Garley, and Garley tried to look him in the eye, but it wasn't easy, and again he wiped his hot face and neck, evasively. Rocklin's voice was doggedly quiet.

'This girl is my wife. And I'll do whatever a man has the right to do to anybody that tries to get a man's wife away from him!'

That was all he said, but they could tell that he was wrestling down the impulse to slap; then he took Clara by the arm and walked out.

On the sidewalk Clara asked, 'Oughtn't we to go get that letter from Aunt Elizabeth? It's in the trunk.'

'She'd let herself be torn to pieces before she gave it up. But they can make things bad if we can't prove your right to marry. I'll take you back to the hotel then—'

When he told what he had in mind Clara said, 'But I must be with you, please, Ken! I am your wife, and I am going, too!'

Garley climbed the stairs with plodding lift of body. He was fat, too fat, and tired inside and out. A couple of slugs of whisky in the Sun-Up in the way to his office had left him sour and dejected. Rocklin was married to the girl, and the fool justice of the peace had said, 'No, I won't issue no warrant! You can go over and do your chargin' an' provin' to the Garden City court.'

The office door, as usual, was open, but he

didn't see Rocklin until he was in the room. Then Rocklin stood up and pushed the door to, and that left Clara visible on the end of the horsehair sofa. Rocklin said, 'We want her aunt's letter!'

Garley said, 'So, hm?' He pulled his head a little to one side and scratched along his neck, then gave his hat a toss toward the table, all leisurely. 'You mustn't blame me.' His voice was plausible. 'I had no choice. Miss Martin insisted. You know how she can!' He was doing his blandest best and explained, 'You don't need the letter now. You are married. Besides,' he added with a half-smile, and indicated the disorderly pigeonholes, 'I don't know where it is.' Then, gravely: 'And I'd like to assure you, both of you, that my personal feelings are not un-friendly. So' – he smiled ingratiatingly – 'would you accept my congratulations?'

Rocklin ignored the friendliness. 'Her aunt'll raise the devil or try to. The letter will cut her claws and shut her mouth. Nothing else will. We want it.'

Garley let his gaze linger on the sling about Rocklin's neck, then said, 'I met Doc Riding. He said you had a bad infection. I'm sorry. A letter is personal property. You wouldn't take it by force, would you?'

'Force or not is for you to say. We've come for the letter.'

Garley saw how it was and sat down

217

wearily in the rocking chair. He tried to seem composed, but the sly glitter in his eyes frightened Clara. Even to be near this man gave her the creeps. He spoke somberly. 'This is robbery. As much robbery as if you were demanding money. You are armed. That makes it armed robbery. I can't stop you, but I can advise that you had better stop. I shall certainly make a report to the court at Garden City.'

Clara plucked at Rocklin's sleeve. 'Ken, we mustn't get into trouble!'

Garley nodded approvingly toward her, but Rocklin pulled his sleeve free of her fingers and told him, 'We're going to have that letter to show the court when you tell how I got it! You lied in saying she wasn't of age, and we'll prove it. So if you won't give it up, I'll look myself. Do you want your papers shucked out and scattered all over the place?'

Garley deepened his voice ominously. 'I have warned you!'

Rocklin turned to the desk, unsure of how to begin where there was no order. The ends of papers stuck out raggedly, and they were dusty and discolored from age. Some of the pigeon-holes were packed, and papers also lay thick on the desk. Rocklin began to shuffle them one-handedly, and he told Clara, 'You know her writing. Come and look these over.'

Garley sat there, fatly solemn, with the chair pushed back on its rockers, and he held it back with lift of toes on the floor. He didn't himself know where the letter was, because he gave little care to orderliness.

Clara didn't want to search among the papers, but she wanted to do whatever Rocklin said. She touched the papers delicately, so as to feel less intrusive. Gritty dust from some of them rasped her finger tips and gave a tingle of shivers, but she smothered down her reluctance to meddle with a man's private letters and half guiltily kept her back toward Garley. She knew that he was trying to catch her eyes and frighten her.

Presently Rocklin pulled at a small drawer and found it locked. He turned on Garley and said, 'Open this!'

Garley's toes gave way and he rocked forward heavily; his big face took on the look of something made out of dough – flabby, gray, lifeless, as if his heart were quitting. Rocklin's 'Open this!' was like a long-delayed and mocking echo from the voice of old Red Caldwell, who had thundered the same words months before.

'Why, Ken! He's sick!' Clara was ready to help.

'He'll be sicker when we find the letter and show the court he knew he lied!'

Garley muttered, 'My heart!' and put a

hand to his breast and sat still. He wished that the encounter with Red Caldwell had cured him of using marked cards, but it hadn't. His voice labored to say, 'My heart does this sometimes,' and he sank back, appearing too weak to move.

Rocklin told him again, 'Open this!' and Clara thought it was brutal. Her glance timidly reproached Rocklin, but he didn't notice. He looked straight at Garley, and Garley got up but he could barely stand. He steadied himself with a hand to the table and drew a key ring. As he selected the key he said, 'All that's in there is some playing-cards. I don't lock my office, and people stick my cards in their pocket. Sometimes we have a little game up here, so I keep cards.'

Rocklin took the key, and Garley sat down again and held his breath. When the drawer was opened it contained nothing but three unused packs of playing-cards. Rocklin at once closed the drawer, disappointedly. He was turning the key when memory whispered, and he paused with a studying look. He opened the draw again.

A card was pasted face down on the outside of each pack to show the type of the deck within, and one of these looked very much like a card that had been found in Caldwell's coat. He couldn't be sure, but he had a thought and looked around quickly and found Garley's eyes wide, staring, and scared.

Without a word Rocklin took the pack that had attracted his attention and put it into his pocket, and Clara said, 'Why, Ken?' in reproach.

He didn't answer her and for a moment or two almost forgot about the letter as he watched Garley with a steadiness that was vaguely accusing. He thought that Garley's eyes were filled with fear, and he almost began to question him but decided that the better way was to find out first if these were marked cards.

Then he continued going through the papers with a methodical persistence that disturbed old stuff that hadn't been touched in years. Clara had the discomfort of a thief who was being watched and wanted to stop, but Rocklin's was a thoroughgoing stubbornness, and he yanked out handful after handful and laid them before her. Many were scattered to the floor, and she would have stopped, but he told her, 'Let him pick 'em up after we're gone.'

Clara found a long envelope addressed in a stiff, thin, hand and said, 'Here it is.' She drew the letter from the envelope, which had been slit at the end, glanced along the first page, and read tremblingly: *Clara was of age about two months ago, but I, of course, shall continue to care for her as for my own daughter.*

She held it out, showing Rocklin, then returned the letter to its envelope and gave it to him.

Clara opened the door, wanting to leave quickly. Rocklin followed, but he stopped in the doorway and faced about.

Garley was hunched in the rocker. No blandness masked his face now, and only the eyes looked alive, for the flesh was a doughish gray, very like death's color. Rocklin told him calmly, 'If these cards are marked, they're going over to the judge at Garden City. And you're going with 'em!'

Rocklin took the Chinaman along and went to Miss Martin's room. When she opened the door he said, 'I've come for my wife's things.' He told her about the letter out of Garley's office, then: 'Now give me what belongs to Clara.'

Miss Martin stepped back with her lips tightly set, her back stiff, her chin up, and she locked her hands in front of her, waist-high, and wouldn't say a word.

The little Chinaman peered about help-lessly, not knowing what to touch.

Rocklin told him, 'All right, bring every-thing! Trunk, clothes, hairpins – everything. Then we'll send back what's not my wife's!'

That brought the old lady around in a resentful fury though she wouldn't open her mouth, but she began to jerk dresses from hooks in the closet and fling them to the floor. He wondered that Clara hadn't killed her long ago.

Clara put things away, into drawers, into the closet, on nails, and Rocklin paid no attention. She washed her face and combed her hair. No man had ever seen her long hair loose and flowing, for that was supposed to be very immodest, like a kind of undressing; but this was her husband and he didn't look at her.

He sat with a lamp burning at a table on which Mrs Carruthers had laid a crisp flowered piece of fringed red cloth to make the room look more gaily bridal, and he was studying the backs of the slick glazed cards that were spread before him. Clara came up behind the chair and put her hands lightly on his shoulders, and he could smell the fresh, clean lavender scent.

'What are you doing, Ken?' She wanted him to let her show interest in whatever he was doing.

'Just lookin'.' His hand ached now and he had been without much sleep for days; his nerves were nagging for a smoke, and it stirred a kind of anger to have this girl so hoveringly close – not at her but at himself for the weakness of wanting to throw down his guard and snuggle her. Anything he did of that kind would be a kind of promise, and he wouldn't make promises that he didn't

223

intend to keep. She was pretty with a warmth of sweetness, but he knew very well that he wouldn't have up and married her if old Miss Martin hadn't come ramping into the room like she did and made a big scene, or tried to. He wasn't sorry he had got into it, for she was nearly helpless in the hands of the old woman and Garley. 'Helpless,' was the word for her, and he liked her fine, but for some reason, even now, he couldn't help thinking of that damned Harolday girl.

He was glad when Cap knocked on the door.

Cap had dressed with care in a black coat and high paper collar and looked awkward, but that was the way he always looked. He bowed stiffly to Clara and called her 'Mrs Rocklin.' She knew now that Cap's shotgun had saved Rocklin's life, for Mrs Carruthers had told her.

Rocklin said, 'I sent for you, Cap, to look at these cards. I can't tell, but I hope they're marked!'

Cap, with much the manner of a scarecrow that had come to life, moved to the table and sat down to examine the cards. It was mysterious and exciting for Clara, and she stooped over the table to watch.

Cap sorted out certain cards and studied the corners of their backs. Soon he said simply, 'Marked, all right,' but it was some time before he studied out the variations;

then he took a quill toothpick from his vest pocket and pointed to the faint telltale differences in the trefoils that indicated suit and value.

Rocklin said, 'How could anybody read them in a game? They're so small.'

'Practice, I s'pose, like reading print.' Then Cap said, 'They're bad things to have around. Do you want to tell me where they come from?'

'Out of Judge Garley's desk!'

Cap didn't show surprise; he never showed surprise, and beyond a slow, stiff nod he made no comment until Rocklin asked, 'What about him?'

Cap rolled another cigarette for Rocklin and one for himself, and he seemed to choose words carefully but as if with no particular interest.

'He showed up here about six year ago, just about the time I bought the Sun-Up. He's allus played some poker, and I've set in games with him and thought him good and never suspicioned. I guess he's smart enough not to be too lucky. For a while he was thick with old Harolday, then they had a fallin' out. Nobody knows why.

'When Red's lawyer died, Red he took Garley for his lawyer in some trouble with a railroad about a shipment, and Garley must've done all right. Ever'body was surprised after Red died to find Garley was

225

executor. Red was a rich man.'

Cap went on rolling cigarettes, giving the ends a tight twist and laying them in a row for Rocklin to have when he wished.

'I'm taking the cards to the judge over at Garden City,' Rocklin said.

Cap told him matter-of-factly, 'Garley'll say you're lyin' about 'em, that's all.'

Rocklin agreed somberly. 'A blackleg will say anything;' then: 'and do it, too.' Cap gazed at him understandingly. Rocklin added, 'So what do you think?'

Cap shook his head faintly. 'He never rode a horse or shot a gun as I know of. He dresses Western, but he ain't. I see what you mean, all right.'

Clara gazed quizzically at each of the men, for they were talking over her head.

Rocklin asked, 'But what about friends to do it for him?'

'Not as I know of. Still, lawyers know a lot of no-good fellers.' Cap tapped the cards. 'Harolday'll be tickled to know about these.'

When Cap had gone Rocklin sat broodingly, and Clara came close and asked with a timid gentleness, 'Why don't you tell me, Ken? What does it mean, these cards? And never having ridden a horse or shot a gun? Isn't it something I ought to know?'

'It'll only upset you.' His look barely crossed her face and went back to the cards.

'But, Ken, I'm not that – that useless. Do

you think?'

He smiled a little without looking at her, and his tone was carefully kind. 'You're from the East and this is West, and things are different and you ain't used to 'em. But I'll tell you.'

He did, and Clara sat tensely and tried not to shudder, but this talk of murder horrified her.

'One thing we do know is Garley uses marked cards which means he's a blackleg. Being Red's lawyer, he made out the will and knew if Red died he'd have charge of things. Being a blackleg, mebbe he wanted it that way.'

Then Clara told him, 'I feel that he would do any evil thing! And, Ken, he doesn't want me to keep the ranch. He wants to sell off the cattle and break the land up into little farms and sell them to people from the East. "Colonists", he calls them. He says that will take time but make lots of money. Aunt Liz wants him to do that, but I am afraid of anything he suggests.'

'I'd be, too.' Rocklin slowly rubbed his bandaged hand and gazed at her with a look as if he didn't see her. 'It goes against my grain to say it, but in your case it'd prob'ly be the sensible thing to do if somebody honest done it. I hear Harolday has some such idea, too, about his ranches. I hear his ideas allus make money. Mebbe you could sell out to him or sort of go in with him in a land company. You're not ever goin' to be happy living in the West.'

Clara said quickly, 'But that pretty Haroldy girl is! Why can't I be like her?'

The name struck him with a faint shock, bringing to mind the gold color of her face and the litheness of her body and the chance he had had and thrown away, and he shook his head. 'She was born into a saddle. She don't know anything else than to ride and boss men.' Then, without seeing the illogic of it, he said, 'And she is not happy – so I hear tell.'

He got up and turned away from her and said that it was time to roll in. He stooped under the bed for the jack and pulled off his boots, then he took a straight chair and turned it over on the floor so that the back slanted to the carpet. After that he drew aside the bedclothes and took a pillow that he put against the inverted back of the chair.

Clara asked, 'What *are* you doing?'

He wouldn't look at her as he explained, 'I can't go off to sleep some place away from you. That would make talk. This is better'n a saddle for a pillow and the carpet's softer'n the ground. I'm used to both and am good and tired to boot, so goo' night.'

'Oh, Ken!'

Then he did look at her, and his face was hard-set and he shook his head. She knew it

228

was no use, at least not tonight; but there would be a tomorrow and other nights, so Clara smiled at him with a gentle, unhurt look and said, 'Whatever you want, Ken.'

She blew out the lamp and undressed. It was a long while before she fell asleep. There was so much to think about and wonder over, and she felt like crying but she wouldn't. *Tomorrow,* she kept thinking, *tomorrow will be different!*

CHAPTER FOURTEEN

When Clara awakened he was one-handedly dripping water at the washbowl and trying to be noiseless with his washing up. He didn't see that she was awake, and she watched for a time, then gaily said, 'Good morning, Mr Rocklin!'

There was a playful lilt to her words that wasn't like what he had thought of her, but he rubbed up about an ear with a coarse towel and didn't smile back. 'I'll get out while you dress.'

Clara pushed the tangled hair from about her face. 'You are still mad because you married me?'

'Mad? Me? No.' He was sober about it and added as he put down the towel, 'I done what I wanted to do.' Then he looked into the mirror and combed his hair. 'Breakfas's ready.'

His unresponsiveness cast a shadow on her face, but she brushed the shadow away with a forced smile and tried to look happy. 'Ken, you didn't like the girl you married, so she isn't that way any more!' That made him look around, listeningly, but he wouldn't smile back at her. 'From the time your wife was a very little girl her aunt Liz didn't want her to have a thought unless she gave it to her. But I had my thought anyhow. I always let her have her way to keep peace. That is all over now. I am going to do as I please, and I want to please you, Ken!'

He thought, *God A'mighty, I can't have this!* Just to look at and listen to the sleepy, tousled, pretty girl sitting up there in bed made him feel weak and kind of breathless, and he knew that she was trying to make him smile but he wouldn't; he didn't dare.

He said, 'I'm hungry,' though he wasn't. But instead of leaving the room he again sat down at the table with the red coverlet and he spread the cards as if restudying them, and what he was thinking was, *This can't go on! I don't want to wind up in love with her!* Not with an Eastern kitten-soft girl. That wouldn't do. It wouldn't work out. She was unlike any girl he had ever known, but by way of self-warning he recalled Hazel and Alice and

Judith. They didn't help; she wasn't like any of them. Now she was enticing in a way that made him feel a fool – and want to be one. He drew on his stubbornness and ignored her.

They went down to breakfast. No woman was there but the motherly Mrs Carruthers, who was waiting on table for the half-dozen men in shirt sleeves and vests, and in the subdued click of tableware and dishes the men turned to stare.

Rocklin hadn't settled himself in his chair before the little Chinaman shuffled in as if scurrying from danger and leaned over Rocklin's shoulder and whispered. Then Rocklin almost knocked the chair over in getting up hurriedly and told Clara, 'You stay here!' He left on the run.

Clara jumped up with a panicky throb and caught hold of the little Chinaman and said, 'Sammy? What is it, Sammy?'

Sammy swung his head up and down and gave her a singsong assurance that everything was all right and for her to stay and eat, but Clara was frightened because she had seen Rocklin's look as he left.

'Where did he go?' she insisted.

'He go black up to loom, missy, but you–'

Clara brushed the Chinaman aside, drew up the front of her skirts, and ran. Sammy followed through the door with a sorrowful air, and he pretended not to hear the men

231

who called at him. Two or three were curious enough to get up from their table and follow, too. It looked like something was happening.

Garley was dressed for the street, even to his wide black hat, as he stood snatching up the cards from the red coverlet on the table when Rocklin, having come on tiptoes, opened the door. Rocklin was unarmed. He hadn't forgotten his gun; it simply hadn't looked right to buckle it on and go down to breakfast in a friendly hotel with a bride. But the bride had so distractedly tumbled his thoughts that he neglected to gather up the cards and put them safely in his pocket. As for locking the door – he had probably never locked a door in his life.

Garley had seen them go down the stairs, and Sammy had seen him go into Rocklin's room; and Sammy liked Rocklin and the pretty missy and he didn't like Garley.

So now when Rocklin came in Garley swung his big face sideways and stood paralyzed, with one hand holding the cards he had gathered and the other spread out graspingly over the remaining cards. His mouth was open, but his breath wouldn't come. Rocklin didn't speak but slammed the door to behind him, and he looked steadily at the fat lawyer as, with backward reach, he turned the key. Its faint click in the silence told what was coming, and much more was told, too, when Rocklin drew the key from the locked door and flung it toward a corner. The silence was lengthened as Rocklin calmly took his bandaged hand from the sling, then lifted the sling over his head and cast it aside.

'Start talking!' Rocklin told him.

Garley spilled the cards from his fingers and onto the floor and stepped back bulkily. He took hold of a straight chair by its back, tipping it toward him, ready to lift it and strike. That eased Rocklin's only fear, for he had thought Garley might swing one of the long coattails aside and draw a gun. His own gun, wrapped about with the belt, was out of sight in the top bureau drawer, and he thought of going for it but really preferred to do what he was going to do bare-handed, even one-handedly.

Garley's big eyes were stretched with dread as he shouted, 'Let me out of here!'

'There's the window! Go any time you like!'

'Let me out or I'll–' He moved the chair, trying to show menace.

'If I shot, you'd be dead and couldn't talk, and you are going to talk, Garley! Talk or go out of that window!'

Rocklin moved toward him, and Garley repeated, 'Talk?' With the quavered intonation of not knowing what the word meant.

'About you, Red Caldwell – and marked cards!'

Garley's heart went right down into his belly, and all the fears that often made whisky turn sour in his throat swarmed over him. The look on Rocklin's face seemed to mean knowledge that justified killing him, and it was made worse, much worse, because this Rocklin had Red Caldwell's eyes and had in them now the blaze that Garley remembered when Red had slapped his face with the splatter of a marked deck. Garley's tongue simply turned traitor on him and he blurted, 'Clint told you!'

Then, as shaken as he was, Garley saw that he had told Rocklin more than he knew. Garley sucked in his breath, and his eyes bulged as he desperately tried to cover up by adding, 'Told lies about me! Clint and old Harolday, damn 'em! They've sworn to ruin me and–'

But his labored cleverness didn't have the right ring to it. Rocklin pointed at the strewn cards on the floor. 'There's what ruined you! What about them and Red?'

The best Garley could manage was: 'I don't know what you mean!'

Rocklin moved toward him, and Garley swung the chair sidewise off the floor, bracing himself to bring it around clublike. The ceiling was too low for an overhand swing. He stepped back and cried, 'Wait!'

Rocklin wasn't waiting, and Garley backed up with: 'Wait! Wait!'

He had backed so far that he was up against the wall now, and Rocklin said, 'Start talking!' and came on.

Garley heaved out the chair and thrust stabbingly with the four points of the legs, and Rocklin's left hand grabbed, caught a rung, jerked, but Garley hung on. Then Rocklin contemptuously swung the chair sidelong from him, making it pivot in Garley's grip. He lurched in close up against Garley, crowded him flat up against the wall, and swung for his jaw with the point of the right elbow. It crunched on Garley's cheek, but a wrenching throb came back into Rocklin's arm, making new pain in his bandaged hand.

The jolt rocked Garley's head, and his hat fell off as he dropped the chair. Rocklin shifted and, with downward glance, gave the chair a splintering kick backward to have it out of the way. As Garley grappled with him a blast of whisky breath came into Rocklin's face. Rocklin jerked his left arm from Garley's grasp and struck the mouth. 'Talk!' said Rocklin, and hit him again.

For all of his heavy flabbiness, Garley had momentary power and the desperation that is strength, and tried wildly to struggle. Their bodies swayed together, bumping over the table, and the lamp thudded on the floor and

235

the chimney shattered, and the crunch of broken glass was under their pounding feet.

Rocklin was hit and hurt and didn't care. He slashed his left fist into the bulbous belly and drew the grunt of a sick man in pain, and the sound pleased him. 'You'd better talk!' Rocklin told him coldly, and again plowed the point of an elbow into Garley's face, this time getting to the nose, which made a blob of blood come. Then the swing of the left went in, overhand and straight, and his rasping knuckles broke the skin on Garley's cheekbone.

The unfamiliar pain dazed Garley, and his throat sobbed for air. He flung his hands and arms about his face and tried to hunch down. Rocklin damned his bandaged hand, the hurt of which made him fierce. He lunged in close with a sagging shoulder and heaved the shoulder up, and the click of Garley's open mouth closing as his head went back had the sound of a steel trap's snap.

'Talk!' said Rocklin, not giving him pause for talk. That would come later. He wanted the need of talking pounded into the black-leg's flesh.

As Garley's head went back Rocklin gathered the broad lapels of the black coat into his hand, drawing them close up under the fat chin, and twisted; then he began shoving with purposeful shift of feet, backing

Garley around, kicking at his shins with boot heels if he wouldn't back, spiking a heel into the top of Garley's foot if he surged forward, all quickly, not letting him get set, and keeping him blinded with pain by jabbing in the point of an elbow if Garley took his hands from his face.

'Talk!' said Rocklin. 'Talk or–'

When Garley felt the low window ledge strike the hinges of his knees he knew what was meant and coming. A blast of terror surged up and his yell was a choked cough, but he wheeled with all of his weight and the forcefulness of fear, circling away from the window, pawing and twisting and jerking. He dragged Rocklin by the grip on the coat lapels then squirmed free, but stumbled backward over the legs of the overturned table and crashed down, splintering off a table leg. That brought Rocklin down, too, and he was rising when Garley staggered up with a club-shaped table leg in his hands.

Rocklin went right in at him, not striking now but wrestling, and the table leg was useless. When he shifted behind Garley he circled the thick neck with his right arm and locked the arm with the grip of his left hand on the right wrist; then he plunged a crooked knee up into Garley's side and heaved down and back, falling back. Garley, off balance and hurt, came over with his feet in the air and shook the building with a flat-back fall,

237

and all the breath was knocked out of him. Rocklin fell, too, in pulling him over, but scrambled to get up. He straddled Garley then dropped and plowed his fingers into Garley's hair. He lifted the head and bumped it on the floor, then he said, 'Talk – or I'll beat you to death!'

Garley with no breath left in him and no strength and no courage, gurgled huskily, giving up, and the suck of his breath rattled in his throat like the suck of a pump when it goes dry.

In the meantime Clara was beating on the locked door and frantically screaming, 'Ken! Ken!' for she could hear the stormy crash in the room. Her voice carried through the hall and downstairs, and men came up on the run. They heard the fight inside and asked her what was up, but nobody could guess, for the little Chinaman had slithered away.

Men tried the door and found it locked, so they beat on it and yelled, 'Open up! Open up!' Some put their shoulders to the door but it wouldn't give. Clara screamed at them to do something and cried, 'They're killing Ken! Killing him!'

Then Dave, of the stagecoach, pushed into the jam. He was covered with the road's red dust; it was in his beard and on his eyebrows and gave a rust color to his sweat-creased clothes. He glowered, demanding, 'Why don't you open it?'

Carruthers, the hotel man, answered loud and helplessly, 'It's locked!'

Others said, 'Locked inside!' and others: 'They trapped Rocklin!' and still others made wild guesses in a confusion of tongues.

Mrs Carruthers tried to get her arms shelteringly around Clara, but Clara wouldn't have it. She was strangely fierce and wild-eyed and cried, 'You're letting them kill him!'

Dave shoved men away as if striking them. 'Locked, is it?' His hoarse voice was contemptuous. 'A'right, git outa my way!' They were crowding back, clearing the door, when the bartender with the white apron about his legs hunched down with an ear to the keyhole. Dave jerked him aside as if throwing him away. 'Keep clear, I told you!'

Then Dave stepped back and hurled himself. His bull-shaped shoulder hit the door, and the door squealed with splintering shrillness as it tore the nails from the lock's face right out of the jamb and the door flew wide open with a bang up against the wall. Dave pitched forward and barely kept his feet as he came to a staggering halt near the center of the room.

There was Garley on the floor with Rocklin on top and his fingers in Garley's hair. Garley had just groaned, 'I'll t-talk–'

Men swarmed in behind Dave, and Clara was among the men. Sudden hope flushed

Garley into the desperate yell of: 'He's killing me!' and he called for help.

Men believed it was true and pulled at Rocklin, and Clara was jostled and bumped because she tried to get in close and she kept asking, 'Ken? Are you hurt, Ken?'

Rocklin got up, shoving sullenly at men's hands and Clara's, too. He turned gloweringly on Dave and said, 'Damn you!'

Dave mumbled, 'Orta!' and looked submissively at Rocklin then eyed Garley. ''F I'd on'y knowed!' he said, and gave his head a regretful shake.

Clara caught Rocklin's bandaged hand and held it in an anguish of tenderness. The cloth was a wet red, and only partly from Garley's face. Rocklin didn't notice that she was squeezing his hand against her breast; he was watching Garley and thinking of what was best. He didn't want Clint's name shouted to the town. Mrs Carruthers put motherly arms about Clara and whispered soothingly, but Clara would not leave.

The voices of excited men beat about the room, asking the cause of the fight. Rocklin didn't say, and they could see by the tightness of his face that he wouldn't. Some were helping Garley to his feet and questioned him, using a tone of sympathy as if he ought to tell them. 'What happened, Judge? What happened?'

Garley sagged against the support of men's

arms and put a hand to his face tenderly. His face was a smear and his thick lips were cut and swollen, too. The smear was on his torn shirt, and his coat was ripped at the shoulder seams and the lining tongued out. He was half crippled, or more than half, for the bones of his foot felt broken where Rocklin's long boot heel had spiked down. Mumblingly he asked men to help him to his room.

Rocklin shouldered in and got before Garley as if to do something more, and the anxious men bunched up to hold Rocklin back. 'You've licked him!' they said. 'Don't do no more!' He stared at Garley, trying to catch his eyes, but there wasn't a chance. Garely's head was down and he leaned heavily on Carruthers's shoulder. Rocklin wanted to keep the truth out of sight; he didn't want men to get hold of Clint's name, for then Clint would hear about it and be hard to find. So Rocklin said with a cold, stern manner of daring Garley to deny it, 'I caught him in here looking for something. Mebbe for that letter that proves my wife is of age!' Then he stepped back.

Two men were helping Garley, and he moved bulkily toward the door, limping. When they were in the doorway Garley stopped, and he didn't look around but wavered out a hand behind him, his voice thick and wrathful. It was hard for his bruised lips to shape up the words, but he said loudly, 'No letter about it! I thought he used marked cards and slipped in here to see. He does! That's them all over the floor!'

A dead hush followed, and the only sound was the scrape and hobble of Garley's feet moving on and the helpfully short steps of those who were giving him a hand. Men looked down at the scattered cards on the carpet with about the same expression as if at so many snakes.

Then Clara said, 'Oh, what a lie!' She began trying to tell where the cards had been found, but Rocklin said, 'Shut up!'

Her amazement protested. 'But, Ken, you know—'

He had turned about and was telling everybody to clear out. They went slowly, some with backward shift of glance between Rocklin and the scattered cards, believing or almost believing Garley.

The last one at the door was Dave, but instead of leaving he pushed the door to and faced about. He took off his hat, not being polite but to rub his hand on the nearly bald spot Doc Riding's razor had left at the back of his head.

'You, too,' said Rocklin. 'I don't want to talk.'

Dave stared solemnly. 'You're goin' to, anyhow!'

Not much of anything could be done

against Dave's burly solidness. Rocklin held the wrist of his hurt hand, for it ached flamingly, and looked at Dave with no interest. Clara came close and put her hands to his arm, but he didn't look at her.

Dave said, 'So you're Old Red's nephy; an' I wonder now I didn't see how you look like him – like when he was younger. An' I hear you two are married. That's good, 'cause the Judys and the like'll git a feller if good girls don't!'

'All right,' said Rocklin with flip of hand toward the door. 'Thanks and good-by.'

Dave took his hat into both hands, stirring out a small puff of dust. 'I'm freightin' for the Fosslers, an' last night that little Mexican out at Stan's quit an' rode in with me. He told me about things!' Dave bobbed down his head, pointing to the spot that still looked tonsured. 'That's why I happened to come up here this mornin' for to say thanks to you an' run into all this ruckus. But *now*,' he added quickly, 'I got more to say.'

'All right, what?' Rocklin's voice was weary and without interest.

Dave's old eyes lighted somberly as he looked about the floor at the scattered cards. 'Garley's, heh?' he asked. Rocklin was stonily noncommittal, but when Dave's look shifted to Clara she nodded furtively.

'A'right,' said Dave. 'Now you lissen. Red got mad at me when I told him he was a damn fool to trust Garley. "'Cause,' I says, "he's a blackleg!" Red he says, "You're crazy." "A'right," I says, "you wait 'n see. I'll prove it!'"

'And did you?' Rocklin demanded, eager now.

'Hold your hosses,' said Dave. 'I'm tellin' you fast as I can. Lots of times I used to make up the mail, clerks bein' busy an' all. I'd seen things come to Garley from a sportin'goods house in Chicago. I knowed what it meant – or could mean. Gamblers got crooked cards from there. Fellers have asked me to watch out in the mail for where things come from to gamblers they suspicioned. I never touched nuthin'; just said if things come from that Chicago place.

'So one day a letter come from there to Garley again. I opened it up to make sure, then I put it all in a letter to Red. And I wrote on a piece of paper I'd robbed the mail to give it to him and I said, "Red, 'less you want me arrested, tear this part up." I mailed it to him here. He was killed before I seen him again.'

Rocklin asked, 'What was in the letter?'

'Garley's? Some printin' an' some card samples. Printin' said, "Best marked cards ever made" – or words like that. Said, "This offer made only to old customers." I marked that part with my pencil. That's what I wanted Red to see. I don't know whether he

244

ever did; he was killed so soon after.'

Rocklin nodded and turned to the window. He trusted Dave, but Dave did get drunk, and just now the fewer that knew the better. Some day he might have to ask Dave to run the risk of admitting that he had pilfered the mails. The Garden City judge would be lenient, perhaps. Now he turned to Dave and asked, 'You mailed it to him here at Santa Inez?'

'Yeah, here.'

Rocklin found it hard to think clearly with a nest of devils using hot pincers on his hand, but it was easy to see that, since the folder had been in Red's coat when he was killed on the way back from Garden City, he had received Dave's message before he went on to Garden City.

'Dave, from what I hear of Red, he wouldn't have wasted any time in jumping down Garley's throat. That right?'

'All spraddled out with spurs on!' Dave agreed zestfully.

'I mean if he had got the letter at the post office here in town, he wouldn't have left town until he had talked to Garley?'

'He'd've chased him out of town!'

Rocklin studied moodily, trying to put two and two together, adding up, and remembered the confessional of 'Clint told you!' Then: 'Who do you think killed Red?'

'Dunno; jus' don't.'

Rocklin considered the risk of such a question, then calmly and bluntly asked, 'Could it have been young Harolday?'

'That fool Clint kid? Drag his tongue in the dust an' it'll leave a snake track, but he wouldn't do a murder.' Dave slapped his leg with the hat, stirring out dust, and growled, 'I'd sooner think it was the Old Man his own self!'

'Are you serious?'

'Well, mebbe not. But he's got some murdered men's ranches, and hankered for Caldwell's!'

'Did he kill them?'

'Somebody did!'

'What ranches?'

'Arly's pa's, f'r one. The Santee.'

'Murdered?'

Thus pinned down, Dave admitted, 'Nobody knows f'r a fact, I reckon. He was missin' a long time, then found at the foot of the Table's bluffs. Some said he'd been shot. Some said nobody could tell, not after a fall like that. I don't know. On'y Arly's maw was a crazy woman ever to marry Harolday! Some say him an' that Arly-girl are goin' to meet head on. That'll be one time he gits the worst of it! Ever'body that has a run-in with her gits the worst of it. I don't care who they are – they'll git the worst of it!' He added almost admiringly, 'I shore did!'

CHAPTER FIFTEEN

Rocklin went directly to the Harolday stables and said to the flat-faced agent who was alone in the office, 'Tell me, where's Clint, do you know?'

'Yeah. The Old Man sent him out to the west ranch day before yesterday. Be back in a day or two 'f not sooner. Anything special?' The agent was grinning inquisitively.

'It'll keep.' He started away, but something flickered in his memory and he turned about abruptly. 'By the way, you mentioned once that both Garley and Harolday had asked you to keep your eye out for my name on the passenger list. That right?'

'Um-hm. Why?'

'Did Garley tell him I was coming, do you think?'

The agent swore in amusement. 'Don't you know about things here? Garley and the Old Man ain't spoke for over a year! They used to be thick, but something happened. And say!' The agent leered confidentially and lowered his voice. 'You sure do know how to tickle the Old Man! I'm s'prised he wasn't mad about your poker-game quarrel with Clint – but taking Arly down a peg just suited him! Then what you done to the Clewses! And now Garley! Why, I'd purt-near bet he'd loan you five dollars – without security!'

The agent was still chuckling inanely as Rocklin went out.

Doc Riding took the blood-wet bandage from Rocklin's hand and said, 'I just got back from seeing Judge Garley.'

'Did he say much?'

'He's in a bad fix. You cut his mouth so that it hurts him to drink whisky! And that boot heel of yours is a dangerous weapon. Yes, he said you are a blackleg.' The doc wiped at the open wound in Rocklin's palm with a piece of cotton. 'I hear you say he was after a paper that proves your wife is of age. I think you both are liars.'

Rocklin admitted quietly, 'That's right.'

'This hurt?'

'Yes.'

The doc nodded, satisfied. 'It'll hurt worse if you don't tell me things.'

'Were you a good friend of Red Cald-well's?'

'In a way. I never had more than three or four really bad rows with Red. Why?'

'You're the coroner. How much of a law officer is a coroner?'

Doc Riding poured carbolic into the palm, then held the palm cup-shaped so the carbolic would soak in good, and said, 'I don't rightly know myself. Why?'

'I won't talk to that Dep'ty Sheriff Jackson. Or to the marshal. I don't dislike the marshal, but I'm not telling him things.'

'Hold your hand still while I get some bandage.' He turned to the cupboard and took out a clean white rag and ripped off a piece: 'All right, what is it?'

'I think I know who has been using that rifle.'

Doc Riding went on binding up the hand. 'I'm listening.'

'Clint Harolday!'

'Clint, hm? Let's hear.'

Rocklin told him, told him everything pertaining to the marked cards and of how, when he caught Garley picking them up off the table, he had locked the door and accusingly flung Caldwell's name at him and Garley had blurted, 'Clint told you!'

The bandage was finished while he talked, and the doc didn't interrupt but returned the hand to its sling; then he poured another drink of whisky and offered it, quietly gesturing for Rocklin to sit down. Doc Riding also sat down, folded his arms, and listened.

Rocklin explained in a slow and careful voice that if you put two and two together and added up, you almost had to think that Garley had made some kind of deal with Clint to get rid of Caldwell. 'Had to get rid of him or get run out of the country!'

Doc Riding looked somberly impressed, admitted, 'I see. Go on.'

'Caldwell's death left Garley in control of the ranch. He couldn't do much that was crooked while Brotherton was alive, so – don't you see?'

'I see. But where does Clint come in?'

'Me. I mean Bowles. Mebbe they thought I was trying to cut in on Red's property and didn't want it that way. Or mebbe Clint just saw a chance to even up what I done to him in the poker game.'

Doc Riding pulled at his leathery cheek. 'Marrying the girl has just about cut the ground clear out from under Garley – that is, if you are guessing right about him.'

'Don't you think I am?'

'Mebbe. Don't know. If somebody shoots you now, I'll be convinced. But go ahead. Why are you so sure it's Clint?'

Rocklin studied. 'Clint's in with Garley somehow. That "Clint told you!" was like holding a match up to a dark place for a minute. Then it went out. I saw enough to know there's something there. And Clint can ride and shoot. Take what happened to Bowles. Somebody sneaked up there and shot a man in a white hat whose back was turned. Had to be somebody that knows the lay of the land. Clint does. Bowles was killed about the same way as Red and Brotherton.

Don't you see?'

Doc Riding rubbed his chin, nodded. 'Good job of figgerin', Rocklin. Yes. You don't think anybody else could fit in all the way round like Clint does, hm?'

'Do you?'

'No-o-o, can't say I do, quite. But you see, I happen to know you've added up wrong somewhere. Clint was in bed with the mumps when Red was shot. And he was over to a dance in the Flat the night Bowles was killed. Horse kicked a man and broke his leg, and I got there about daylight. Clint was still there, dancing. And it just happens that Jim was killed midafternoon a day or so later. And that afternoon Clint come for me to look at a sick horse down at the stable. The Old Man had gone over to the ranch, the vet was drunk again, and Clint knew his father would be meaner than ever if the horse died. So I went. I don't much like Clint. He's a spoiled fool kid with a bad temper. The Old Man pampers him one day and is mean with him the next. He's had to lie to Harolday from the time he was a little shaver or have the tar whaled out of him. He still does.'

Rocklin gazed glumly at the doc and felt bad, but said stubbornly, 'I still think Clint knows something.'

'And I think you'd better keep your eye on the Clews bunch.' Doc Riding's voice was quiet, kindly. 'And if you've guessed right about somebody not wanting you to cut in on the ranch, you're going to get shot. In the back, too. So be careful.'

Rocklin stood up, put on his hat. 'Could Garley have used them?'

'I don't know. You've guessed so far wrong about Clint that if I was you I'd be awful careful about anybody else. The one thing certain is the Clewses are a bad bunch and they'll lay for you.'

'Another thing is certain, Doc. Garley *is* a blackleg! 'By.'

He went down Doc Riding's stairs and turned west, going back to the Harolday stable.

Juan Romeras was standing with a shoulder against the wall under the archway and took the small cigarette from his lips. His greeting was cool, and he gave Rocklin a long stare that seemed to glisten with dislike. Rocklin returned the *'Buenos dias, señor'* and passed by. He had heard that whenever you saw Juan, Arly wasn't far away and wondered about that but wouldn't ask.

Harolday was in the office now. 'Mornin',' he said, and the look from his flint-gray eyes was like a weight that he laid on Rocklin's face. It made him feel that maybe Harolday thought he had come to borrow the five dollars – without security. 'You and the judge had a run-in, I hear.'

Rocklin used short words to tell how it was; then: 'I'm taking your advice and going to Garden City.'

'My advice?'

'Yours, about going to the district court.'

Harolday locked his hands behind him, commented tonelessly, 'That'll about finish Garley, won't it?'

'Hope so! And if they hadn't broken in the door I'd have had the whole truth out of him this morning. I'm not through trying.'

'"Whole truth"?' Harolday repeated, and stared inquiringly.

'It's a muddle to figger, but all signs point to Garley. He can't ride or shoot, so mebbe somebody did it for him. There's no loyalty in him, so he'll say who if he's coaxed enough. I tried this morning. I mean to try again. Come to think of it, I want to book three seats on the stage!'

'Three?'

'I'll take Garley with us tomorrow!'

'Mebbe he won't want to go.'

'He'll go – or tell everything he knows here in town before witnesses!'

'Um-hm, I see.' Harolday slowly swung his head up and down, understandingly. Then a shine came into his glassy eyes and he smiled, or at least showed his teeth. 'Rocklin, you're about the smartest man that's showed up in this country for a long time! Cute of you to marry that girl! And *three* seats, yes!'

253

Rocklin didn't like the sound of it, for Harolday seemed approving the slyness of marrying the Caldwell girl and thereby getting control of her property.

Pap Fossler found Rocklin on the sidewalk before the Honeycomb and took him down to meet the 'boys' – men now, with families – who had built Pap's little store into the trading-center of the Santa Inez country.

While Rocklin talked with the younger Fossler, Pap thievishly dipped a handful of hard candy from the bucket into his pocket and looked gleeful because he thought he hadn't been seen.

'It's all as much his as ours,' said the Fossler boy, 'but Pap likes to think he's getting the best of us. About .38-.40s. Doc Riding was asking some time ago, too. I didn't think to tell the doc that Sam Haynes has got one. He used to shoot rats with it back there in the warehouse, but we ask him to quit that. Poison's cheaper and don't scare customers!'

Sam Haynes carried out a sack of oats from the warehouse's cavernous dimness and stowed it in a nester's wagon; then, as the wagon pulled away, he stood on the edge of the platform and waved flirtatiously to the nester's tiny daughter who had her mouth and apron pocket full of Pap's candy.

'Yeah,' said Sam, rolling a cigarette for

Rocklin, 'I got a .38-.40. Had it since I was a kid. Put my initials on the butt with brass tacks. That and my saddle was about all I carried off the ranch when we lost it. We knew Dad had borrered but never imagined any ten thousand dollars. But Harolday had his note and cleaned us out.'

Pap pulled at his whiskers and said, 'A powerful lot of money, ten thousand dollars!'

'Y'see,' Haynes went on, 'we just run our cows on the open range, but Harolday he got punchers to homestead and deed over to him. You uncle done it, too. Not legal, but the only way a man can hold his range, I reckon.'

Pap said, 'Tell him how Red was dickerin' to buy your ranch.'

'W'y, nothin' to tell Pap. Dad was ailin', and Red and him talked some of a deal. Then Dad was called to the door one night and shot and the man rode off. We never had any real suspicions. There's allus some drunken puncher that's been fired, some hothead you've fussed with over a brand, some nester you've run off from a water hole he's tried to fence. Been ten year now.

'About the rifle – I brought it down here to kill rats a couple years ago, but I ain't shot it in for a long time. Get it if you'd like, and show it to you.'

Rocklin said, 'Never mind,' for there was

255

no possibility of suspecting Sam Haynes's frankness; but Sam said, 'I'll be right back.'

He came back empty-handed, with a puzzled but not angry manner, and shook his head worriedly. 'Darned thing's gone!'

'Stole?' Pap asked incredulously.

'Case is still there, but the gun's sure gone. Box of shells, too. No tellin' how long ago. Yesterday 'r last year – I wouldn't know. Lord, we never think of anything bein' stole around here, do we, Pap? Somebody could've pitched it outa the window back there, then gone around an' picked it up. Gives you a queer feelin' to think somebody would steal!'

When they left the warehouse Pap offered Rocklin a piece of candy, then said, 'I was hopin' Sam might tell you about how Red acted up when Harolday foreclosed. Red tried to get Sam and his maw to fight that Harolday note. Red said he bet Harolday couldn't prove he'd ever loaned any ten thousand. Red said he bet it was more like a thousand and Harolday raised the note after Haynes was killed.' Pap chuckled. 'When Red didn't like somebody he didn't care what he said!'

'What did Harolday say back?'

'Nuthin'. What could he say without havin' a fight? Nobody wanted a fight with Red, an' Harolday won't quarrel with anybody.'

'He quarreled with Garley, didn't he?'

'Oh, that. Over a lawsuit, I reckon. Nobody knows.'

When Rocklin was going back to the hotel he again passed the stables, and Juan was still there with a shoulder against the wall as if he hadn't moved for an hour or more, and perhaps he hadn't. His greeting was politely cold but his stare seemed to warn Rocklin of dislike.

Rocklin stopped short, gazed at the taciturn old Mexican, and said quietly in Spanish, 'Señor, it appears that you do not like me.'

Juan replied, very quietly, too, 'Señor, that is true!'

'Then, if you please, let us have an understanding. I do not dislike you. Why do you dislike me?'

Juan told him, 'I have known for years that some day you would come, señor, and I am sorry!'

'That I would come? How can that be true?'

'That some day some man would come who would do what you have done to the señorita. The man's name is of no importance. It is not your fault your shadow is black!' Rocklin listened, scowling his puzzlement; then, strangely, Juan added, 'I believe in God, señor!'

'Who doesn't?' Rocklin asked simply.

Juan shrugged a shoulder. 'Permit that I roll

257

a cigarette for you.' He rolled it deftly, gave it to Rocklin, and offered a lighted match. Then: 'It is now too late, señor, to wish that you had never come. I do not blame you, but I fear that I must hate you. Good day, señor.'

That was a gracious enough dismissal and the cigarette was a token of good will in spite of the words; but, for all of his sympathetic understanding of Spanish people, Rocklin didn't know what to think and he wondered if Arly had told Juan some untrue thing about the night at the cabin on the Table.

The hotel man had moved Rocklin and Clara to a back room, and the back windows overlooked a pigpen where shotes were fattening on hotel slops, and near the pen were ramshackle sheds, a chicken house, and a midden of broken dishes, tin cans, rubbish.

When he came in Clara sat quietly and regarded him with staring silence. There was a disconsolate look about her; she had been crying, but her eyes were dry now. He closed the door, and anger boiled into the guess. 'Has that old aunt of yours been at you?'

Clara shook her head. Her dark eyes were lustrously sad and her mouth was set to keep it from quivering, yet she sat erectly as if she wouldn't be weak; then she asked in an aloof, troubled voice, 'Ken, where have

258

you been?'

He could tell that there was a catch to the question, for suspicion of some kind showed in her stare. He pitched his hat to the floor, studied her face, and felt that the old aunt must have been setting traps. 'I went to Doc Riding.' He moved the bandaged hand in the sling, showing her. 'Then I went to the stage office and booked three seats for us to go to Garden City. Then–'

'Three?' Her tone hit the word queerly, as if it fitted in with her suspicions.

'We are taking Garley. He doesn't know it, but he is going! Then I went down to Fossler's store to ask some questions and saw some men. On the way back I stopped at the Sun-Up and said hello to Cap, then come back here.'

'And no one else?'

'"No one else" – what?'

Clara gazed at him reproachfully. 'There is always something so weak about a lie! And I wanted to remember you, always, as strong and honest!' Her voice became low and tense. 'Ken, I know that you have been with that Harolday girl!'

He pondered that, then asked, 'Who said I had?'

'I have talked with her, Ken!' Clara waited expectantly, but he had a listening frown and also waited. He could see that she was trying not to go to pieces, and there was

259

much for him to wonder about, but he knew that it would all come out pretty soon without his having to ask.

Then Clara said with labored, tense quietness, 'Now I know that you married me because – because–' Her hurt was too strong to be suppressed, and she cried at him in a desperate, choking way, 'I just won't believe you did it for money!'

'I'd sure hate to have you.'

'Well, then, then you were just *sorry* for me. It had to be one of the two, because you love Arly Harolday!'

The surprise shocked his face into a hardened look, and he couldn't imagine how she had made a guess like that. It wasn't true, of course, but he didn't offer a denial. Arguing was something he never liked, not with a woman, and he merely looked at her.

'Be honest with me, Ken! Oh, please be honest!'

He sat down on a chair within arm's reach of her. It was a straight chair with a cane bottom, and he drew his long legs back alongside the chair uncomfortably. 'What all did she say?'

'That she loves you!' Clara waited with eyes questioning, but he wouldn't say anything, so Clara added, 'That you love her, too!' He had a look of calmness that he didn't feel, and she lost patience, demanding, 'Why don't you say something?'

'Did she make out I married you to cut in on the ranch?'

'No, she didn't. But what else was I to think after all she told me? I mean' – Clara corrected hastily – 'I had to think that – which I won't, just won't, Ken! – or that you did it because – well, she said that you two had a quarrel, and so you just married me – well, just married me because you were mad at her, and that it didn't mean a thing – your marrying me!'

He picked his words in a slow, cold voice. 'I oughta know best what I mean.'

Clara's hands fluttered out impulsively toward him, but she drew them back into her lap and said rapidly, with feeling and a kind of challenge that he saw was not going to be easy to answer, 'No, no, Ken! You don't act as if you even liked me! And you certainly don't love me, Ken. You haven't said so. You haven't kissed me. You won't look at me. You draw away as though I am repugnant to you. And of course you would feel that way if you loved someone else! And, oh, Ken, I can't really blame you because I can see how it would be if I had to be near some other man, any man but you – I would loathe him!'

There seemed nothing he could say. How tell a girl that he wouldn't look at her because she was lovely and he was uneasy and susceptible and afraid; that he was trying honestly to use good sense and keep

261

his emotions hobbled; that he did like her and liked her a lot, but love was something else, raised hell with people, and he didn't have it and didn't want it; and he felt that way partly for her own sake, too, because the West would ruin her Eastern daintiness and make her unhappy with its loneliness and hardness and cruelties; and she couldn't be happy, not with him in the West – and he wouldn't go East? He could feel those things and think them, but he couldn't say them.

But Clara's look and silence required that he say something. He spoke coolly. 'I never showed any love for her as I know of. Nor her for me, so–'

'Oh, Ken, that isn't true! You even showed her my letter! I had asked you to destroy it, but you gave it to her! She knew what I had written and she said it was "sweet" of me.' Having Arly call her "sweet" seemed rather an insult. 'She told me you gave it to her!'

Rocklin left his chair and walked to a back window and looked through, eyeing the pile of tin cans without noticing them. He was remembering Hazel and Alice and Judith, how they could twist things up and get the best of a man; and now Arly had taken what he had meant as an insulting slap and turned it into evidence of – 'love,' she called it, and Clara was convinced. He said absently, 'It wasn't like that.'

'But she knew by heart everything that was in the letter, Ken. So you must have given it to her. Didn't you?' Then, sorrowfully: 'Please don't lie to me. Whatever the truth is, Ken, it won't be as bad as a lie – as for you to lie!'

He turned about and was half mad but kept cool, and Clara's eyes didn't waver. He said, 'I tell you it wasn't like that! She had a fellow try to steal it. I took it away from him and I tore it up in little pieces, and I was so mad I told him, "Take it to her!" That's not exactly "giving," is it? Then she put the thing together. I ought've burned it, but I didn't. But I didn't give it, not like she's made you think!'

He felt that would settle something, but it didn't, because Clara ignored the explanation and told him, 'You went to work for her though Mr Brotherton had hired you. He sent for you and paid you and needed you. He told me he needed you. But you – you wanted to be with *her!*'

Rocklin studied her face and said sternly, 'That's not being honest to your own self! Not when you heard her hire me there in Garley's office. Did that sound like "love"?'

Clara nodded. 'The way she explained it, yes! She wanted you – wanted you near her, but she wasn't sure then just how you felt about her, and she thought you might refuse, so she said her father wanted you. I recall how quickly you accepted! And you did seem pleased, Ken!'

Rocklin stared at her glumly. 'No use talking if you want to look at it that way. Anything else?'

'Much else!' Clara was stirred, hurt, resentful. 'She didn't put you to work at all, but sent you off to a cabin, alone. Then she came, alone. And you two were together. She said so. What do you say, Ken?'

Clara was begging him to deny it. He didn't, not just then, for he was muddled by Arly's saying an untrue thing of that kind. A strange girl and without shame, it seemed. He remembered the warning that she would get even with him somehow, no matter how, and he wondered what the devil she could have told Juan and why had she told Clara such a parcel of lies? Was it malice – or had she meant what she seemed to mean when she came out of the wet night and to the cabin?

'Is that true, Ken?'

'I don't know.'

'"Don't know"!'

'Like the other things, it may be fact, but I'll be damned if it's truth!' He went up close to Clara and stared down sternly. 'She sent me up there with Bowles for a guide, and he stayed longer than he was supposed to – and got killed by mistake for me. There was so little "love" in my head I thought that

264

was why she'd sent me – so somebody could kill me easy. All right, then she did come and she stayed all night, and I thought she hated me. Nothing happened to change that way of thinking. She said she'd come to tell me Brotherton had been killed and I was to go to your ranch. And I did. Now she's come in here with a lot of lies and raised hell with you!'

Then Clara stood up, a lonely and saddened figure but resolute as she faced him. 'She wasn't angry, Ken. She was quiet and earnest and – and convincing. I am sorry I accused you of being with her today, but she said that she was going right out and find you. That you belonged to her, and that there wasn't anything I could do about it. And – and she made me feel that way, too!'

'So I'm like a horse with her brand on me, hmm?' he murmured somberly.

'And I am not really blaming you, Ken. Honestly I'm not. I asked you to marry me, and that was shameless; but I know now that I loved you even then. I must have – and I knew it so soon afterward! And it was fine of you to pretend that you didn't do it out of pity. I can't be what is called a "rival" to her. She's too pretty and vivid and strong. I wish I were like her. She loves you and so do I. It is for you to say something, Ken.'

He said, 'She don't love me!'

'You sound as if you wished you could be sure!'

He frowned meaningly. 'And just when I'd begun to think you didn't have a cat-claw streak like other women!' His eyes hurt her, and Clara was sorry she had said a thing like that. He took his time, thoughtfully, then said, 'Right now the only thing I feel like saying is, "Let's not talk about it." If you could look inside of me and see what I don't know the words for, it would be all right, or purt-near. I wish you could. She's either a little crazy or she's out to get even with me. I don't know what's the matter with her.

'But now you lissen close. If you want me to go away from you, all right, I'll go. But no matter how you feel, you'd better let me finish with Garley. Then I think you ought to sell the ranch and go back East – where you belong.'

Now Clara took her time, thoughtfully, then she said, 'I suppose that I ought to be brave and proud and insulted and go away from you. But I do appreciate your thinking about my welfare. I really do, Ken. And I know that I do need you, need your advice and help. So may we keep it as a friendly – well, like a friendly business relationship? Is that it?' She forced a smile and listened.

He said, 'Whatever you want.'

CHAPTER SIXTEEN

When the supper gong rang Clara said, 'I couldn't possibly eat, but you go down to supper.'

She wasn't pouting and she was trying not to look sad, and he felt sorry for her and thought, *Damn Arly!* He had worked it out in his own mind that Arly was a bad one. Any way you looked at her, she was no good – a shameless liar and a shameless girl. And not really pretty. Lithe and tense, with a bold brightness in her eyes and a twist to her tongue that would drive a man mad. He thought the worst he could of her, unaware that it gave him an excuse for deliberately thinking of her.

In the dining-room Doc Riding was among the men at the table and there was much talk, but Rocklin had little to say, very little.

The town had learned from Cap that the marked cards were not Rocklin's, which disposed of Garley's accusation; but Doc Riding said it took a devilish smart man to have thought up such a good comeback at a time like that. He stressed the 'devilish.'

Rocklin ate hurriedly and pushed back his chair, leaving.

In the hall he turned toward the stairs, and Clint was there in the dimness with his arm on a newel post. The oil lamp on the wall wasn't much brighter than vague moonlight, but it was enough to show that Clint wasn't wearing his calfskin vest, and the handkerchief about his neck wasn't silk, but the hatband had a sliver gleam.

'Hello,' Clint said a bit doubtfully, but Rocklin returned, 'Howdy,' quietly and without stiffness.

'I didn't want to talk to you in there before people, so I waited out here.' Clint was offering friendliness, almost overfriendliness. Rocklin suspected that it might be meant trickily, but he was glad to find Clint back in town. Then Clint went on in the hurrying way of one who has studied out a little speech and is afraid he may forget. 'Lissen, I don't hold a grudge for that run-in we had!'

'Suits me,' Rocklin told him. 'I don't like grudges.'

Clint looked relieved and grinned a little. 'I'll admit I was mad as hell when I heard how Arly hired you, but–'

'Your father hired me.'

Clint's grin widened. 'Little you know!' His nervousness was going away, unless the womanish talkativeness was another phase of nervousness. 'That was just Arly's way of doing things! You can't never tell what she's up to! Like now, in sending me to say she

268

wants you to come over to the house right away. I don't know what she wants, only she wants to see you alone. And she couldn't, not alone, if she come to the hotel. So she sent me.'

Rocklin had no intention of going near Arly, but he did want to put Clint in a corner and make him talk, and would coax if he could but use force if he must; so he asked consideringly, 'Can't you make a guess? You must have some kind of idea.'

Clint now seemed to have a kind of babbling readiness for talk. 'You never know what she's up to! But her and the Old Man have just had one hell of a big row over to the house. Juan was out in the hall, so I couldn't listen. But mebbe,' Clint went on, as if making his best guess, 'she wants to tell you what the Old Man is up to in planning that land company again.'

'Land company, hm?'

'Makes her mad to think about turning range land into farms!'

'Why would she want to tell me?'

'Why, you practically own Caldwell's K C now, don't you? You won't want nesters swarmin' in, will you?'

'Come along upstairs. My wife's up there. She owns the ranch.'

Clint replied willingly. 'Sure. I've never met her.'

They started up the stairs side by side.

'Land company?' said Rocklin. 'But a man has the right to do with his own land as he likes, hasn't he?'

'His, mebbe.' Then Clint added glibly, 'But Arly claims the Santee from our maw, and it's in the Old Man's name. He won't let go and she won't give up – and she'll get it somehow. You'll see! I want her to have it. It's all she wants out of him, and then I'm to have everything else when he cashes in!' His tone had a callous hopefulness, almost the expressed wish that his father would soon die.

They were now at the top of the stairs. Rocklin paused, asked, 'How can all that have anything to do with me?'

'You mean her rowing with the Old Man?'

'That's it, yes.'

Clint poked a finger toward Rocklin's breast. 'You're a lot like Red Caldwell was. Mebbe she thinks you're enough like him to stop the Old Man like Red did a couple years back. Red said, "Now you look here, Harolday. You know what I'd do to a man that set fire to my range. Or brought in the hoof-and-mouth on purpose! Or poisoned water! Or run sheep! So don't you start bringin' in nesters!"

'That,' Clint went on, 'made the Old Man back down. He won't quarrel. I don't think he's easy scairt, but quarrels hurt business and he's good at business. He knows how to look ahead and wait!'

'But he did quarrel with Garley, I hear.'

Clint half laughed. 'Yah, the Old Man thought he was doin' something purty cute, but the judge got the best of him!'

'How was that?'

Clint half laughed again. 'I can't tell you. Wouldn't do. But the joke was sure on the Old Man!'

They were going down the corridor now. 'How old are you, Clint?'

'Twenty, purt-near. Why?'

'Being so young, I'm surprised Garley lets you know about things that he hides from other people. 'Specially when he's not friends with your father!'

Clint stopped short. 'What'd you mean?' he asked, suddenly tense. 'I don't know what you're talking about.' His voice was sulky. That was his way of covering up; not a very good way, since it showed that something was being covered up.

It was too dim here for Rocklin to have a good look at his face, but the words had bull's-eyed. He knew it was a gamble as to whether or not Clint could really tell something about marked cards, Garley, and Red Caldwell; and all day, or ever since the talk with Doc Riding, fluctuating doubts had made him wonder if the wily old blackleg had confided in the vain, bad-tempered boy. But Rocklin meant to find out, no matter what it took.

'I'll explain in a minute just how it is,' Rocklin told him quietly. 'Here we are.'

A slit of lamplight lay under the door, and Rocklin fingered the knob.

As he pushed the door open Clint's eyes made an uneasy grab at Rocklin's face, trying to guess what he had in mind; but Rocklin pointed. 'My wife.'

Clara was by the table with sewing in her lap. The needle paused in the cloth as she looked up in mild surprise at the coming of a visitor. Clint took off his hat and stepped inside.

'Clara, this is Clint Harolday,' Rocklin said, and closed the door and stood there, and they didn't know that he was guarding the door.

The Harolday name gave tension to Clara's face; it was a young and pretty face and held Clint's surprised attention. She said, 'How do you do, Mr Harolday?' as if not sure of the name. She wasn't sure why anyone with that name would be brought into the room, and her glance quickly inquired of Rocklin, but there was no response. He was eyeing Clint.

Clint had a polite way with women, and he said, 'Pleased to meet you,' and smiled. But she didn't smile back and wasn't even looking at him, and when Clint followed her stare and turned around a throb of nervousness came up into his throat. He knew that he was in for something bad; he had seen that kind of look in Rocklin's eyes before and had knuckled under there in the Sun-Up and emptied his pockets of poker winnings. Now his sudden dread was as great as then, or greater.

Clara exclaimed anxiously, 'Why, Ken, what is the matter?' and arose from the chair.

Rocklin told her, 'Set down and keep quiet.' He sounded harsh, then said slowly and with a warning in his tone, 'Clint, Garley and me had a little talk this morning, and your name was brought up.'

'M–My name?'

'Your name!'

Clint's lips went dry; he was rattled and tried not to show it, but there was a stutter to his 'W-What did he s-say?'

'Lots! Mebbe you heard that I beat hell out of him.' And he was telling Clint that he would do the same to him, too, here and now.

Clara had sat down, but she pitched her sewing to the table and got up again with the anxious protest of: 'Oh Ken, what now is wrong?'

He told her, 'Keep away,' but she came up close, for she saw Rocklin's anger, and put her hands tightly to his arm, begging, 'Please – please, Ken!'

Clint turned to her with a bewildered hurt

air and said, 'I don't know what he's talking about! Honest, I don't, Mrs Rocklin!'

That air of abused innocence settled it in Rocklin's mind, and he shook Clara from him, jerking his arm free, and hit Clint as hard as he could, and was coldly purposeful about it. He felt there was no better way than a crack on the jaw to straighten out Clint's crooked tongue, and he was very much aware that it was all a gamble as to how much Clint really knew. But the dice had been spilled out; the throw would soon be added up.

Clara trembled back with much the same shocked look as if he had hit her, and dismay stared out of her wide, dark eyes, then she looked pityingly toward Clint. He sagged against the wall with his hand to his face. The blow had hurt. Clara cried out at Rocklin, 'Oh, that's foul and cowardly, and I never thought you would do such a thing!'

Rocklin again pushed her aside. 'Keep out of the way!' He knew the uselessness of trying to explain to her and, having started on Clint, he had to keep pressing in; so he reached out, gripped Clint's shoulder, shook him roughly. 'You'll tell it and tell it all, or I'll beat hell out of you!'

Clara said, 'Oh, what kind of man are you? I never thought – thought – a mere boy, too!' She couldn't go on.

'You never thought what?' His eyes were

somber, for her tone hurt and her look hurt worse than her voice. She didn't reply, and he said, 'There's been murder – more than one! And he knows about them. And he's going to talk. So you keep quiet and out of the way!'

That, in spite of all Doc Riding had said, was the guess that Rocklin had made. He was stubbornly standing to it, and he was telling it to Clint as much as to her, and he turned and watched Clint.

Clint was moving from the wall and held his hand to his face and dragged his feet. Clara's gaze followed him pityingly, and Rocklin's look followed him, too, not pityingly.

Clint was moving as if in a kind of stupor; he was trying to get as far from Rocklin as he could, and he went across the room and turned about to sit in the chair that was before the back window. They heard a gun fire and the report sounded faint and thin, but Clint lurched up stiffly with backward jerk of head and upward fling of arms, and his eyes flew open in a dazed, senseless stare, and his mouth was wide and silent.

For a moment he stood in grotesque motionlessness, his back in a bend as if it had been rammed by a great knee and his arms aimlessly overhead. He had gone between the lamplight and the back window, and the thud of the bullet into his flesh, the brittle clink of the broken window, and the thin bang of the gun were one sound. Then Clint went down, falling backward with seeming slowness, and he struck the seat of the chair, seemed trying to sit there when all of his bones were broken, but his body drooped forward and he pitched head first to the floor.

Clara cried moaningly and started to run toward him, but Rocklin's arm swept out and his hand took hold of her with a force like anger and jerked her back and close up against him at the wall beside the door. 'Don't get between that lamp and window!'

For a brief, tense moment his arm enfolded her; then he said, 'Stay here!' and opened the door into the dark hall and closed it quickly behind him to cut off the light, then he turned to the rear window. He raised the window and leaned forward on the ledge and peered down.

The ground was splotched with the deep shadows of sheds and rubbish piles, and here and there the shimmer and glint of tin cans caught the starlight; and in the stillness he could hear the sleepy, questioning grunt of a pig. He strained, searching for movement, but nothing moved. He decided that whoever had fired must have run instantly, and not on horseback, for he would have heard hoofs. Nobody was out there now; nobody would wait this long – not after sending a bullet from the darkness into a man's back.

An unalarmed man's voice called from the kitchen porch below, 'Hey, who's shootin' out there?'

Then a woman's voice, not so clearly, said, 'Hope it's not somebody after a polecat again! The last time – whew!'

Rocklin leaned farther through the window and called, 'Mrs Carruthers?'

'Yes. What you shootin' at? And who are you?'

'Rocklin. Upstairs. If Doc Riding is still down there, send him up. And you'd better come!'

When he returned to the room he left the door wide and went by Clara without noticing how she looked at him.

Clint lay between the table and the chair with a drunken twist of body, and Rocklin squatted down and stared at the dead boy's face. He remembered, without feeling any reason for remembering, Juan's 'I believe in God, señor!'

Then Clara came toward him staringly, and she steadied herself with a hand to the table and said, 'You are to blame!' He stood up and started to speak, but she moved back, keeping away from him, and said, 'How could you?'

'You mean I had him shot?'

All in a breath she said, 'Oh, no, no, not that – but the way you looked and acted and struck him – it was as if you wanted – wanted something dreadful to happen to him!'

Rocklin eyed her broodingly and didn't say anything.

Then there was a trample of feet in the hall.

CHAPTER SEVENTEEN

Now they were waiting for Harolday to come.

Clara had let Mrs Carruthers lead her away, and Carruthers stood in the door, keeping men out but talking with them worriedly.

Only Doc Riding, Pap Fossler, and Cap were in the room with Rocklin, and he said very little after telling them: '...said Arly wanted to see me and guessed it was something about the ranch. He come up here with me and went to set down over there. Got between the light and the window.'

Pap said, 'How could anybody take Clint's shadder f'r yours?'

Rocklin didn't reply, but Cap guessed, 'Somebody as knew this was his room an' waited for him. When they saw a man's shadow they thought it was him. That right, Doc?'

Doc Riding took the cold pipe from his mouth, set his hat far back on his head, looked at his watch. 'I suppose. Looks like more than the Clewses gettin' even, though. Comes too pat on top of – you know what I mean?' What he meant was the beating Rocklin had given Garley, but only the doc knew about the suspicions that Rocklin had had of Clint. He felt that Rocklin hadn't told them all there was to tell about tonight but wouldn't question him here and now. The doc's crusty saddle-leather face was troubled. He said, 'If it's another .38-.40–' but he didn't finish.

Cap gave Rocklin a cigarette, and Rocklin said, 'Thanks,' and when he leaned to the match that Cap held he saw Juan. Carruthers had admitted him into the room, for Juan was like a member of the Harolday family, and he had entered so quietly and stood so unobtrusively by the side of the door that Rocklin hadn't noticed his coming.

He had never seen Juan before with his hat off, and, though he was old, his hair was long, smooth, black. Rocklin set his eyes against the steadiness of Juan's look, and for a long moment he uncontrollably suspected this old Mexican. He believed that if for any reason Juan felt it was his duty to kill he would do it, or try, and wouldn't need hate to make him – no more than an executioner needs it. *But in the back?* Rocklin couldn't believe that, not of a man who had said, 'I believe in God, señor!'

Rocklin spoke to him, and Juan crossed the room readily, long-legged, light of foot. Asked what he made of it, Juan shook his head, not replying otherwise. Asked if he had known that Arly sent Clint, Juan again shook his head, adding, *'Eso no lo sé.'* He didn't tell that Arly, in a rage this afternoon, had fired him, ordered him out of the house, never wanted to see him again, had called him names, among them *pendejo!* She had never called him 'coward' before; that is, not without smiling, and it was all in a quarrel over this man Rocklin during which she had stormed ragefully and he had said nothing unkind in return.

There was a stir at the door and men clustered in, filling the room. Carruthers himself moved along at the side of a wide-eyed youth in torn overalls who was holding a rifle. Doc Riding reached out with: 'Let me have it, Tommy.'

Tommy talked a blue streak, on and on, repeating his story. 'Us kids was lookin' around out there – sorta pokin' around – Bud he give me a shove – y' know, jus' in fun – an' I bumped up agin the side of the chicken house – then my foot struck sumpin' an' – this gun! Like it had been shoved under the chicken house, but the butt stuck out a little an' I stubbed agin it–'

Doc Riding threw the lever and an empty fell. The murderer hadn't even take time to reload; he had been in that much of a hurry to get rid of the gun. Doc left the breech-block down as a safety precaution and turned to the lamp. 'See?' he asked Rocklin, who was looking over his shoulder. Rocklin nodded. It was a .38-.40, and along the right side of the stock was the dim outline of *S.H.* The brass-headed tacks that had formed Sam Haynes's initials had been pulled and something rubbed on that darkened the wood, but the imprint of the tack holes and heads remained.

Pap Fossler spoke in piping excitement. 'Sam's, all right! Somebody stole it – he don't know when! Said so today!'

Cap went on from there in his slow, cool way. 'I reckon there's not a rifle in the country that somebody wouldn't know whose it was. So this feller stole the gun so if he had to get rid of it in a hurry like tonight – and it was found, nobody would track it back to him. That's why he must've stole it from Sam.'

Many voices were adding their speculation. 'He shot and chucked it quick an' lit out!'

'Two or three jumps, then he could act like nuthin' happened – if he wasn't carryin' a rifle!'

281

'Mebbe he come right back into the hotel an' had him a drink!'

'Mebbe he's standin' right here now in this room!' When that was said uneasiness ran over men's faces, quieting talk, and unfocused suspicions looked out of men's eyes and into friends' faces.

Doc Riding raised his voice in rough friendliness and gestured impatiently. 'Well, clear out! Clear out, boys!' Carruthers urged them, too, and they moved with slow scuffle of dragging feet out into the hall and most of them went on down into the barroom. 'Shut the door,' said the doc.

Carruthers shut the door, then said, 'But I think I'll go along, too, Doc.' He explained mildly, 'The bartender may need some help.'

When he went out Doc Riding turned the key in the door to bar the curious and looked at his watch. 'Harolday ought've been here long before this.' He glanced about to ask if Juan could explain, but Juan had gone, too.

After that the doc eyed the rifle that was lying on the table. 'How long ago, Pap? Stole, I mean?' Pap shook his head. Then the doc counted on his fingers and asked, 'Could it have been over seven months ago?' They knew that he was referring back to Red Caldwell.

Rocklin said, 'From what I gathered by how Sam talked, yes. The case was there, so

Sam never missed the gun.'

Doc Riding studied the rifle without touching it, an old gun with rust scars that oil had covered, a piece of filed-down penny that had been set in for a front sight. Then he turned and looked over toward the bed where Clint's body lay under a blanket and on a slicker to save bedclothes.

Cap moved in his stringhalt way to see who was trying to force the door, then he stepped back and Harolday lurched in. He was wearing spurs and kept his hat on, and his hands were behind him. A slow-moving man, called Fred, from the stable was with him; and Fred took off his old hat and said in a hushed, awkward mumble, 'I knowed he'd just started for the ranch, so I rode out an' overtook 'im.' Nobody seemed to hear.

Doc Riding indicated the blanket, and Harolday peered toward the bed. He was gaunt and stooped, with neck out-thrust, and stood still and didn't say a word. Pap mumbled, 'Bad!' sympathetically, and looked kindly at the man he didn't like, that no one liked. There was a new look of old age cut into his face, and the flint-colored eyes had a brightness that must have been pain, but he didn't open his mouth. Nobody had ever seen Harolday shaken before.

In the stillness Fred muttered, 'He jus' wouldn't b'lieve me when I told him! Said I was crazy!'

283

Doc pointed to the rifle. 'Kids found it under the chicken coop. Stole from Sam Haynes; nobody knows when.' The doc tossed his hand helplessly. 'I'm guessing it's the same gun that's been used all along.'

Harolday's thin, hard mouth tightened as he gazed toward the rifle; he appeared to be studying it, but as if he wouldn't touch the thing. Then he began to look all about with an air of searching, and when he found Rocklin's face the search seemed ended. His eyes were not expressionless now; they had hate in them, and Rocklin thought, *I don't much blame him!*

It took some time for Harolday to speak, and his voice was hoarse and trembling, for the words struggled against coming and hurt his throat. 'What was my boy doing up here?' His voice charged Rocklin with blame; almost, it seemed, with guilt.

Rocklin rubbed out the cigarette, stroked the bandaged hand a time or two, glanced toward the rifle, playing for time to thin out how much to tell. Fred slowly fumbled his hatbrim through his fingers and eyed the bed slantwise, not wanting to look directly. It was so quiet that the doc's pipe made a rattling bubble, so quiet they seemed listening to the bubble. Doc took the pipe from his mouth and held it in the cup of a palm.

There was a lonely and weary drag on Rocklin, like too much weight, in having to make up his mind whether or not to tell it all. Clint was dead; Rocklin wished now that he hadn't hit him, but to do it over again he would hit him again. That was the way he had to tell it.

He put a foot on the seat of a chair, rested the elbow with the sling on his raised knee, and looked straight at Harolday, but he hadn't said ten words before running feet reached the door and it was flung open.

Arly stopped and sent a swift look across the face of each of them. 'Juan just told me!' she said.

Juan followed close behind her, and when he came in he took his stand against the wall and Fred locked the door. Rocklin saw how steadily Juan was watching him, knew there must be some reason for it, and darkly suspicious thoughts of Juan again stirred faintly in his mind; but somehow they wouldn't stick.

Arly had come just as Juan found her at home, bareheaded, in a long, loose, bright cotton dress that reached the low shoe tops and had wide pleats. Running had shaken the curls of her dark hair into a tangle, and her breast heaved. She stood straight and tense and looked for a long moment frowningly at Harolday. He had glanced about when she rushed in but didn't look at her again. They all could tell that Arly was about to say something, and they waited, for she was breathing hard; then the words flew out like sound shocked from her by the mystery and mercilessness of it. 'In the back, too!'

Doc Riding moved a chair, touched her arm. 'Set down, Arly.' She sat down, and the doc added, 'He's just telling your father how it happened.'

Arly's face changed; she hesitated, then corrected coldly, 'He is telling Mr Harolday.' She looked steadily toward Harolday, and the way she said it cut down on all of them as something that just oughtn't be said, not at a time like this, not in that tone.

Doc Riding clucked in reproof, and Pap pulled nervously at his beard. There wasn't a particle of recognition when she met Rocklin's eyes, and he thought, *She'll hate me in a minute!* He couldn't tell whether that would give him relief or be something that he didn't want.

He didn't put his foot on the chair seat now but ran slow fingers through his hair and let the hand fall. 'Clint come here tonight, and said Miss Arly sent him.'

He paused, questioning her, and Arly said with quiet firmness, 'I did.'

Then Rocklin's look went toward Juan, and Juan's black eyes tightened so inscrutably that it was with effort that he quit staring at Juan and again looked straight into Harolday's glower and continued.

'Clint was standing about where Juan is,

then he started for a chair over there by the window. That put him between the lamp and the window. When he turned his back to the window he was shot.'

Then Rocklin added slowly, making each word fall deliberately clear, 'I don't know whether he was shot by mistake for me – or to shut him up!'

That had about the same startling effect in the room as if another gun had gone off. Pap gave a nervous jerk and peered excitedly, and Arly rose from the chair with lips parted, and it was moment before she could gasp, 'What can you mean?' Doc Riding knew now how Clint's name was coming into it, and he was sorry for Rocklin. Harolday stiffened, then said bitterly, 'You're lyin'! You are lyin'! To shut *him* up?'

'That's right.' Rocklin was calm about it and slow-spoken and wasn't to be hurried. Everybody's face was strained in a hushed, listening look, and Harolday trembled. His hands were not behind him now but were knotted into fists, and he pressed them against his stomach.

'But, Ken, what do you mean?' Arly asked, and there was friendliness in her voice, a full tone of it.

'I'll tell from the beginning,' he said, and looked directly at Harolday and kept on looking at him and at no one else. 'This is the way things, lots of things, have shaped up. You'll see how they all fit in.'

'I lost my coat on the stage, coming. At the Caldwell ranch Jim Brotherton give me a coat of Caldwell's. Later I learned it was the one he had tied on his saddle when he was shot.'

Arly sat down and leaned forward and stared, trying to draw Rocklin's eyes to her, but he went on speaking only to Harolday. 'In that coat was samples of playin'-cards and a printed letter saying they were marked and being offered only to regular customers.'

He didn't see Pap shaking his head re-proachfully and saying, 'Tut tut tut!' at the idea that Red Caldwell would touch such things.

Harolday broke in, shouted, 'What's that to do with Clint?'

'Keep listenin',' Rocklin said, and drew a deep breath. 'Yesterday I got married here in town.' That wasn't easy to say, not with Arly looking at him, and he felt strangely hot about the face. It wasn't much easier to add, 'Garley and the Martin aunt said Clara Caldwell wasn't of age and that I knew it and I was marrying for her money. And they tried to have me arrested.'

That part was over and he breathed more freely, but he wouldn't look at Arly. 'We knew Garley had a letter that proved facts about her age and we went to his office, and when he wouldn't give it up I set out to find

288

it anyhow. In looking, I run across some fresh decks of cards locked in a drawer I made him open. I thought one deck looked like a sample of the cards that was in Caldwell's coat, so I took it. I couldn't tell if they was marked, and I had Cap come to see. He found it was a crooked deck.'

Cap said quietly, 'That's how it was.'

'But Clint – Clint?' Harolday's voice was low and hoarse and he was sweating, and they could hear his breath.

Rocklin said, 'I'm coming to him. This morning when I went down to breakfast I forgot the cards. Something happened to make me go back up, and Garley was in the room, stealing the cards. I'd already figgered there must be something between him, marked cards, and that printed letter in Caldwell's coat. I locked the door and told him so. I said I'd beat hell out of him if he didn't talk.

'He let go all of a sudden with "Clint told you!" – like it had been scared out of him. Then he shut up and I beat hell out of him, and he would've talked but folks busted in the door.'

Then Rocklin paused and passed his hand over his head and glanced about, and nobody moved. Their eyes were set with the steadiness of waxen faces, and every eye was on him. The tips of Arly's fingers were tightly pressed against her cheeks, making her face look thinner, but her eyes were wide; and he had the feeling, perhaps imagined, that she was glad her name had not been brought in with the cards that were found in Caldwell's coat. He fiddled for a moment with the edge of the sling, drawing out the creases, then he told Harolday, 'I've found out since, no matter how, that the printed letter and crooked card samples was sent to Garley – only Caldwell got 'em first!'

'What's all that to do with Clint?' Harolday roared, and he was shaking all over.

'You'll hear,' said Rocklin. This was hard going. The boy was dead. 'Tonight, when he come here, Clint was chipper and friendly till I asked about Garley, and then he got sulky. When I saw he was trying to lie out of it I hit him. He had to know something for Garley to be scared Clint had talked, and I told Clint I'd beat it out of him if he didn't tell me, and I would have. I was letting him set down to think it over and–' Rocklin looked at Arly and pointed toward the window. 'That's how it happened.'

For a moment her eyes met his and she didn't seem mad, and she cried in a sharp voice, quick with warning, 'Look out, Ken!'

Harolday was coming at Rocklin, but the doc was near, and he and Cap and old Pap clustered up in front of him with their hands out and talked restrainingly. Harolday shouted wildly, 'He hit my boy!' He kept on saying it and raised his voice to a kind of yell and wouldn't be quieted.

Then Arly spoke with a blazing directness. 'You've beat Clint up at times all his life for less, lots less! I feel dreadful about Clint, but you know how he would lie, and there was no other way to make him tell the truth!'

That brought a sudden quiet, almost as if they all held their breath to see how quiet they could be. Rocklin was surprised at her and thankful, too, though he did feel it was a callous way to speak at such a time to old Harolday, but it shut him up. Doc Riding turned to her and said, 'Shush, Arly! Not that way, not here, not now!'

Arly said, 'I know Ken is telling what's so, even if I can't quite believe a fool boy like Clint was into a mess with a man like Garley; but he's a mean, cunning old devil, so maybe he did drag Clint into something.' She rose out of the chair, saying, 'I think we ought to march right in there on Garley and let Ken make him talk!'

The doc said, 'Set down, Arly. Set down and hold your horses.'

Harolday shook a bony hand at Rocklin and shouted, 'I believe you had my boy murdered! I've got good reasons to believe just that!'

All of which didn't mean a thing to Rocklin except that Harolday was half crazy, and he could think that sympathetically. Harolday looked it, too, for his eyes were wild and his face was twisted, and he didn't appear to know what he was doing. Doc Riding got up close and took hold of his arm and said, 'Steady, now. Let's stick to plain sense! We know how you feel and you can't help it, and nobody's blaming you, but don't let yourself go to pieces because–'

Rocklin didn't hear what else the doc said. Cap had rolled and lit a cigarette and was offering it, and Rocklin nodded his thanks. Cap said, 'Poor old devil. Bad.' Rocklin nodded. He wanted to look at Arly, but he didn't want anybody to see him looking at her, so he looked at Juan. The old Mexican was not watching him now; he was watching Arly, and there wasn't much to go by, but Juan's Indian-like face had an expression of sad tenderness.

Rocklin was studying the tip of the cigarette to think things over when Harolday suddenly pushed the doc aside and shouted furiously, 'There never was anything for Clint to tell you!' Harolday's voice had a peculiar sound, hoarse and desperate, and he talked wildly but with halting pauses, as if a gush of feeling clogged words in his throat. He said in effect that once when he was out of town Garley told Clint he had to see him. Garley had had a quarrel with Red Caldwell over cards and was going to leave the country because he was afraid of Red.

But Garley held some notes from people and knew that if he left the country he'd never collect.

'I was the only man in town with ready money, and even if we wasn't friends, he wanted me to take up the notes at any discount I said. Clint sent me word out to the ranch, and I sent back word I wouldn't touch anything Garley ever had his hands on. That's all Clint ever knew!'

Then Harolday began cursing Rocklin, and Rocklin had felt that maybe he had it coming; but Doc Riding again got before Harolday and said earnestly, 'Here, now tell me, that was about how long a time before Red was killed?'

Harolday turned his eyes on the doc with a look of trying to burn his face, but all he said was, 'I don't know!' But Cap was also asking, 'After that, didn't you think of how Garley'd talked when Red was killed that way?'

Harolday glared at Cap with wrathful pondering and choked up, and though he looked as if he was going to say something, all he did was to shake his head; and that made a listening quiet in the room.

It was into this quiet that Arly suddenly thrust the knifelike words: 'You all know he wasn't sorry when Red was killed!'

Pap growled, 'Arly!' in a surprised, hurt tone. The stableman, Fred, let his hat slip from between his fingers, and Doc Riding scowled at her. The doc knew that she was hard to handle when she got the bit between her teeth and, even if he didn't like Harolday, the man was suffering now and Arly oughtn't to be mean.

Arly said, 'You men, all of you, make me tired!' She was addressing all of them, and there was a bright look in her eyes and she went on swiftly. 'It's been awful and horrible to have Clint killed. It was that way when Bowles was killed, too – and for the same reason! Somebody was trying to shoot him!' She pointed at Rocklin. 'But you know – every one of you! – that he' – she pointed at Harolday then – 'didn't like Red Caldwell and was afraid of him, and I won't say he was glad when Red died, but I will say he wasn't sorry!'

They could tell that she wasn't through, and Harolday faced about and glowered at her and called her a 'fiend,' and shouted, 'Shut up!' He looked wild enough to jump and try to strike, but Arly sat there and eyed him with a kind of wicked serenity. Pap came close to her and said, 'N-Now, Arly!' about as he would have spoken gentlingly to a horse that he was afraid of.

'You men!' Arly said scornfully. 'He's just admitted he hid the truth about Garley – and had Clint help him hide it! Any honest man would have told what he knew! Told it to the district court. But he kept still about the quarrel and cards, and Garley got his big dirty hands on everything Red owned!'

Now they were all looking at her, Harolday, too, and listening in a kind of unnerved way; and nobody thought of saying, 'Shut up!' It would have been about like telling the wind to stop. She wasn't saying a thing more than the doc and Cap had had at the back of their heads, but she was bringing it out in the open, then and there, and they wouldn't have done that, not at a time like this before Harolday.

She looked right at Harolday as she said, 'But of course Mr Harolday will have some kind of explanation! After all, he hasn't done anything illegal. He never does! When he pulls a mortgaged bed out from under some sick woman he always does it legally!'

Doc Riding said, 'Arly, for God's sake!' and right away wished he hadn't spoken, for she turned on him.

'You know it's so! You know poor old Mrs Potter was sick when that damn Deputy Sheriff Jackson foreclosed on her and moved her off the bed so he could take it! On what's called a "chattel mortgage!" Don't you stand there and look at me that way, Doc Riding, when you know as well as I do it's the truth!'

The doc didn't look at her but fumbled his pipe out of his pocket and looked down at it.

Arly's eyes whipped toward Harolday and she went on. 'I'm going to tell you – all of you! – what he said to me today. He said my mother married him because she owed him so much that she couldn't pay him back any other way! So, he says, I have no legal right to the Santee ranch! "Legal!" Oh, how he loves the law!

'Legal or not, Mr Harolday, I'm warning you here and now before these people that I'll have that ranch, right away and in my own name, or I'll–'

Juan's long legs were moving up with noiseless stride, swiftly, and from across the back of her chair he clapped down a hand on her mouth. *'Callate tu!'*

Arly didn't struggle or even pull at his hand, and when he removed his hand she sat just as quietly as though she had finished what she intended to say. In a way she had, for everyone knew what would have come flying out if Juan hadn't shut her up.

Harolday was no match for her, and Rocklin wondered if any man could be. She wasn't even excited, but a kind of deliberate fierceness had struck out, over and over; and there wasn't much of anything that anybody could do about it – except choke her.

She had drawn Harolday's wrath from Rocklin to herself, though perhaps not purposely. Clint had said they had been into a hell of a big row, and this was some more of it. Harolday didn't try to answer her, and Rocklin felt sorry for him even though Arly may have been telling facts. He surged away from Doc Riding, saying, 'Have my boy sent home!' He rushed to the door and jerked blindly at he knob, but the door was locked.

Fred stooped and turned the key and followed Harolday out.

CHAPTER EIGHTEEN

A half hour later Rocklin was alone with Doc Riding, Arly, and the inscrutable Juan. Arly had moved to another chair and sat with an elbow on the chair's arm, her palm against her chin, looking steadily at nothing. Juan's shoulder was still against the wall, touching it lightly, for he stood straight.

The doc wanted to talk with Rocklin and suggested, 'It's late, Arly. Juan, you had better take her home.' Then to Arly: 'Or don't you want to go home after – you know?'

Arly moved her eyes slowly, reluctant to give up her thoughts and speak of other things. 'Why? Because of what I said to him?'

'After what had just happened, yes.' The doc jerked his head toward the shattered window. 'Harolday was already a broken man. You laid it on, mean.'

'What did I say that wasn't so?' she asked with rising inflection.

Doc Riding shook his head, for her quiet way of asking it carried a challenge, and he didn't want to stir her up. He merely said, 'Clint,' to let her know his feeling about the time and place.

'Clint?' she murmured, and was thoughtful. 'He could be sweet. Harolday didn't want him that way.' Her eyes leveled at Doc Riding. 'Be sure of it, he had told Clint never to mention anything about Garley and his quarrel with Red. I know that man!'

Then Doc Riding smiled at her grimly. 'You can be unfair, little lady.'

Arly nodded. 'If I want to be, yes.'

The doc didn't say anything more to her, and Arly returned to her moody thoughtfulness, with a far-off stare at nothing, and a manner of patient waiting.

The doc fingered his pipe, glanced toward her, then questioned Rocklin with a look; and Rocklin silently conveyed, 'I don't know what she wants,' but he was afraid that he did. As he carefully filled his pipe the doc asked, 'So you're going to lug Garley over to Garden City tomorrow?'

'The sooner the better, don't you think?'

'Yes. Begins to look as if Garley's hands were pretty damned dirty – or worse!' He put a match hoveringly to the pipe bowl, puffed, then blew out the match. 'Which still

298

don't tell us who shot Clint. No, nor why.'
He gazed at the rifle. 'Funny,' he said, meaning mysterious, tragic, terrible. He pulled at
his weather-scarred cheek, then said, 'Well,
good night.' He took up the rifle but paused
with a long look at Arly, and she didn't
notice, for she was staring at nothing, broodingly. He opened the door and looked back,
not sure that he ought to leave; then he
closed the door and they could hear him
walk away.

Arly stood up and glanced toward the
door. 'Lock it,' she said. Juan turned the key
and resumed his stand by the wall. Endless
waiting didn't tire him. Her eyes were staringly on Rocklin as she moved slowly with
gentle sway of long, wide-pleated skirt and
came to where he stood. When she stopped
she was almost against him, and she looked
up steadily, waiting. Rocklin's eyes went
away from her in an uncertain glance at
Juan, and Arly said quietly, 'He knows I love
you. He knew it before I did!'

There wasn't a flicker in Juan's expression
that gave a sign of approval or disapproval,
but Rocklin's guess was that the old Mexican didn't like it.

She stood there close before him, wide-
eyed and waiting, and he didn't move and
he didn't say anything. At last Arly spoke
softly. 'I love you, Ken.'

Rocklin shook his head at her and seemed

soberly calm, but that wasn't the way he felt, for his impulses were in a turmoil and his ears burned. He knew that she knew what she was doing to him, but nevertheless now he didn't think of her as a shameless girl. Never in his life had it been so hard for him to talk, and all he could say was, 'I am married, Arly.'

'But didn't your wife tell you?'

'Yes.'

'Well, then?' It was scarcely more than a whisper breathed on his face, and a shy coaxing glinted in her eyes. She wasn't the same girl, not at all in any way, that he had ever seen before, for now she looked meekly happy and submissive, and he thought, *Damn her!*

'Well, then – what?' he asked, and knew that was an awkward and stupid thing to ask, but it was the best he could do. Now her face wasn't thinly tense; it didn't seem even thin, and she was beautiful and knew it and knew that he knew it; and he felt helpless, and she knew that, too. No woman before had ever been like this with him, but his stubbornness came up and locked his jaw and he wouldn't give way to her; however much he wanted to, he just wouldn't, and that was the way it was going to be. And he had to say something defensive, so he said harshly, 'You told her a lot of lies!'

But Arly merely shook her head at him

and murmured, 'No, Ken, not one.'

'Why, you're lying now to say that because you told her—'

Arly came in interruptively quick. 'But you *did* work for me though Jim Brotherton had hired you!' Her voice was quiet and reasoning. 'And you *did* give me her letter to read! And I *did* go to the cabin and stay all night with you!'

'None of it was the way it sounds, and you know it!'

He was glowering at her now, and Arly knew why and didn't mind, and she admitted, 'That's very true, but I didn't lie, Ken. Not really, did I? And I love you and you know it. And you love me and I know that, too. So?'

'I am married.' He said it low and stubbornly.

'She can't hold you, Ken!'

'As long as she's my wife she'll hold me!'

Arly's eyes flinched narrowingly, and she studied that and scrutinized his face, then she told him, 'You don't love that girl, Ken. She is sweet and pretty and nice – nicer than me! But she isn't *me,* and that's what counts! And you didn't marry her for her ranch, not you! You couldn't. You married her to take care of her. To keep that aunt of hers and Garley from robbing her. You did it because she is sweet and honest and helpless. And besides, you were mad at me! Didn't you?

301

Answer me, Ken. Didn't you?'

Rocklin calmly said, 'No.'

Arly stared at him queerly, and a new look came into her face, a kind of happy flush; then she whirled about suddenly, spinning the pleated skirt, and she cried out at Juan in rippling Spanish, 'See! He *is* worth stealing!'

Juan answered briefly and with sharpness, 'He speaks Spanish!'

Arly swirled about again and faced Rocklin, and her 'Do you?' was a little startled. His eyelids dropped and rose, and Arly regarded him thoughtfully as he said, 'I am trying to recall if you ever told me that you did not understand Spanish. But no, you never have; so you fooled me but not deceived! I like it that you do.'

This was all too much for him. He felt exhausted and was bewildered, and he wished that she would go and he wanted her to stay. Bad, shameless, tricky, wild-tempered, and whatever else she might be, it somehow didn't matter now. There was reason in plenty to believe all those things of her, but she was so much more, too, and her body was like a flame offering warmth to him, and he wanted it. He was married and wished that he wasn't, but he wouldn't give way, just wouldn't. His stubbornness was like that. Now he stared across at Juan.

Arly told him, 'You needn't look at Juan.

302

We've been all through this, me and Juan! And he has made me believe that if I could steal you, you wouldn't be worth having! And I can't, it seems. But I'll get you; I'll get you somehow, Ken. You'll see!'

The doorknob rattled, but the key was turned in the lock and a fist struck on the door and Clara called, 'Ken? Oh, Ken! Are you in there?'

He answered, 'Yes,' and Juan opened the door.

The blood went away from Clara's face as she stood there, shocked; then she walked in, and the blood gushed back to her face with the flush of sunburn. 'Helpless,' Arly had called her without disparagement, but now her quietness seemed strength.

Arly merely said, 'I wanted to talk with Ken, and people have been coming and going all evening.' It was put as simply as that, without embarrassment and without challenge; and she looked ready to leave but not as if retreating. There was a moment's silence, and when Clara didn't speak Arly said, 'Good night, Clara. 'By, Ken,' without seeming to expect a reply. Juan opened the door and she went out, and he closed it, following her.

Clara stared at the closed door, then turned toward Rocklin and stared at him. She looked more hurt than angry, and he had to say something, but the best he could do was a dull: 'I don't know what you think.'

'You ought to!' Then she sat down, weakly glad to sit. She didn't look as if she were going to claw him to pieces, and that made him sorrier for her. She was one person that he felt he ought to do anything in the world not to hurt; she was so young and fine and gentle and lovely. A better girl than that damned Arly, really; and even Arly knew it. But she wasn't Arly.

Clara said quietly in a faraway voice, 'A little while ago Mrs Carruthers heard from Doctor Riding what that poor Harolday boy knew and how important it was – and that you did right. I felt ashamed of how I had acted, and I came to say so. I just hadn't understood.' Then she moved her hand helplessly, and her dark eyes reproached him though her tone didn't. 'You do love her, don't you, Ken?'

'You and me have talked that out once today.'

'I thought at first that it was perhaps just because she is so Western in boots and hat and short skirts and rides so well, but she *is* pretty.' Then: 'And she said that she loved you, didn't she, Ken?'

His face was stony. He didn't want to hurt Clara, but he didn't want to be dragged to the branding-fire and have anybody's ownership burned on his hide, so he wouldn't say anything.

'And, Ken, she seemed happy. Here in this room where her brother had just died she looked pleased!' Clara paused, but he wouldn't reply, so she asked; 'You must have said something that made her happy, Ken.'

'I sure didn't try to.'

'Did you – did you take her in your arms, Ken?'

'Wouldn't I lie about it?'

'Would you? I don't think so, but I don't really know. You must have done something! And at a time when she ought to feel dreadful! Alone in a locked room; my room, too!'

'You saw we weren't alone.'

'That Mexican – what does he care?' She didn't expect him to answer that, and he didn't try, but he wished that she knew how very much old Juan did care; but if he tried to tell her it would sound weak and defensive.

'So, don't you see, Ken, I can't keep up even the pretense of my marriage any longer? Not even though I do – do need you – your help and – and–' Her voice sank away, losing itself among unsaid things, and she gazed at him steadily.

He took up a cigarette butt and put it in his mouth, then he picked a burned match and splintered it with his thumbnail. He held the splintered end over the lamp chimney until it took fire, and he lit the butt and drew deeply on the smoke.

305

'Clara, I'm not going to wrangle with you, but things are not like you think. I don't know why she looked what you call happy. I just don't know. She did talk to me like a girl oughtn't. All I said back to her was I'm married.'

A staring pause lay between them, then Clara asked, 'Ken? Y-You didn't kiss her?'

'No.'

'But you must have said – done – something? She told me that I couldn't hold you, and just now she looked as if she knew that I couldn't. Don't you see?'

'She said that to me, too. I said as long as you were my wife you'd hold me!'

'Ken!' Clara jumped to her feet with misunderstanding happily aglow on her face.

He was caught, bogged down, and felt helpless. All he had been trying to do was to show that he hadn't let Arly make a fool of him, and Clara eagerly misread his meaning and her eyes shone with trustful happiness. And he had to let it stand that way, at least for the present; it would be brutal even to try to explain now, because Clara snuggled wearily against him, and the pressure of her body hurt his hand, but he let it hurt. Then she smiled up with tears in the corners of her eyes and she said, 'Kiss me, Ken!'

He kissed her.

CHAPTER NINETEEN

It wasn't quite sunup when Rocklin and Carruthers went to Garley's door, and Carruthers knocked hard and called, but there was no answer. 'He's a hard sleeper, the judge is.'

'Try the door.'

It was unlocked and they went in, but no one was there. Rocklin lit the lamp. The bed was rumpled. Carruthers said, 'I never knowed him to get up so early before.'

Rocklin guessed, 'He got out last night. The bed's mussed from him usin' it yesterday. I oughtn't have waited till morning.' He eyed a couple of empty quarts and a pint or two. 'From them I'd think he was too overloaded to move.'

'The judge can hold a lot.'

'Look around and see if he packed and carried off much of anything.'

Carruthers poked about the room. 'No, don't 'pear like it. Valise is here. Things still in the drawers, even his razor.'

When Rocklin went down to the stage office to say that he and Clara would not take the trip to Garden City today he learned from the agent that Harolday had already left for the Flats to get a farmer who preached on Sundays to come in tomorrow for the funeral.

Doc Riding looked tired out. He hadn't yet been to bed, for a nester was waiting in the office last night and took him over to the Hesico, but the kid was dead before they got there.

'Ho hum,' said the doc, and stretched his arms with a studying look at Rocklin. 'So Garley hunted a hole, has he? All right, let's unwrap your hand. What did that girl want last night?'

'She just wanted to ask about some things.' Rocklin put out his hand. 'I don't figger Garley's gone very far. They don't know anything down at the stable about a rig or even a saddle horse going out. 'Cept the buckboard Harolday took out to bring back a preacher. That makes me think he's still around close by. He couldn't walk far!'

'Hardly walk at all. So mebbe somebody has carted him off to keep you from catching him!'

'Find out who and we'll learn something!'

'Mebbe,' said the doc. 'What kind of things did Arly want to know about?'

Rocklin said, 'That bandage is stuck, Doc. Hurts.'

'No such thing. I used a scalpel on you and it didn't hurt as much as you make out now. Hold still! It's the question that hurts!' He eyed Rocklin with a grim smile. 'Don't you think I know how to diagnose?'

Rocklin, too, forced a sort of smile. 'Then why do you have to ask questions?'

'I don't. Arly's in love with you and wants you to leave your wife!'

Rocklin felt a jolt of surprise and set his face stubbornly, not wanting to talk about it, meaning not to talk. The doc let silence slide by and went on with the dressing. Each was waiting for the other to say something, and Rocklin tried. 'Nobody would help Garley get away that wasn't mixed up with him.'

The doc came back with: 'That's right – but what about Arly?'

Rocklin thought it over. 'Did Juan tell you?'

'No. Juan never tells me anything.'

'Then who? Did she?'

'No.'

'How did you guess, Doc?'

'I didn't guess.'

'You had to – unless it was Clara. Was it?'

'Your wife? I didn't know she knew. You must be in a sweatbox!'

'Nobody else knows!'

'You're wrong. But I half thought that somebody was lying about it until just now when you confessed.'

'Who told you, Doc?'

'Harolday.'

Rocklin didn't say anything, he just waited; and after a time the doc said, 'Harolday was at the stable when I rode back from the Hesico and he asked if he could come along up here with me to explain about last night. Said he felt he'd made a bad impression last night. Particularly wanted me to understand how it was.

'He's a secretive old coot. I never expected he'd loosen up to anybody, but he did this morning, quite a bit. Last night, finding Clint dead – that smashed him all up inside. But he'd been having a hell of a time with Arly. She's ripped into him to have the Santee deeded over to her. Accused him of having a land company in mind and getting ready to break up *her* ranch. He hasn't, he said. "Not definitely" – that's the way he put it. In their quarrel one thing led to another until Arly up and told him that she was in love with you and that she was going to have you and that she was going to have the Santee to take you to.'

Rocklin nodded glumly, remembering Harolday's glare. 'No wonder he hated me!'

'He told me he was sorry he'd said you had Clint shot; but last night, all of a sudden, he had felt just that way about it. Said it just popped into his head that mebbe you figgered that with Clint out of the way – Arly – everything would be hers. Understand?'

'That is,' Rocklin growled, 'I suppose after I'd shot him, too?'

'I guess he was a little out of his head.'

'I thought so.'

'Matter of fact, I was sorry for him last night. This morning, too – even more. He's bad hurt.' Doc Riding waved toward a chair. 'Set down and we'll have a drink. He told me he hadn't had any dealings with Garley, not in the least. "On his honor", he said.' The doc added speculatively, 'Whatever that means.'

'Well, it is funny he never told anybody about Garley and Red having a quarrel over cards.'

'Oh, not so funny,' said the doc, and Rocklin couldn't tell from his gruffness whether or not the doc was sarcastic. 'He explained about that. He said he supposed Garley and Red had patched things up. Said if they hadn't, Red would never have let the will stand making Garley executor. Plausible, don't you think?'

'Arly said he would have an explanation.'

'You like that girl, don't you?'

Rocklin asked, 'Don't you?'

The doc shook his head. 'I don't like her trying to steal a three-day-old husband! Neither does Harolday. He said it was – I don't recall the words, but he meant that it was a shocking offence to Christian morals and decency. He didn't say, but I judged he

311

thought it was a lot worse than selling a bed from under a sick widow. And, by God, she was sick! But let's stick to the subject. What about Arly? Do you think she'll get you?'

Rocklin felt like squirming but didn't; he sat still and thoughtful and looked levelly at the doc and said, 'No.'

The doc spun the whisky in his glass and watched it swirl nearer and nearer the top. When a bit went over the brim he quit spinning it, then said, 'I'll make a little bet that she does.'

Rocklin told him, 'I don't like to talk about things like that.'

Then the doc's gruff voice took on a purr of friendliness. 'Of course you don't. But I know Arly. You heard her just the same as say that she'll kill Harolday if he didn't give her the ranch. And he's scared. He knows she'll do it. She'll do anything that she wants to do.'

Rocklin said 'Yeah,' believingly.

'The only thing to do with Arly is to let her have her own way. Do that, and she'll give you the best of it, every time. Fight her and you lose – every time! I've never known anybody like her. So she'll get you – unless she changes her mind about wanting you. I don't know. She's never been in love before.'

Rocklin said slowly and stubbornly, 'I'm not leaving my wife – not as long as–' Then he stopped. 'As long as she needs me,' was in his mind. He almost said, 'As long as she

312

wants me.' That wouldn't sound good either, so he let the sentence stand unfinished.

The doc waited awhile, then said, 'Go on. As long as – what?'

'Nothing.'

'You're a liar.'

'Mebbe so. I don't know. I can't talk good and I don't want to talk at all. Not about women. And we oughta be talking about who used that .38-.40.'

'You're right,' the doc agreed. 'You have to find Garley. Have to! We know his hands are dirty from marked cards. I think they've also got blood on them. We know enough to make a good guess as to why he may have had Red killed. Then mebbe he got afraid that Jim Brotherton was on to him. Or would be! As for you – mebbe somebody thought you'd try to cut in on the ranch. That was when Bowles was killed – by mistake. Last night when they shot Clint mebbe it was because that somebody thought you had cut in on it by marrying the girl, and that you could and would make a lot of trouble. Looks right now like Garley was behind it all. A man that'll cheat at cards is not going to be honest with a dead man's property, not if he can help it. One good way to help it is to get rid of the heiress's husband, who's a tall, broad-shouldered fellow with a bad temper.'

Rocklin said, 'I've not got much of a temper,' and was earnest about it.

'No? You forget I'm a doctor. Had to patch up some of the fellows you've argued with. One thing's certain, Garley didn't use that gun himself. So who did? Mebbe some of the Clews bunch. Could be, but I don't think so any more. Not after last night.'

The town knew that Garley had crawled into a hole and helped look for him, but it soon seemed certain that he was not in the town; then the wonder was as to how he had got away and where he had gone.

Harolday didn't name Garley but did say that he would offer a reward of one thousand dollars for the man who shot Clint; however, no dodgers were printed.

Rocklin told the shorthanded Lee Frank to hire some more men on the ranch. 'Whether or not we find him, Garley is all through, and the court at Garden City'll approve putting on enough men to run the ranch right.'

Rocklin rode about the country, much of the time alone. Friends warned him to be careful, and he took the precaution of not letting anybody know where he was heading, and it seemed to work. Three days later his hand was out of the sling but still bandaged, and he hoped he wouldn't have to do any left-handed shooting. He couldn't practice because he couldn't reload one-handedly. And he knew it wasn't safe to carry six bullets in the single-action Colt's cylinder, for any kind of accidental blow on the hammer might fire the gun – but just on the chance of having an extra shot if he needed it, he took the risk.

Hearsay kept him in the saddle. For instance, it was reported that Garley had been seen at Tolin's, down beyond the Flats; but Tolin chewed a green alfalfa stalk and said, 'W'y no, mister, not here; but he was seen over to Wessler's, so I heard.' Wessler's was ten miles east, and there Rocklin learned, 'Nope, not around here. But I'll tell you, he once done some lawin' f'r Toby Smith down on the Helaker place, and some of the boys say they heard he stayed the night there.'

And so it went.

About the middle of the week he met Pete in town. There was still a trace of discoloration on Pete's eye, and he drawled, grinning, 'She keeps makin' fun of it. An' by the way, she says she's agoin' over to Garden City to see the doin's when you go.'

'How does she know when I'm going? I don't!'

Pete shook his head. 'I'm on'y sayin' what she says. But I'll bet she does. You wanta lose your shirt?'

Rocklin said, 'No.'

'An' have you heard they're hirin' old Dave back to drive stage? One fellow made a coach into kindlin'-wood over at Injun Wells, an' another stove up the horses bad.

So Dave, he's agoin' back on the seat.'

One day Doc Riding told him, "F I was you, I'd have Clara go be friends with her aunt again.'

'Not me, never! I don't want her to get her hands on that girl again.'

'All right, have it your way, Ken. But old lady Martin is a mighty sick woman. With lots of grit. She's told me what's the matter with her. And she's known for years that she couldn't be cured, and she's suffered like hell and never whimpered. But that's what's made her so snappish and mean, I guess. She takes it out on people. I don't think she'll ever get out of bed again. The shock of so many things happenin' – and all. She's furious that Garley fooled her. And she don't want anything to do with you.'

'Suits me fine. But if it's that way, and Clara wants to – I wouldn't want her to feel too bad about what she didn't do if her aunt died.'

'That's the way I thought, too.' The doc went on. 'If I was you, I'd take Clara over to Garden City and see Judge Benn. Settle, or at least begin to settle, Garley's hash. Then keep after him. He's sure to know about murder – more than one – and he'll tell if caught.'

On a Saturday morning Rocklin went into the stage office to book two seats for Monday, and Harolday was there. His gaunt frame was more bowed, the wrinkles in his face had deepened, his glassy eyes had a stern and smoldering stare, and he looked steadily at Rocklin, then dropped his eyes to the ledger. He didn't look up when Rocklin left.

The flat-faced agent nervously said, 'They're going Monday, Mr Harolday,' and was ignored.

Presently Harolday closed the ledger. 'I've got to ride out to see a fellow about money that's owing. I won't be back mebbe until tomorrow.' He went out, walking slowly, his hands folded behind him.

The agent scratched his head. He didn't know of any account that was overdue, and the Old Man had a biting way of letting him hear about such things.

Later in the morning the agent spoke to a Mexican youth, one of the Romeras tribe who had been hanging around town for a week, and the boy headed his pony for the Santee.

The air was pleasantly cool and the street empty when Clara and Rocklin went toward the stage office a little before six Monday morning.

The stage was in the street at the front of the office, and a drowsy hostler held the leaders' heads. Harolday stood at the office door in an attitude of bleak loneliness, his hands behind him, and glowered sullenly; then he looked at his watch and went inside, and they could hear him call through the side door, 'Hey, Dave! Time to roll!'

Dave came from under the archway with the whip in his hand and pulled at his floppy hat brim, saying, 'Mornin',' to Clara.

'I'll ride for a ways with Dave,' Rocklin explained, and helped her into the coach. She didn't say all right; she did not say anything, and he ought to have noticed that she did not want him to leave her alone. There were no other passengers.

Dave let the whip fly with the sound of a gun firing, and as the stage whirled away the drowsy hostler flung up his hand in a lazy gesture of good-by. Dave sat bulkily motionless with the reins threaded through his curved fingers, enjoying the wind on his face and the throbbing pull of the eager horses, the rasp of the spinning wheels that stirred the dust in the quiet morning air. Rocklin tried a few words, but Dave wasn't ready for talk, and so they rattled on.

They rocked along for five or six miles, then Dave's foot gave the brake a gentle push as they pulled down under a high bank along the road where scrub oak cast a dense shadow. Clara put her face through the window eagerly, thinking that Rocklin was coming to be with her inside the coach; but he didn't notice her, and she heard Dave say, 'This is where Red was killed. Thought you'd like to see!'

Clara shuddered her hands to her face and sank back on the seat, refusing to look; things that had to do with anger and violence and sudden death made her feel sick.

Rocklin looked all about, then: 'Who do you guess, Dave?'

'Git up!' said Dave, and the stage rolled on. He drove for a while silently, then: 'No guessin' about it! Garley had to kill 'im or git run outa the country. So don't argy!'

'But there was Brotherton, too. Bowles and Clint – both by mistake for me. All killed the same way. Looks like with the same gun. Wasn't Garley that did all that shooting.'

'Mebbe not, mebbe not. But you catch 'im and make him tell you who!'

'Uh, hadn't thought of that. Thanks,' said Rocklin.

An hour later they took a kinky turn and pulled up before a small log-cabin store at Indian Wells. Off to one side of the store was a smashed-up stagecoach. A cheery little old man hobbled out to give Dave a letter to mail, and he fixed a queer look on Rocklin, then asked squeakily, 'You're the Rocklin feller, ain't you? C'd guess from that hat an' yore head. Think you'll ever cotch the judge, mister?'

'Mebbe.'

319

As they went on Dave pointed backward with the whip butt. 'After that coach back yonder smashed, Harolday sent f'r me. He said not to remember my row with that Arly-girl. She'd told me that when I was hired I was hired to do what the people as hired me wanted done, no matter what, an' if I didn't want to do it, I could quit. So I quit.

'The boys at the stable tell me that then she give the Old Man hell for lettin' me quit. Said he'd wish he hadn't! Said I wasn't old an' wore out like she'd told me I was. If that ain't jus' like a woman – that woman, anyhow!'

Dave took the lines and whip into one hand for a moment and reached for his chewing-tobacco. 'We druv off this mornin' an' left two passengers that didn't show up. The Old Man he said to roll out on time to the minute, an' that's what I done.'

'The clock at the hotel was slow,' said Rocklin. 'We barely made it, though I thought we had plenty of time.'

'I set my watch by Harolday's this mornin'.'

CHAPTER TWENTY

Stan saw the dust roll up at Holman Pass and he yelled nervously, 'Here she comes a'ready!' An old unwashed man with a scraggly beard and a cross-eyed look stared toward the dust; then he hitched up his baggy trousers, pulled his slouch hat forward, and peered off cross country. Stan peered in the same direction, asked jerkily, 'What you goin' to do, Briggs?'

'We hold that stage 'r you know what'll happen to us. An' you're in this as much as me!'

Stan knew and he didn't like it. The stage was thundering down the long, gentle grade, and the dust made it look as if it raced through a smoldering fire. Somehow he and Briggs had to keep the stage from going on, though Stan unhappily didn't in the least want it to stay at his place.

When the stage rolled in Stan stayed out of sight, but Briggs gave a whined greeting as he jogged up to the leaders. Dave called out wrathfully, 'Whar's my relay?'

'W'y, you'll have to be a little patient, Dave. I had 'em up an' ready to harness, but two of 'em bolted when I took 'em to water.

I'll go round 'em up.' Briggs was eyeing the woman's face at the coach window.

Dave stepped down from the seat and said things, and Briggs protested with discouraged humbleness. 'Think I c'd he'p it, Dave? An' there's a lady hearin' how you talk!'

Dave said, 'A worthless ol' damn ruff'an hearin', too! Put the two you got in an' I'll go on. I ain't goin' to wait while you ride around all over the pasture catchin' 'em.'

'They ain't even harnessed yet, Dave. But I'll go git Stan to help me!'

Briggs clumped up to the house on the run. Stan had peeked from the window and now was having a drink of his own bad whisky. 'Don't keep 'em here – not with that girl!' he begged in a shaken voice. 'We got to let 'em go!' Stan choked on the whisky and wiped his mouth uneasily.

Briggs's ugliness glinted at Stan. 'You jus' git 'em outa the way f'r couple minutes. Unnerstand?'

Rocklin had helped Clara from the coach. Stan bowed and scraped apologetically, but that did no good, for Dave gave him hell. Briggs called out, 'I'm hurryin' – I'm hurryin'.' And Stan said how sorry he was and invited them into the house out of the sun.

Dave said he didn't mind the sun but would take a drink, and Rocklin said that he didn't want a drink but would like a word or two with Stan.

Clara held her skirts well off the floor when she went in, and she sat on the bench in shrinking distaste of the uncleanness all about her. It looked so much worse in daylight, or she had been too dulled by weariness to notice when she was here before. Now there were sour, frowzy smells that she hadn't remembered, and she could see cobwebs bunched in corners of the low ceiling. Dust lay thick on the floor, and there was a buzzing swirl of bluebottles and some thumped the dirty windows. From the open door of the kitchen came the stale odor of burned fat that stirred her nearly to nausea.

Rocklin sat by her and watched Dave take his drink at the one-board bar, glad to see that it was only one drink.

Stan came shuffling up and showed his teeth in an uneasy grin at Clara. 'You was good to me,' he said, as though gratitude gave him the right to some kind of familiarity. His undershirt looked as if it had been hung over a smoky fire before he put it on, and his slack mouth sagged open, letting the words drip. 'You was good to me,' he repeated.

Dave moved up with spraddle-legged bulkiness. 'Why you got that ol' Briggs around here?'

'Help's hard to git, Dave.'

'Call him help?' Dave snorted.

Then Rocklin said, 'Stan, mebbe you've

323

heard that I'm running the Caldwell ranch now.'

Stan gave an approving smirk toward Clara. 'Yeah, I heard you married her.'

'Tell me where that K C hide came from!'

Stan's eyes shifted from Rocklin's face, came back uneasily, and he spoke with a hangdog whine. 'I thought all that was settled.'

'Your part is. But don't you know it was salted down on you so Jackson could find it? Get credit for catching a rustler? Somebody was throwing you to the wolves!'

'No, hones' – no, they wasn't,' Stan mumbled.

'Huh, I can tell you who,' Dave said. 'It was that ol' Briggs out there. You forgit I laid here a couple o' days with a busted head and heard talk. He owns a little place over in the willows, ten-twelve miles across yonder somewhere.'

'Oh, he done it friendly,' Stan insisted. 'He brought the yearlin' over 'cause he said that much meat 'ud spoil on him and I c'd use it here.'

Rocklin's look was a weight on Stan's face, and he wondered if Stan in a simple-minded way believed that or was afraid of Briggs. 'All right, I'll talk with Briggs.'

Stan whimpered, 'An' he'll think I told on 'im!'

Rocklin's eyes hardened. 'I'm running a

cow ranch!'

Clara put out her hand in a worried gesture, uneasy from the way Rocklin looked. 'Ken, please don't make trouble over that now. You just mustn't!'

When the horses were hitched Briggs scratched his cheek and said, 'I'm awful sorry about holdin' you up, Dave.'

'Shut up!' said Dave.

The stage moved slowly, for Dave had tired horses now. Briggs looked after it, hitched up his trousers, rubbed his nose with the back of his wrist, and started to laugh. 'If Dave don't break his own neck, he'll mebbe try to break mine!'

Stan said, 'I reckon I orta tell you Dave knowed you fetched me that cow that time. He jus' now told that Rocklin. So 'f they both come here – Rocklin he may start talkin' about that cow.'

A flurry of oaths came out of Briggs's mouth. 'Then I ain't stayin'! Jager an' them may be drunk agin an' not show up atall! Me, I'm goin' now!'

Clara sat quietly with her hands in her lap. Here was the chance she had wanted to talk with Rocklin, and she had dressed as prettily as she could and had studied out words that she hoped would bring a full and pleasant understanding.

'Ken?' she said, and reached for his hand. Then her throat tightened in eagerness to be persuasive. 'Ken, we will sell the ranch and go back East and have a big farm. Horses and cattle, where there are trees and the grass is green the year round. Wouldn't you like that?'

'You don't like the West.' He wasn't asking but made the statement, quietly.

'No, Ken. I do not like the West. I have tried, but there is a loneliness about it and a lack of comfort and – and so much danger!'

'I'm 'fraid you and me don't have the same ideas.'

'Ken, then it was just because you felt sorry for me? I know it was!'

'Well, then you know what ain't so. I liked you. I still do. Always will. But a farm to me would be about like a big jail. Fences make me mad. The only good of a gate is to break it up for firewood. What you call loneliness is to me a kind of peaceful feelin'. I don't know more about comforts than I've had, so I'm satisfied. As for what you call "danger" – nobody can get away from that in one shape or 'nother. If you don't get hurt you get sick. So it all works out about even, East or West. About the worst I've ever been hurt is from the nick of a beer bottle. There are beer bottles in the East.'

'You know what kind of danger I mean, Ken.'

'Getting shot at? That's part of living, too. Out here men do mebbe get shot more than

326

back East. But back East I bet more men die of being sick. I'd rather be shot than bad sick.'

She was thinking of Arly when she asked softly, 'What kind of a woman would she have to be, Ken?'

He studied that moodily. 'I don't know that any woman could make me want her more'n I want my own way. There are some women that make you feel a little like you do when you've had too much to drink, and then you get overhappy and excited. The next morning you see what a fool you've been!'

Clara gave him a weary smile. 'I wouldn't know about that!'

Then the coach toppled as if turning over, and both of them were thrown headlong toward the front seat. They fell together in a cramped huddle on the floor and were shaken and bumped as the coach continued to lurch. Clara screamed, and Rocklin told her, 'Don't yell like that – you'll scare the horses worse! A wheel's come off!'

Dave had been driving at a walk on the up-grade, and the stage swayed with easy motion and whimpering creak. He was nursing tired horses, and it would be another fifteen miles before he got a fresh relay; so he sat hunched bulkily with elbows to knees and the lines laxly held between the fingers of one hand as his glance drifted along before the team. The grade's curve was now to the right, and the earth sloped away from the right side of the road.

Suddenly the coach tilted steeply forward to the left and dropped.

Dave jerked his foot from the brake slot, and his broad boots lashed out to search the floor board for something to brace against as he slid forward and slantwise off the seat, shortening the lines in his hands to yank back as he called a loud 'Whoa-a-a-whoa-up!' Whether or not the stage was going over, Dave held to the lines.

The near front wheel had rolled off and the coach joltingly lurched down on the front axle, pitching so close to the wheeler's heels that the wheeler jumped; and that set the other horses off and they hit their traces, plunging and rearing.

Dave's boot heels had lodged against the floor board's side strip, and he settled himself in a kind of squatting crouch on the slanting floor with knees braced against the dashboard and his back against the front seat; and he swore in a loud, soothing voice and put all of his weight into the pull on the shortened lines. The drag of the axle helped to make the leaders haw, and Dave yanked to keep them headed toward the high side of the road. The axle was gouging the earth like a full plow and sent up a swirl of red dust as the horses struggled on with wild sidling jumps that nearly had the coach off the road; but Dave held them with powerful steadiness, and they could not run but they did plunge and rear, backing and filling.

Rocklin told Clara to hold fast and stay quiet and left her sitting on the floor of the coach. He kicked open the door on the raised side and slid through, getting struck by the swing of the door as the horses plunged.

He picked himself up out of the dust and ran forward to the leaders' heads and took a left-handed hold on their bridles and helped Dave steady them. When they were fairly quieted he went around behind them and unhooked their doubletree from the tongue. The stage was now cramped very close to the road's edge, and Dave came down off the seat with a blur of dust in his eyes and unhooked the wheelers' traces.

Now if they did run away they would run only with their harness.

Dave took a chew of tobacco, kicked the axle with his heel, glowered back down the road. Rocklin asked, 'So you don't think it would do any good for me to look along the road for the nut?'

Dave snorted, spit, looked toward Clara, and didn't say what he felt like saying, but merely, 'Never had a flanged nut come off before in my life. That means it was took off. Mebbe Briggs learned I knowed about that cow an' it's just his ornery-mean way of gittin' even.'

Rocklin wasn't convinced. 'But we come a long way from there, Dave, before the wheel slipped.'

Dave bobbed his head. 'Half mile or more. We come slow. Till right about here the grade was to the left, an' that kep' 'er on. Here we turned right an' pulled 'er off.'

'Mebbe I'd better take a little walk back and have a talk with Briggs. But if I don't get the nut?'

'We'll all set right here till somebody fetches one!'

Arly and Juan were walking their horses around the curve at the foot of the hill, but when they saw the stalled stage Arly came on the lope. She swung from the saddle before the horse stopped, and she didn't stagger but held her balance by a little short-stepped run that put her by Clara's side. Her high-headed horse braced itself on stiffened forelegs and stopped with the reins on the ground, then poked out its small ears inquiringly toward the stage horses as if asking, 'What you fellows been up to?'

Clara stood in the deep red dust with the long skirts heavily about her feet, and she was perspiring and worried and felt help-less, and her hat was lopsided and the black cotton gloves were dirty, her dress all askew, and a button was gone from the waist. She hadn't thought about how she looked until Arly came, but now she flushed at standing bedraggled before this Harolday girl who was trim and neat in the wine-colored corduroys and bright, loose-fitting waist.

Arly's eyes flashed anxiously. 'What's happened?'

Juan had reined up and got off with long-legged stride and stood by his horse, and his wrinkled, Indian-dark face had no expression whatever.

Rocklin's face was set, with almost a sullen firmness, and he wished that Arly wasn't here, probably because he was so uncomfortably glad that she was; and in the days past he hadn't tried to forget her, for trying wouldn't have done any good; but he had pride, and stubbornness, too, and this blazingly willful girl seemed to think that she could drag him around like a roped calf, but he'd be damned if she could.

'Nut come off the axle an' let us down!' Dave said, and then he said more than that. Women or no women, he used what he thought were suitable words to accuse Briggs, telling what he'd do if he got his hands on him.

Arly cut in, 'I'd help you but he's gone, Dave. Down yonder we saw a man loping cross country, and Stan said it was his helper quitting. He was afraid you would come back!'

331

Dave looked at Clara and growled, 'He might've killed us all! Look how banged up she is.'

Clara said, 'Oh, I'm all right,' and didn't smile, and she tried to adjust her dress without seeming to.

Arly walked around the coach and glanced down at the axle. 'Dave, Juan can ride back to Indian Wells and bring a nut from the wreck there. That'll take three or four hours. We can all go back to Stan's and wait.' She went to Juan and spoke with him for a minute, then he raised his hat to her, lifted himself into the saddle, reined about, and rode off.

Dave flung out an arm backward. 'You can all go. I'll stay here. 'Ud rather be alone anyhow. When the wheel's on I'll come back down, water the horses, pick up him an' her.'

Then Arly turned to her pretty horse and shook the dust from the end of the reins and said to Clara, 'You can ride Belle.'

Clara had never been on a horse in her life, and for a moment she was pinched by the suspicion that Arly knew it and was playing a trick to make her look ridiculous. Her fingers fumbled where the button was missing on her waist and she asked protestingly, 'Ken, must we go back to that horrid place?'

He moved his hat, setting it lower on his

forehead. 'Be easier than waiting here.'

'But I don't mind walking.'

'Won't be easy,' he told her.

'You'll ruin your shoes and dress, too, walking,' Arly said quickly. 'They're button shoes and nice. And I've never had a pretty dress like yours. Fashionable, I mean. And, oh, how I've wanted one! I went so far as to order material over at Garden, then changed my mind – for where could I wear a dress that was so long I had to carry part of it in my hand while I had it on my back! So I ordered a new saddle instead. And don't need it, either.'

Clara found it very confusing, the way Arly rattled on. Arly didn't seem to remember that they were enemies, and she wasn't in the least embarrassed and she seemed completely friendly; and there wasn't even a glance toward Rocklin as if she wanted him.

'–so climb up there on the wheel hub and lift your skirts and Ken will help you get into the saddle and–'

Clara made up her mind that she would ride, just to see what it was like; and Rocklin steadied her on the wheel hub, and she raised her skirts and petticoats and lifted a foot across the saddle, then she clutched the horn and slid across the seat and pushed hastily to get her skirts down low over her legs.

Arly took Clara's foot and guided it into

the stirrup and gave her leg a quick little pat and said, 'There! That's the way. Slip your other foot in like this one. That's better than walking in a long dress.'

Clara clutched the horn with both hands. It didn't seem better than walking; she was so high from the ground and felt that she might fall off at each slow step the horse took.

Rocklin fell behind, looking or pretending to look for the nut that might have been dropped. He was also keeping away from Arly; he wasn't going to let her, or Clara, think that he wanted to be near her. And in a way he really didn't; he couldn't understand her or himself, but he wasn't going to let himself be a fool about her; and besides he was not going to let Clara feel any more hurt about her than he could help.

Arly walked beside the horse, and after a time she looked up and smiled at Clara. 'You may hate me, and I suppose you ought to, and I don't blame you, but I like you!' Clara gazed down at her and was wide-eyed and speechless.

'You,' said Arly, 'are so sweet and honest and gentle you make me feel ashamed – a little. Not much, but enough to make me wish I was more of a lady. That is, sometimes I wish it. Not when I'm mad!' She stared up, half smiling, with something wistful in the smile. 'Doc Riding says I'm nothing but a savage. Just selfish and mean and don't care what I do as long as I have my way.' Consideringly: 'I don't know how to be any other way, but I would rather be like you. I would, honest I would!'

Clara's heart leaped high and colored her cheeks with a happy flush, for she believed that it was Arly's way of telling her that they weren't rivals any more and that she wouldn't do anything more to get Rocklin away from her.

When Clara got off the horse at Stan's she breathlessly half fell, for she tried to keep her leg covered as she drew it across the saddle, and Rocklin couldn't give her much support with the hand that was so stiff the fingers wouldn't close.

Stan shuffled up with almost a drunken manner, and Arly's words jumped at him. 'Did you know what Briggs was up to?' He swore that he hadn't known, and his eyes went scooting about the ground, afraid to lift and meet hers. She demanded, 'Where's that nut?'

Words labored in Stan's scrawny throat. 'I dunno, Miss Arly. Hones'. I didn't know nuthin' about it a-tall.' His glance sidled toward Clara and he jerked his thumb. 'I wouldn't do anything to hurt her, you know I wouldn't, not after–'

'Oh, shut up!' Arly said, irritated by his maundering. 'Put my horse in a stall and

335

take off the saddle.' As Stan started to lead the horse away Arly hooked her arm in Clara's, saying, 'Come on. Let's see if there's any pop.'

Clara didn't draw away but turned and said, 'Come on, Ken,' and she sounded relieved and pleased. He didn't know what to think and felt muddled by the strangely sudden friendliness between these girls. The better to think it over for a minute longer he looked at the ground as if searching and presently stooped and picked up a twig, as if that was what he had been looking for; then he followed slowly and still didn't know what to think.

Arly didn't find any pop bottles behind the bar but she did find a fresh sack of tobacco and papers. 'I'll see if I can roll Ken a cigarette. A horse fell on Juan a couple of years ago and I learned to roll them for him. Oh, never quite right but–'

CHAPTER TWENTY-ONE

As soon as Stan led the horse into the shed at the edge of the stable Jager lurched close up and cursed him. 'Why didn't you let *him* bring that horse?' The hatchet-faced Bob jerked the reins from Stan's fingers and leaned close, also accusingly. 'Yeah, w'y didn't you? Been over with by now, an' we'd be on our way!'

Three saddled horses were already crowded there. The Clewses and Wally, coming cross country, had dipped into an arroyo to remain out of sight when they saw Juan and Arly coming down the Holman grade; then they had intercepted Briggs, heading for home, and learned what he had done to the stage. After that they raced in here to hide and wait, sure that Rocklin would come back, perhaps alone, to look for the nut.

It was dim in the stable even with sun streaks cutting through cracks, and it was hot and the manure was steamy-strong, and Stan put a hand to his throat to ease its tightness. 'She tol' me to bring it. He can't unsaddle with a hurt hand.' Stan's eyes wavered through the dimness to where Wally squatted by a crack, and a sunbeam slanted across his knotted face. Stan pantingly dragged at words. 'With them girls here, you boys won't now, will you?' He was asking Wally, but Wally had a sullen look and didn't say anything.

Jager let go with an obscenity that meant he didn't care how many women were about; then he drew a crushed package of fine cut, fingered some of it into his mouth, and rammed the package back into his hip pocket. As he wiped the loose tobacco from his lips with the flat of his hand he stared down at Wally.

Bob said gleefully, 'Hey, Jager, lookee!' Arly's holster with the small revolver was on the saddle horn, and the quirt was looped there, too. 'Been like her to use 'em on us! Now her claws is cut!' Bob chuckled in a nervous, tickled sort of way.

Wally, still on his haunches, took up a straw and broke it. They had intended to be inside the house when the stage rolled in. Briggs was to keep the driver outside, and Stan was to get Rocklin inside. When it was all over Stan would have had to tell about it in the way they wanted it told. They hadn't known that Clara was coming along, and now the Harolday girl had shown up, too. Wally didn't like the women being here. 'They might get hurt.'

Jager moved closer and said, 'We can't back out now. And what you so scairt of?'

Wally stood up. He was hunky and muscular with a scar on his knobby face that gave him an ugly look. 'Yeah? Lissen, Jager. All of us agin one feller with a crippled hand don't go with "scairt." The women make it bad. They're goin' to tell how it was done.' Wally's voice changed softly. 'You just said "scairt" to me. Lissen, Jager. This Rocklin he gun-whipped you in front of the town – an' done as bad to Bob. Yet you two want me to help

– an' him one-handed! Mebbe it's you that's scairt!'

Jager scowled. 'You're talkin' reckless!'

Wally said, 'I'm feelin' reckless!'

Stan got over among the saddle horses because this was beginning to look serious. Bob edged around behind Wally. He and Jager had often said that sometime Wally would go too far in talking back mean to them and would have to be shown, and Bob's glance kept asking if this was the time, but Jager didn't notice.

'Uh – yeah? Just what you got in mind, Wally?'

Wally told him, 'You orta walk in there an' make Rocklin start it. Hurt hand 'r not, he will, quick. I've seen how he does! Then you do what you've come to do – 'f you can! That's what I think!'

Clara was trying to learn to roll cigarettes, too, and Arly sifted tobacco flakes into the paper for her. Arly's weren't very good, but Rocklin was glad for the smoke; and now she was saying to Clara, 'Squeeze your thumbs down as you fold it over.' Clara spilled tobacco over the table, and Arly pulled the sack's mouth wide and carefully distributed a little more along the paper and gave more advice.

Rocklin wasn't watching; he was looking down at the floor, still trying to think. This

339

Harolday girl, without any longer seeming to try, was making good her threat that she would make him want her. He wasn't going to admit that to himself even, but there it was. She was bad-tempered and tricky and selfish, and somehow all that didn't matter. And he couldn't understand what had happened between the girls. They were now very like friends, almost as if everything unpleasant had been forgotten. Arly seemed perfectly natural, treating him as she might have treated any other man that she merely liked, and was at ease and wholly unembarrassed. Perhaps she had changed her mind about him. *Be like her,* he thought. *Changeable and flighty as a bat!* And he saw how it would be if he fell in love with her when she fell out of love with him, and he smiled to himself a bit crookedly. *Hell, she don't know what love is!*

He heard footsteps in the kitchen and accepted them as Stan's coming the back way, and he didn't look up until a voice said, 'High-ee?' brightly.

Bob Clews sagged against the kitchen doorway with his thumbs through the armholes of his vest in a studiedly inoffensive posture, and he grinned at Rocklin. 'Nice day, heh?' Bob added with a nervous cackle.

Rocklin sat still, but Arly swore in startled Spanish and jumped up, giving the bench a thrust with her legs that moved it and jarred the unfinished cigarette from Clara's fingers.

Rocklin kept his eyes on Bob and dropped the cigarette to have his hand free, and he shifted on the stool just enough to get his legs from under the table.

Bob was saying, 'I hear you're lookin' f'r Judge Garley, hm? That right?'

Rocklin knew, of course, that this meant trouble. He wasn't sure what kind of trouble, for Garley's name made it sound as if Bob wanted to dicker, maybe sell out Garley's hiding-place; but more likely he wanted to take Rocklin into a trap on the pretense of showing it. He and Arly were both distrustfully studying Bob's slack, thin face when Clara cried out and made a stablike gesture toward the front door.

Arly wheeled about. 'Jager!' she said, and then: 'Whipsawed!' She moved with purposeful swiftness, getting around the table and back of Rocklin, and she faced toward the two men at the door. 'And Wally Russell, too!' Then scornfully: 'Why so few?'

Jager was just ready to come in, and Wally was behind him but not real close. She had caught the Jager moving with a stealthy strut. Two guns dangled on his hips and his face was thrust forward in cunning alertness, not quite smiling, and the squint of his close-set eyes had a mean certainty. He stopped in the doorway as Arly's words went at him like something thrown. 'So you're trying to shoot another man in the back, Jager!'

They hit and hit hard, and Jager hunched a little as a man does when about to come in close and strike, and he swore at Arly and told her, 'Git outa the way!'

Arly said, 'I won't!'

Rocklin had got up off the stool with a glance behind him as soon as he heard Jager's name, then his look snapped back to watch Bob. 'Whipsawed!' told it, and he was worse than cornered. He couldn't make it a fight, not even a hopeless fight, for the girls were in the line of the cross fire and he had a heart-heavy awareness of his left-handed awkwardness. The best he could do right now was not to turn his back on Bob. There wasn't a place in the room that would offer any kind of shelter, even if he could reach it; and by himself he didn't stand a ghost chance against three men but must try to get as many as he could, and he especially wanted Bob Clews.

Arly was talking and talking fast and kept on talking. Her hands were stiff down behind her as if she held something concealed, and her head was up and there wasn't anything about her that looked like fear. 'I'll not get out of your way,' she told Jager, 'and if you touch me I'll kill you!' She couldn't have seemed more assured if she held a gun.

Then at once she said, 'And you, Wally Russell! You've come down pretty low, you have, since the time you carried that snake-bit kid twenty miles to Doc Riding!'

Wally's look soured as his tight, small eyes shifted toward the back of Jager's head; then he stared at Arly for a moment, and after that he glanced at Clara. She had stood up and was pressing back against the wall at the end of the bench with her hands to her cheeks in a way that pulled her dark eyes staringly wide.

Jager moved a step or two and stopped. Arly had called, 'Ken, keep your eyes on that–' She used a Spanish name for Bob Clews that was a scorcher. 'I,' she said, 'will take care of this–' She used English words for Jager, and they were the kind to blister a man's face, and she didn't say them in a wild temper but with the sound of picking each word because it fitted and they were the worst that she knew. Then she kept her eyes on Jager as she called, 'You've turned bad, Wally, but not bad enough to want to hurt *me!* Make Jager play his hand alone and I'll make him crawl!'

She was groping for some manly weakness in Wally. He had moved to one side of the doorway and now he wet his lips, trying to say something, but he didn't; and his small, deep-set eyes peered across at Bob, flicked toward Jager, returned to Arly, then again he looked at Clara.

Clara was saying, 'I can't stand this! I just can't stand it!' She didn't know what she

343

was saying or that she was saying anything as she huddled against the wall.

Then Jager began to sidle a little toward the center of the room; but Arly moved, too, facing him, and her arms were stiffly down with her hands behind her. He could read the menace in her eyes, but of course she was bluffing. Her taunts made him furious, but she was also baffling because she seemed so unafraid. Jager's eyes flickered questioningly toward her concealed hands.

'Lettin' him hide behind a woman's back!' was the best Jager could say, and Arly told him echo-quick, 'You're crawling before a woman's face!'

Bob had his shoulders away from the wall and he had taken his thumbs out of the vest armholes and kept his hands lifted, shoulder-high, surrendering, for Rocklin's fingers were on the gun. He hadn't drawn it; he didn't dare, because Jager would start shooting – Arly or no Arly – and there was also Wally behind him. He knew, or thought he knew, what Arly was up to; she was trying to work on Wally's pride and shame, make him keep out of this, and so lessen the odds; and by holding Jager off with reckless talk she was giving Rocklin time to do something.

He weighed chances and hated the security of being behind a woman's skirts; but it was real security, at least now. And he was up against a hard choice. Bob was near enough to make it an easy shot, the next thing to point-blank, but you couldn't shoot a man with his hands up; just couldn't. It was tough to figure. If shooting started, the girls would be in sure danger. Clara's voice reached him now in the low moan of: 'Oh, God!' and he could tell that she was sinking back on the bench and he heard her thump down as if in a faint. He thought steadily, *If I jump over toward the bar there won't be so much cross fire on them!* But first Rocklin said, 'Unbuckle that belt and drop it!' Tense as it was, with half seconds maybe making a lot of difference, he had to use the chance to disarm Bob. 'Damn you, be quick!' Rocklin told him, for Bob's hands moved slowly and his fingers lagged at the buckle.

And all the while Arly was lashing Jager with her tongue. '–in the back! That's the way you shot Jim and Bowles and Clint!'

'I never!' said Jager, and Arly said, 'You're lying!'

Words seemed her only weapons, and she used them flailingly. Suddenly she said, 'You touch me and Wally'll kill you!' She didn't look toward Wally, but Jager did for an anxious instant, and Wally scowled sullenly and didn't deny it.

Then Jager raised his voice with: 'I ain't aimin' to hurt you, but you git away from him or–'

She wouldn't listen. It was as if she thought every word spoken was that much time gained, and she stabbed for the places that hurt. 'You've been gun-whipped before the whole town! Now you're crawling before a woman! If you get out of here alive, you'll sneak off and steal a horse or burn a barn! If you want to get out of here alive, Jager, turn tail and run! You know how, Jager! You've done it before!'

Jager's face was a scorched red. He was a killer and he had done bold things, even if the cowardly pleased him about as well; but this girl was a devil and gave him a sense of dread even as she goaded him. Jager felt that he just couldn't stand any more and he shouted, 'Shut up, you!' and started to rush at her, but he stopped, for the fear suddenly flashed into his mind that she was deliberately taunting him into striking her because she believed that Wally would then kill him!

Jager backed up a half step and twitched his eyes toward Wally, and all he saw was a sour, unreadable scowl. Arly edged toward him with: 'You're yellow, Jager! You're a coward and know it!' The shift of her feet brought her nearer and nearer, and she raised her voice to tell him, 'You're nothing but a barn burner, a horse thief, a jailbird! Not even smart enough to stay out of prison! Not even brave enough to push a woman out of your way!'

When she said that she wasn't an arm's reach from him, and Jager couldn't stand it. He swore at her and started to clap one hand to a gun as he struck out with the other fist in a sweeping blow to knock her aside and get at Rocklin. But Arly exploded into cat-quick movement. She jumped right at him with a clenched fist swinging, and the hand opened in front of Jager's face and splattered a handful of cigarette tobacco into his mouth, into his nose, and blindingly into his eyes.

Jager howled as if smeared by fire and turned away and slapped fingers and fore-arms at his eyes. He stumbled backward with writhing bend of body and coughed and stamped his feet and cursed and sneezed.

The empty tobacco sack fell behind Arly as she rushed at him with lowered head, and she clawed a gun out of its holster before Jager knew what she was doing; but it was a big gun and her hands were small, and in her haste she didn't have a good hold and it slipped from her. Jager clutched out unsee-ingly and got hold of her arm high up near the shoulder, and he cursed out threats of what he meant to do and jerked to bring her up close. '—break ever' bone in yore damn body!' was what Jager roared.

Arly didn't try to get away. Instead, when he yanked at her, she lurched yieldingly and tried to get to his face with her fingernails, and did. That made Jager howl, and he ripped her blouse and hit her in frantic pawing to thrust her back from him and he couldn't.

Guns were beginning to go off now with crashing echoes, and Arly screamed at Rocklin with a sound of triumph encouragingly. Jager, sightless and frantic in the midst of the shooting, beat at her, trying to get free; but she was quick and strong and wouldn't give way and didn't care if he hurt her, and she kept at him like a wildcat at some big, blinded dog. When he drew the other gun to club her, for he couldn't see to shoot, Arly simply scrambled in closer and locked her arms about his arm and set her teeth in his forearm and wouldn't be shaken off.

Jager cried out with a kind of crazed pleading. His eyes were sightless, on fire, and watering as if he wept. She hurt him fiercely with all the rage of her temper and lithe strength, and he was in terror, blinded and afraid of the gunfire. As they swayed and trampled, Arly clamped a foot behind his foot, hooking her small silver spur under the long shank of his boot. When he fell it was with as much suddenness and as hard a jolt as if his heels had been jerked forward from under him. The revolver was twisted in his hand and it fired when its hammer struck on the floor.

The room was already filled with smoke

haze, and gun echoes reverberated like small thunder.

Rocklin's look had been holding Bob as if he were on the end of a pitchfork, but Bob fumbled with the belt buckle, and a part of his slowness was because his fingers were shaky. He knew Rocklin would kill him if he tried tricks, and Bob didn't have that kind of nerve. Then the gun and cartridge-studded belt thumped to the floor, and Rocklin was saying, 'Get away from it! Back up!' when Arly jumped at Jager, flinging the tobacco into his face.

Bob backed up with hands up, and that carried him through the doorway a step or two into the kitchen itself; and Rocklin, trying to look both ways at once, jumped forward, meaning to take possession of the gun Bob had just dropped. But he had got a glimpse of Arly struggling with Jager and had no idea that she had thrown herself at the big cutthroat. His instant wrath believed that Jager had struck her and she was striking back, and when with scarcely more than half a glance forward again he saw that Bob Clews was gone, at least was out of sight, Rocklin whirled with his gun leveled waist-high. He saw that Wally was standing by the wall and not moving. His hands were empty, and he wasn't even looking at Rocklin but at the fight out in the room.

The small girl and the big man were in a

swirling flurry of legs and arms, with faces flashing into a glimpse of view as they rocked out across the room; and Rocklin saw that he must thrust the gun's muzzle hard against Jager's body if he would be sure of not hurting her. And he meant to do just that.

He ran towards them, and a gun roared behind him. As Rocklin dropped with a twisted sprawl he thought it was Wally who had fired, but Wally's hand was still empty and he was peering across toward the kitchen doorway. Too late now for Rocklin's wish that he had shot Bob Clews, hands up or not; and as he rolled over a second bullet gouged dirt up out of the floor near his head and ricocheted from the floor's shale-like hardness.

Rocklin, flat down, thumbed his hammer and fired quickly, but it wasn't good, and the agonized warning went through his thoughts, *Aim careful!*

Bob stood in the kitchen doorway, leaning forward with his arm at full length, and his thin face was set in a strained look as if trying to put the thrust of his muscles behind the bullet. *He can't help but kill me!* whipped coolly through Rocklin's mind; and Bob was sure of that, too, but overeager and not cool, and he fired twice more, rapidly. Dust spurted inches away from Rocklin, missing.

Rocklin's right leg was flat down. He felt no pain in it, only a vague kind of numb warmth, and one part of his brain was wondering if he could force himself to stand, but he wasn't ready to try. His other knee was drawn up, and he lifted his weight on his right forearm, leveling out the revolver. Stubbornly he meant to line up the sights however long it took and not trust to snap-chance luck. His handicap couldn't be overcome in any other way, and this took no appreciable length of time as clocks count time; but there was the strain of having to do consciously what ought to have been instinctive.

Bob sensed the deadliness of the pause that was taking aim and he jumped backward, firing as he went, to scoot again to the side of the kitchen door and be concealed. *Right in the belly!* was Rocklin's thought without thinking about it as his finger squeezed; and he knew that it was good, though Bob went out of sight as if jerked by an invisible rope about his waist, falling as he went.

Arly dropped to her knees on the floor beside Rocklin and hovered there with her hands to his cheeks, and a question was so anxiously in her eyes that she seemed afraid to give it words.

He sat up, keeping the leg straight, and said, 'No, not bad at all. Just in the leg.'

Arly said, 'Where?' and began to look.

Her blouse was torn from her and hung in rags about her shoulders; the wine-colored

351

corduroy skirt was loose from the wide belt; there was a boil-sore bruise on her forehead, and her mouth was cut and her hair a tangled mess, but beauty glowed like a light in her face.

Wally strode by with sullen lurch and disappeared in the kitchen.

Rocklin jerked his head. 'Did he shoot Jager?'

'No, but I believe he would have! Jager carried a shell under the hammer. It went off when he fell and he shot himself. We've had luck!'

'Luck, hm?' He groped down below his knee where the pain was coming, but that was an unconscious gesture, for he wasn't noticing the pain. He was looking at Arly. 'Luck?' She seemed so small and slender now, just an anxious little girl with happy tenderness in her staring eyes; then a swift change came for a moment in her expression as she put her teeth edge to edge and told him earnestly, 'I'm glad I can be *mean!*' Then she half laughed and caught at his hand.

Wally came back, walking heavily. He stopped, gave Rocklin a nod. 'You got him!' He moved his fingers awkwardly about his mouth and looked at Arly. He tried to say something, but it wasn't easy; then he blurted, 'I'm gettin' outa the country! Long as I'm around here folks'll remember I was one of the bunch and blame me for things I don't do. I never much liked Jager or Bob – neither of 'em – but we fitted in. Your axle nut is under the water trough.' Now he frowned at Rocklin. 'That Judge Garley is over to Injun Wells waitin' for us to ride in an' say you're dead!'

'Where'bouts over there?'

'Back of the store. He's been livin' there!'

Then Rocklin asked, 'Was it Jager and Bob that did Garley's killings for him?'

'Not as I know of, and I'd've knowed. We've been hangin' out over at Briggs' place. The judge he hunted us up some days ago 'cause we all had it in for you. Later he sent word you'd be along today in the stage. Alone, he said. He never said she'd be with you.' He twisted toward Clara. She was huddled in loneliness on the bench with her hands clenched together up under her chin as if that was the only way she could hold up her head, and fear was still in her eyes. 'Me,' said Wally, 'I don't fight women!'

Rocklin didn't think much of the statement and let it pass without giving the approval that Wally wanted, but Arly smiled at him and said, 'Why, I knew that, Wally!' She hadn't known anything of the kind, but to have her say it brought a slow, pleased look onto his knobby face. 'That's why I wasn't afraid of Jager!'

'You ain't afraid of nuthin' – an' never was! Well, good-bye.' He went out, hurrying.

353

Rocklin got up with Arly's help and sat on a stool, then she took his foot up under her arm, turned her back to him, and pulled off the tight boot. Blood had drained into the boot. She pushed his hands away when he began to draw up the pants leg and did it herself, gently. He had been shot just below the knee.

'Bob's the worst shot I ever saw,' said Rocklin. 'Purt-near as bad as me!'

'Jager could shoot! I knew I had to get his guns off of him somehow!'

Clara watched staringly, with a dead numbness in her throat, as Arly tore rags from her tattered waist and wiped at his leg.

'We'll find that nut,' Arly said, pitching away one rag and jerking another from the torn waist, 'and have Dave head around and take us back to Indian Wells. If Juan finds Garley there – be too bad for Mister Garley!'

'Juan?'

'Juan's always polite, but Lord help you if he doesn't like you! He has never liked Garley.'

'Nor me.'

Any lifted her eyes and smiled. 'You – Juan? Little you know.'

'He told me so.'

'He liked you, but he didn't like my being in love with you! He made me promise to quit wooing you. And I did – why, didn't

354

you notice? He said it was shameful. Said I had no pride – me! He said – but I told you this before – he said if I could steal you, you wouldn't be worth having! And I believed *that*, so I stopped trying, but–'

Arly shut up and gave a little start as if suddenly awakened, for Clara was coming toward them with a slow, trancelike blankness. Rocklin looked at her, and his face tightened in dread of what was gong to be talked about.

Clara came close, passing right by Arly as if not seeing her, and she gazed at him and seemed waiting for him to speak first; but she wasn't, and she put out a hand and touched his shoulder and tried to smile and could scarcely speak. Her voice was very low and sincere. 'Ken, I understand now. Oh, I do! It just couldn't be any other way, not after – after today!' Then she turned quickly to Arly and said, 'You were glorious!' She grabbed Arly and hugged her. 'I'm not jealous – not now – not in the least. I just am not! Only how I do wish that I could be like you!'

Then it was Arly whose tongue was so numb that she couldn't say a word and the glisten of tears shimmered in her eyes.

CHAPTER TWENTY-TWO

The stage was about halfway back to Indian Wells when it met Juan, and Dave stopped with rasping whine of brakes.

Arly swung the coach door open to lean out, and when Juan reined up alongside she talked rapidly. He saw the ragged nakedness about her shoulders and the bruises on her face, and he saw Rocklin's leg propped up on the seat before him, and for a long moment Juan studied Clara's weary anxiousness and perhaps wondered that she clung to Arly's hand with trustful liking.

Arly told what they had been through, then Juan untied the serape from the back of his saddle and gave it to her, saying quietly, *'Poco a poco voy comprendiendo"* but there was no telling just what or how much he was beginning to understand, because there was nothing readable on his wrinkled dark face.

Juan then changed horses, putting Arly's saddle in the boot, and tied his own tired horse on the lead rope behind the stage.

When the stage stopped before the log-built store the little old man hobbled out, not cheerily now, and screeched, 'What happened, Dave? W'y you back?'

'Ax'dent,' Dave told him, then harshly: 'Come here, you!'

Juan was helping the girls out of the coach, and the storekeeper queasily sensed that something was wrong, very much wrong. It was in the quietness of the girls, in Juan's black stare, and in Dave's hoarse: 'You stay right out here!'

Arly had thrown the serape over her shoulders, crossed it on her breast, and fastened the long ends under her belt. She didn't seen to care how she looked and whether or not the bareness of her shoulders was concealed.

Dave and Juan helped Rocklin out of the coach. His leg was stiff now and hurt, but he wasn't noticing as he balanced himself on one foot by keeping an arm on Juan's shoulder and stared down at the little storekeeper and told him, 'Garley is here!' No question about it; Rocklin simply made the statement, and the storekeeper instinctively started a denial but broke off and began to explain.

'I couldn't help myself! I didn't want 'im, but—'

Rocklin said, 'We've come for him. Where is he?'

Dave and Juan supported Rocklin between them as they went into the small, dim store, and Dave moved a keg for Rocklin to sit on,

357

and he sat there with the stiff leg out before him.

The storekeeper pointed to a back-room door and said, 'In there!' and again tried to explain why he had concealed Garley, but Dave told him, 'Shut up!'

Juan went to the door and didn't knock but opened it without a word; then he looked in and stepped in, disappearing from view, and they could hear Juan say quietly, 'Come out into the store, if you please.'

A moment later Garley came out and Juan was behind him. Garley was in stocking feet and not wearing a coat, and his white shirt was no longer white. He was unshaven, and the bruise marks of Rocklin's fist still showed on his face. His clothes were baggy, for he had lost weight and he had been drinking, been drinking for days. Worries had eaten all of his strength away, and his big eyes looked like empty holes. He gazed toward Rocklin as a man with a rope on his neck might look at the hangman, now without hope and without hatred, just soddenly helpless.

Rocklin said at once, 'So Harolday shot Clint, thinking it was me!'

Clara hadn't expected anything of that kind and gave a low cry. Dave put an arm about her, but Arly had guessed what was coming and she twisted a corner of the serape and stared at the floor.

'And Bowles, too!' Rocklin added.

Garley groped for a backless chair and sagged down and looked at his hands.

Rocklin said, 'Tell about it!'

Garley started to lift his head but didn't. It seemed too much effort. He said, 'Yes,' and nodded. Then he mumbled, 'When Red threatened me I wanted to leave the country, but people owed me money.' Wearily: 'I need a drink.'

Rocklin gestured, and the little storekeeper hobbled quickly to pour from a jug into a tin cup and took it to Garley. Garley didn't even say thanks, but drank a deep swallow or two and coughed, then held the cup with both hands between his knees and his hands shook.

He said, 'Once me and Harolday were friends.' His voice was strained and low, and having said that, he stopped, studying memories; and nobody told him to go on. The silence itself was pressure enough. 'But I found out if a man died owing him money he'd raise the note. We – we quarreled over that.'

Dave scowled. 'I bet you quarreled 'cause you gouged him over how much he paid you for helpin' to cheat the widow!'

Garley raised his eyes but didn't seem to care. Nothing mattered now. His eyes dropped to the cup, then he emptied it with another gulp or two and held it for a moment, but the cup slipped to the floor and he didn't notice. His head bobbed a little, but there was nothing to show whether he was admitting what Dave had charged or was deciding to tell all that he could.

'Red would've killed me,' he said mumblingly. 'Harolday wasn't in town. I went to see Clint at the house. He wasn't well – was in bed. He knew why me and the Old Man had quarreled. "Joke," he called it. Uh – joke?' He paused, studying the word's ugliness; then: 'I told him I'd had a row with Red over cards and had to get money somehow so I could go away. He sent out word to Harolday, and the Old Man come. We had a talk. He said he'd work out something for me if I'd help him get hold of the Caldwell ranch. He never said he'd shoot Red. I wouldn't've agreed to – to that.' Garley looked up, trying to see a little sympathy on somebody's face, but there wasn't any. Nobody believed him; nothing he could say defensively would do any good now. He was nakedly without even a tatter to hide behind.

It was Arly who asked, 'How much did Clint know?'

Garley fumbled at his face with an unsteady hand. 'I don't know. I don't think he believed it was his father. He didn't think the Old Man would shoot anybody. He called it just lucky for me that somebody waylaid Red. Red had quarreled with such a lot of men. Clint did know that the Old

360

Man was after the ranch and that I was helping. We would've fixed up a land company but–' he gazed dully at Rocklin then – 'but you come to town.'

Rocklin asked, 'Was Brotherton killed because he sent for me?'

Garley said, 'Partly. It scared Clint and the Old Man when you come, though I'd told 'em you were coming. Harolday was afraid of Brotherton, and he thought all the blame 'ud be put on Jager. Specially for shooting you. And he had to get you out of the way. Anything you did was bad for his plans. Then after what Arly said to him about you – he thought he'd shot you there in the hotel, and he went back to the stable and started for the ranch. That's how he worked it – shoot and get away quick, clear away. Pretend not to know anything till he was told. How'd you ever get on to him?'

Rocklin almost didn't reply, then he said, 'It was pretending you and Harolday weren't friends that had people fooled. But this morning he set his watch ahead to send off the stage before other passengers showed up. Usually he'll hold a stage if they're late. That fitted in with the Clewses showing up at Stan's to catch me – alone. You sent them there. So it added up that you and Harolday were working it together.'

Rocklin looked toward the little storekeeper, and now again he began trying to

361

tell how it was with him. 'I owed Harolday some money and he said the judge was innercent! That's why I kep' him – I didn't know nuthin' about what they'd been doin'! I thought the judge was innercent.'

Juan had moved quietly to the front door and stood there for a moment; then presently they heard the sound of hoofs going away fast. Dave hurried out and came back, mystified. 'Juan – he's rode off, hell-for-leather!'

Arly cried, *'Que ande con Dios!'* All eyes swung questioningly at her, but only Rocklin understood that she had referred to death – to one who was about to die. Arly put her knuckles to her mouth and nodded, and her voice was a whisper.

'Yes, I know what's coming! I – I know Juan!'

Harolday was at home before the table where he worked up his accounts. The large square iron safe that guarded his notes and mortgages and cash on hand was open beside him. He had been counting his money, as he often did when he wished to feel pleased, but today the money might have been any kind of cheap metal, the mortgages mere paper. He twisted about in the chair and stared through the window behind him and slowly twiddled his watch charm. His tired, gaunt face looked skintight on the bone, and all he could do was wait.

The house was quiet and his nerves were tensely alert, but he hadn't heard a footstep when the door opened. Harolday jerked about with a hand going toward an open drawer in the table as if to protect his gold. A tall figure came in quietly, closed the door, and stopped there. Harolday took his time staringly and at last asked, 'What is it, Juan?'

Juan removed his hat. 'Señor, I have come to kill you!' Harolday didn't move. His hand still rested inside the drawer and he gazed steadily at Juan; then: 'Garley?'

'Yes, señor.'

'Don't you know Garley is a liar, Juan?'

'Yes, señor, often!'

'Then why – why won't you give me a chance to – to–'

Juan said softly, 'To use the gun you have in your hand, señor?'

Harolday flinched but his arm remained rigid. 'Juan, you have always hated me!'

'That is true. I have long suspected that you killed my señorita's father. Now I am sure of it!'

Harolday lurched up suddenly and leaned across the table, leveling the gun; and even as Harolday fired Juan was saying coolly, 'I believe in God, señor!' And when that was said he had drawn his revolver.

As Rocklin came through the Emporium door Pap Fossler sidled away from the candy bucket and joggled up to meet him. Pap thrust out his hand. 'You're purt-near a stranger, Ken! Want the mail? Yeah, letter f'r you. Nice big square un. Yeah.'

Pap hurried around the counter to the post-office pigeonholes and from the one marked *Santee Ranch* he drew papers, circulars, a stock journal, and a large square envelope addressed to Mr and Mrs Kenneth Rocklin.

Rocklin ripped it open with a thumbnail. Another envelope was inside, and inside of that one was an engraved card that announced the engagement of Miss Clara Isabella Caldwell of Danvers, Massachusetts, to—

'How's Arly? How's she gittin' on these days, Ken?'

Rocklin was carefully, almost tenderly, returning the card to its envelope, and he smiled slowly. 'Pap, she's tamed at last. That new man out there on the ranch can sure handle her. Anything to please him. She even gets down on her knees to him. The little redhead is purt-near six months old now, and he's boss – and he a'ready knows it!'

The publishers hope that this book has given you enjoyable reading. Large Print Books are especially designed to be as easy to see and hold as possible. If you wish a complete list of our books please ask at your local library or write directly to:

The Golden West Large Print Books
Magna House, Long Preston,
Skipton, North Yorkshire.
BD23 4ND

This Large Print Book, for people
who cannot read normal print,
is published under the auspices of

THE ULVERSCROFT FOUNDATION